PENGUIN BOOKS

THE QUANTITY THEORY OF INSANITY

Will Self's other books include the highly original novellas *Cock and Bull* and, most recently, *My Idea of Fun*. Both of these are published by Penguin.

The Quantity Theory of Insanity was one of the most highly acclaim-ed debuts of 1992. It won the 1993 Geoffrey Faber Memorial Prize and was shortlisted for the 1992 John Llewellyn Rhys Prize.

WILL SELF

———

THE QUANTITY THEORY OF INSANITY

PENGUIN BOOKS

PENGUIN BOOKS

Published by the Penguin Group
Penguin Books Ltd, 27 Wrights Lane, London W8 5TZ, England
Penguin Books USA Inc., 375 Hudson Street, New York, New York 10014, USA
Penguin Books Australia Ltd, Ringwood, Victoria, Australia
Penguin Books Canada Ltd, 10 Alcorn Avenue, Toronto, Ontario, Canada M4V 3B2
Penguin Books (NZ) Ltd, 182–190 Wairau Road, Auckland 10, New Zealand

Penguin Books Ltd, Registered Offices: Harmondsworth, Middlesex, England

First published by Bloomsbury 1991
Published in Penguin Books 1994
1 3 5 7 9 10 8 6 4 2

For K.S.A.S. who knows the stranger
truth behind these fictions

CONTENTS

However far you may travel in this world, you will still occupy the same volume of space.

Traditional Ur-Bororo saying

The North London Book of the Dead

I suppose that the form my bereavement took after my mother died was fairly conventional. Initially I was shocked. Her final illness was mercifully quick, but harrowing. Cancer tore through her body as if it were late for an important meeting with a lot of other successful diseases.

I had always expected my mother to outlive me. I saw myself becoming a neutered bachelor, who would be wearing a cardigan and still living at home at the age of forty, but it wasn't to be. Mother's death was a kind of a relief, but it was also bizarre and hallucinatory. The week she lay dying in the hospital I was plagued by strange sensations; gusts of air would seem personalised and, driving in my car, I had the sensation not that I was moving forward but that the road was being reeled back beneath the wheels, as if I were mounted on some giant piece of scenery.

The night she died my brother and I were at the hospital. We took it in turns to snatch sleep in a vestibule at the end of the ward and then to sit with her. She breathed stertorously. Her flesh yellowed and yellowed. I was quite conscious that she had no mind any more. The cancer – or so the consultant told me – had made its way up through the meningitic fluid in the spine and into her brain. I sensed the cancer in her skull like a cloud of inky pus. Her self-consciousness, sentience, identity, what you will, was cornered, forced back by the cloud into a confined space, where it pulsed on and then off, with all the apparent humanity of a digital watch.

One minute she was alive, the next she was dead. A dumpy nurse rushed to find my brother and me. We had both fallen asleep in the vestibule, cocooned within its plastic walls. 'I think she's gone,' said the nurse. And I pictured Mother striding down Gower Street, naked, wattled.

By the time we reached the room they were laying her out. I had never understood what this meant before; now I could see that the truth was that the body, the corpse, really laid itself out. It was smoothed as if a great wind had rolled over the tired flesh. And it, Mother, was changing colour, as I watched, from an old ivory to a luminous yellow. The nurse, for some strange reason, had brushed Mother's hair back off her forehead. It lay around her head in a fan on the pillow and two lightning streaks of grey ran up into it from either temple. The nurses had long since removed her dentures, and the whole ensemble – Mother with drawn-in cheeks and sculpted visage, lying in the small room, around her the loops and skeins of a life-supporting technology – made me think of the queen of an alien planet, resplendent on a high-tech palanquin, in some Buck Rogers style sci-fi serial of the Thirties.

There was a great whooshing sensation in the room. This persisted as a doctor of Chinese extraction – long, yellow, and divided at the root – felt around inside her cotton nightie for a non-existent heartbeat. The black, spindly hairs on his chin wavered. He pronounced her dead. The whooshing stopped. I felt her spirit fly out into the orange light of central London. It was about 3.00 a.m.

When I began to accept the fact that Mother really was gone, I went into a period of intense depression. I felt that I had lost an adversary. Someone to test myself against. My greatest fan and my severest critic and above all a good talker, who I was only just getting to know as a person – shorn of the emotional prejudices that conspire to strait-jacket the relationships between parents and children.

When my depression cleared the dreams started. I found myself night after night encountering my mother in strange situations. In my dreams she would appear at dinner parties (uninvited), crouched behind a filing cabinet in the office where I worked, or on public transport balefully swinging from a strap.

She was quite honest about the fact that she was dead in these dreams, she made no attempt to masquerade as one of the living, rather she absorbed the effect that death had had on her personality much the way she had taken the rest of the crap that life had flung at her: a couple of failed marriages and a collection of children who, on the whole, were a bit of a disappointment to her.

When I tried to remonstrate with her, point out to her that by her own lights (she was a fervent atheist and materialist), she ought to be gently decomposing somewhere, she would fix me with a weary eye and say in a characteristically deadpan way, 'So I'm dead but won't lie down, huh? Big deal.'

It was a big deal. Mother had banged on about her revulsion at the idea of an afterlife for as long as I could remember. The chief form that this took was an extended rant aimed at all the trappings of death that society had designed. She despised the undertaking business especially. To Mother it was simply a way of cheating money out of grieving people who could ill afford it.

She had told me a year or two before she died that if it was at all possible I was to try and give her a kind of do-it-yourself funeral. Apparently the Co-op retailed one that allowed you to get the cost of the whole thing down to about £250. You had to build your own casket though and I was never any good at anything remotely practical. At school it took me two years to construct an acrylic string-holder. And even then it wouldn't work.

So, after Mother died we arranged things conventionally, but austerely. Her corpse was burnt at Golders Green Crematorium. My eldest brother and I went alone – knowing that she would have disapproved of a crowd. We sat there in the chapel contemplating the bottom-of-the-range casket. One of the undertakers came waddling down the aisle, he gestured to us to stand and then moved off to one side, conspicuously scratching his grey bottom, either inadvertently or because he considered us of no account. Electric motors whirred, Mother lurched towards what, to all intents and purposes, was her final resting place.

A week or so later when I was going through more of Mother's papers I found a newspaper clipping about the DIY

3

funeral. I threw it away guiltily. I also found a deposit book that showed that mother had invested £370 in something called the Ecological Building Society. I phoned the society and was told by a Mr Hunt that it was true. Mother had been the owner of a seventh of a traditional Mongolian *yurt*, which was sited for some reason in a field outside Wincanton. I told Mr Hunt to keep the seventh; it seemed a suitable memorial.

Meanwhile, the dreams continued. And Mother managed to be as embarrassing in them as she had been alive, but for entirely different reasons. With death she had taken on a mantle of candour and social sharpness that I tended to attribute to myself rather than her. At the dream dinner parties she would make asides to me the whole time about how pretentious people were and what bad taste they displayed, talking all the while in a loud and affected voice which, needless to say, remained inaudible to her subjects. After a while I ceased trying to defeat her with the logic of her own extinction; it was pointless. Mother had long since ceased to be susceptible to reasoning. I think it was something to do with my father, a man who uses dialectics the way the Japanese used bamboo slivers during the war.

About six months after Mother's death the dreams began to decline in frequency and eventually they petered out altogether. They were replaced for a short while by an intense period during which I kept seeing people in the street who I thought were Mother. I'd be walking in the West End or the City and there, usually on the other side of the road, would be Mother, ambling along staring in shop windows. I would know it was Mother because of the clothes. Mother tended to wear slacks on loan from hippopotami, or else African-style dresses that could comfortably house a scout troop. She also always carried a miscellaneous collection of bags, plastic and linen, dangling from her arm. These were crammed with modern literature, groceries and wadded paper tissues.

And then, invariably, as I drew closer the likeness would evaporate. Not only wasn't it Mother, but it seemed absurd that I ever could have made the mistake. This late-middle-aged woman looked nothing like Mother, she was dowdy and conventional. Not the sort of woman at all who would say of effete young men that they 'had no balls', or of precious young women that they 'shat chocolate ice cream'. Yet each time the fact that

Mother was dead hit me again, it was as if it hadn't really occurred to me before and that her failure to get in touch with me over the past six months had been solely because she was 'hellishly busy'.

When I stopped seeing fake Mothers in the street I reckoned that I had just about accepted her death. Every so often I thought about her, sometimes with sadness, sometimes with joy, but her absence no longer gnawed at me like a rat at a length of flex. I was over it. Although, like Marcel after Albertine has gone, from time to time I felt that the reason I no longer missed Mother with such poignancy was that I had become another person. I had changed. I was no longer the sort of person who had had a mother like Mother. Mother belonged to someone else. If I had run into her at a dinner party fully conscious, she probably wouldn't have recognised me. My mother was dead.

All of this made the events that transpired in the winter of the year she died even more shocking. I was walking down Crouch Hill towards Crouch End on a drizzly, bleak, Tuesday afternoon. It was about three o'clock. I'd taken the afternoon off work and decided to go and see a friend. When, coming up the other side of the road I saw Mother. She was wearing a sort of bluish, tweedish long jacket and black slacks and carrying a Barnes & Noble book bag, as well as a large handbag and a carrier bag from Waitrose. She had a CND badge in her lapel and was observing the world with a familiar 'there will be tears before bedtime' sort of expression.

The impression I had of Mother in that very first glance was so sharp and so clear, her presence so tangible, that I did not for a moment doubt the testimony of my senses. I looked at Mother and felt a trinity of emotions: affection and embarrassment mingled with a sort of acute embarrassment. It was this peculiarly familiar wash of feeling that must have altogether swamped the terror and bewilderment that anyone would expect to experience at the sight of their dead mother walking up Crouch Hill.

I crossed the road and walked towards her. She spotted me when I was about twenty feet off. Just before a grin of welcome lit up her features I spotted a little *moue* of girlish amusement – that was familiar too, it meant 'You've been had'. We kissed on both cheeks; Mother looked me up and down to see how I was weighing in for the fight with life. Then she gestured at the shop window she'd been looking into. 'Can you believe the prices they're charging for this crap, someone must be buying it.' Her accent was the same, resolutely mid-Atlantic, she had the same artfully yellowed and unevened dentures. It was Mother.

'Mother,' I said, 'what are you doing in Crouch End? You never come to Crouch End except to take the cat to the vet, you don't even like Crouch End.'

'Well, I live here now.' Mother was unperturbed. 'It's OK, it's a drag not being able to get the tube, but the buses are fairly regular. There's quite a few good shops in the parade and someone's just opened up a real deli. Want some halva?' Mother opened her fist under my face. Crushed into it was some sticky halva, half-eaten but still in its gold foil wrapping. She grinned again.

'But Mother, what are you doing in Crouch End? You're dead.'

Mother was indignant, 'Of course I'm dead, dummy, whaddya think I've been doing for the last ten months? Cruising the Caribbean?'

'How the hell should I know? I thought we saw the last of you at Golders Green Crematorium, I never expected to see you in Crouch End on a Tuesday afternoon.' Mother had me rattled, she seemed to be genuinely astonished by my failure to comprehend her resurrection.

'More to the point, what are you doing in Crouch End? Why aren't you at work?'

'I thought I'd take the afternoon off. There's not a lot on at the office. If I stayed there I'd just be shuffling paper back and forth trying to create some work.'

'That's an attitude problem talking, young man. You've got a good job there. What's the matter with you? You always want to start at the top, you've got to learn to work your way up in life.'

'Life, Mother? I hardly think "Life" is the issue here! Tell me about what it's like to be dead! Why didn't you tell any of us you were having life after death in Crouch End? You could have called . . . '

Mother wasn't fazed, she looked her watch, another crappy Timex, indistinguishable from the last one I'd seen her wearing.

'It's late, I've got to go to my class. If you want to know about life after death come and see me tomorrow. I'm living at 24 Rosemount Avenue, in the basement flat, we'll have tea, I'll make you some cookies.' And with that she gave me the sort of perfunctory peck on the cheek she always used to give me when she was in a hurry and toddled off up Crouch Hill, leaving me standing, bemused.

What I couldn't take was that Mother was so offhand about life after death, rather than the fact of it. That and this business of living in Crouch End. Mother had always been such a crushing snob about where people lived in London; certain suburbs – such as Crouch End – were so incredibly non-U in Mother's book of form. The revelation that there was life after death seemed to me relatively unimportant set beside Mother's startling new attitudes.

I probably should have gone and told someone about my encounter. But who? All a shrink could have offered would have been full board and medication. And anyway, the more I told people how real the experience had been, the more certain they would become that I was the victim of an outlandishly complex delusionary state.

I had no desire to be psychiatric cannon fodder, so I went off to see my friend and had a fulfilling afternoon playing Trivial Pursuit. Just suppose it was all for real? I had to find out more about Mother's resurrection, she'd always been so emphatic about what happened to people after they die: 'They rot, that's it. You put 'em in a box and they rot. All that religious stuff, it's a load of crap.' Setting aside the whole issue of the miraculous I really wanted to see Mother eat humble pie over this afterlife issue, so much so that I went through the next thirty-odd hours as if nothing had happened. It was an exercise in magical thinking. I figured that if I behaved as if nothing had happened, Mother would be waiting for me, with cookies, in Rosemount Avenue, but if I said anything to anyone, the gods might take offence and whisk her away.

Rosemount Avenue was one of those hilltop streets in suburban London where the camber of the road is viciously arced like the back of a macadamised whale. The houses are high-gabled Victorian, tiled in red and with masonry that looks as if it was sculpted out of solid snot. Calling it an avenue was presumably a reference to the eight or so plane trees running down each side of the road. These had been so viciously pruned that they looked like nothing so much as upturned amputated legs. Poised on the swell of the road I shuddered to myself. What had brought these macabre images into my mind? Was it the prospect of my second encounter with a dead person? Was I losing my balance? Examining myself I concluded in the negative. In truth suburban streets, if you look at them for long enough, always summon up a sense of mortality – of the skull beneath the skin. The Reaper always waits behind the bus shelter. You can see his robe up to the knee; the rest is obscured by the route map.

The basement of No. 24 looked rather poky from the street; I couldn't see in the windows without going down into the basement area. Before I could do so Mother appeared clutching a tea strainer in one hand. 'Are you going to stand up there all afternoon? The kettle's boiled.' Death had done nothing to dampen down Mother's impatience. She still carried around her a sense of barely repressed nervous energy; in a more active, physical age Mother would have probably broken horses, or gone raiding with the Bedouin.

I noticed as I stepped into the flat that Mother's name was under the bell. For some reason that shocked me. I felt that Mother ought to be incognito. After all it was pretty weird her being alive after death. What if the Sunday papers found out? It could be embarrassing. I said, 'Mother, why have you kept your name? Surely if you're going to go on living in London you should change it? Aren't the people in charge of death worried about publicity?'

Mother sighed with exasperation. 'Look, there aren't any "people in charge of death". When you die you move to another part of London, that's all there is to it. Period.'

'But Mother, what about that performance at Golders Green? Weren't you in that coffin?'

'All right I'll admit it, that part of it is a bit obscure. One minute I was in the hospital – feeling like shit, incidentally – the next I was in Crouch End and some estate agents were showing me around this flat.'

'Estate agents! Dead estate agents?'

8

'Yeah, they were dead too, the whole thing is self-administered, a bit like a commune.'

Mother's eschatalogical revelations were beginning to get to me a little and I had slumped down on a sofa. My new vantage point jolted me into looking around the flat. I'd never seen a piece of elysian real estate before. What struck me immediately was that Mother's final resting place, if that's what it was, was remarkably like the flat she'd spent the last ten years of her life in.

There was the same large room with sofas and chairs scattered round it. There was a kitchenette off to one side, and high double doors at the end of the main room led to the bedroom. Through another door at the back of the room I could see a set of french windows and through them a small, well-kept garden. The flat was furnished haphazardly with odd posters and paintings on the walls and a lot of books; some shelved, others stacked on tables. A set of half-corrected proofs lay on the arm of a chair.

The principal difference was that whereas in the past it had been photographs of my brothers and me that had stood, either framed or mounted in plastic cubes, scattered around on the available surfaces, now the impedimenta that betrayed Mother's affections were entirely unfamiliar to me. There were photographs of people I had never seen before. Young men who looked rather too smooth for my taste. And other, older people. A jolly couple grinning out from a particularly ornate silver frame looked like Cypriots to me. I picked up a postcard someone had sent Mother from Madeira of all places and scanning the back recognised neither the bright feminine hand, nor the scrawled male salutation and signature.

I was shocked by all of this, but kept silent. Once again I felt sure that if I pressured Mother she would tell me nothing substantial about the afterlife.

The kettle boiled. Mother filled the pot and placed it on a tray, together with cups, sugar, milk and a plate of my favourite chocolate chip cookies. She brought it over and placed it on the low table in front of where I sat. She poured me a cup of tea and offered me a cookie. The conversation lapsed for a while. I munched and Mother went into the kitchenette and opened a can of cat food. She let a couple of black kittens in from the back garden.

'New cats, I see.'

'Uh-huh, that's Tillie and that's Margaret.' The cats lurked and smarmed themselves around the furniture. I wondered idly if they were familiars and if my mother had really always been the kind of witch my father had said she was.

I started browsing through the books. They weren't the same as her mortal collection – I had those – but they covered the same ground: Virago Classics, a lot of Henry James and Proust in several different editions, scores of miscellaneous novels, books on gardening and cookery. By now I was quite openly looking for something, some clue. I couldn't admit it to myself but once again Mother was managing to rile me as much dead as she ever had alive.

I went over to the phone table. There was an address book lying open which I started to flick through idly. Again there were the same kind of names, but they belonged to totally different people, presumably the ones in the photographs, the ones who sent cards. Mother had always struck up acquaintances fairly easily. It wasn't so much that she was friendly as that she exuded a certain wholesome quality, as palpably as if a vent had been opened on her forehead and the smell of bread baking had started to churn out. In my view this wholesome quality was the worst kind of misrepresentation. If there had been such a body as the Personality Advertising Standards Commission, Mother would have been the subject of numerous complaints.

There were phone directories stacked under the table – phone directories and something else, phone-directory-shaped, that wasn't a phone directory. I bent down and pulled it out by its spine. It *was* a phone directory. *North London Book of the Dead*, ran the title; and then underneath: *A–Z*. The cover was the usual yellow flimsy card and there was also the usual vaguely arty line drawing – in this instance of Kensal Green Cemetery. I started to leaf through the pages.

'So, you're not here five minutes and you want to use the phone,' said Mother coming back in from the kitchenette.

'What's this, Mother?' I held up the directory.

'Oh that. Well I guess you might call it a kind of religious text.' She giggled unnervingly.

'Mother, don't you think it's about time you came clean with me about all of this?'

We sat down at the table (similar melamine finish, similar blue, flower-patterned tablecloth) with the *North London Book of the Dead* in between us.

'Well, it's like this,' began Mother. 'When you die you go and live in another part of London. And that's it.'

'Whaddya mean, that's it?' I could already see all sorts of difficulties with this radical new view of death, even if I was sitting inside an example of it. 'Whaddya mean, that's it? Who decides which part of London? How is it that no one's ever heard of this before? How come people don't notice all the dead people clogging up the transport system? What about paying bills? What about this phone book? You can't tell me this lists all the people who have ever died in North London, it isn't thick enough. And what about the dead estate agents, who do they work for? A Supreme Estate Agent? And why Crouch End? You hate Crouch End.'

'It could have been worse, some dead people live in Wanstead.'

'What about the people who lived in Wanstead when they were alive?'

'They live somewhere else, like East Finchley or Grays Thurrock, anywhere.'

'Mother, will you answer my questions, or won't you?'

'I'll just get another cup of tea, dear.'

I wrung it out of her eventually. It went something like this: when you die you move to another part of London where you resume pretty much the same kind of life you had before you died. There are lots of dead people in London and quite a few dead businesses. When you've been dead for a few years you're encouraged to move to the provinces.

The dead community are self-administering and there are dead people in most of the major enterprises, organisations and institutions. There are some autonomous services for dead people, but on the whole dead services operate alongside 'live' ones. Most dead people have jobs, some work for live companies. Mother, for example, was working for a live publishing company.

'OK. I think I've got it so far, but you still haven't explained why it is that no one knows. Now I know I could shout it to the rooftops. I could sell my story to the tabloids.' I was getting quite worked up by now, hunched over and absent-mindedly gobbling chocolate chip cookies with great gulps of tea. I didn't even notice the kittens eating my shoelaces. Mother was imperturbable.

'The funny thing is, that very few people seem to meet dead people who they know. It just goes to show you how big and anonymous the city really is. Even when people do meet dead friends and relatives they don't seem inclined to broadcast the news.'

'But Mother, you've always had an enquiring mind, you always thought you'd rot when you died. Why haven't you got to the bottom of all this? Who's the main man? Is it the "G" character?'

'How should I know? I work, I go to my class, I feed the cats, I see a few friends, I travel. I'm not clever like you, if I do reflect on it at all it seems wholly appropriate. If I had spent days trying to visualise the afterlife I probably could have only come up with a pale version of the very real Crouch End I'm now living in.'

'What class?'

Mother gestured at the phone directory. 'The people who compile the phone book hold regular classes for people who are newly dead. They run through the blue pages at the beginning of the book and explain the best and most appropriate ways for dead people to conduct themselves.'

'I should imagine that there are a lot of newly dead people who are pretty badly traumatised.' I probably said this with unwarranted enthusiasm. I was still trying to look for the gaping holes in Mother's suburban necro-utopia.

'Oh no, not at all. Put it like this: most people who've had painful illnesses, or are lonely, are only too relieved to discover that instead of extinction they're getting Winchmore Hill or Kenton. The classes only go to underline the very reality of the situation. There's something immensely reassuring about sitting on a plastic chair in a cold church hall reading a phone book and watching a pimply youth trying to draw on a whiteboard with a squeaky magic marker.'

'I see your point. But Mother, you were always so sparky and feisty. It's out of character for you to be so laid back. Aren't you curious to get the whole picture? What happens in other cities? Is it the same? If dead people move to the provinces after a while don't these areas get clogged up and zombified? There are a million questions I'd like the answers to. You always hated groups and here you are submitting to indoctrination in a religion ostensibly run by dead employees of British Telecom. Why? For Christ's sake, why?'

'Yeah, it is kind of weird, isn't it. I think death must have mellowed me.'

We chewed the fat for a while longer. Mother asked me about my sex life and whether or not I had an overdraft. She also asked about the rest of the family and expressed the opinion that both my brothers were insane and that some gay people we knew were 'nice boys'. All this was characteristic and reassuring. She let me take a closer look at the *North London Book of the Dead*. It was genuinely uninspiring, based entirely on fact with no prophecies or commandments. The introductory pages were given over to flat statements such as: 'Your (dead) identity should hold up to most official enquiries. Dead people work in most major civil service departments ensuring that full records of dead people are kept up to date. Should you in any instance run into difficulties, call one of the Dead Citizens' Advice Bureaux listed in the directory.' And so on.

Somehow, reading the book calmed me down and I stopped harassing Mother with my questions. After an hour or so she said that she was going out to a party a friend of hers was throwing. Would I like to come? I said, 'I think I can probably do better than socialising with dead people,' and instantly regretted it. 'Sorry Mother.'

'No offence taken, son,' she smiled. This was completely uncharacteristic and her failure to get violently angry filled me with dismay. She let me out of the flat just as a small wan moon was lifting off over the shoulder of Ally Pally. I set off towards Stroud Green Road buzzing with weird thoughts and apprehensions.

That night I thrashed around in bed like a porpoise. My duvet became saturated with sweat. I felt as if I were enfolded in the damp palm of a giant ... Mother! I awoke with a start, the alarm clock blinked 3.22 a.m., redly. I sat on the edge of my bed cradling my dripping brow. It came to me why I should be having such a nightmare. I wanted to betray Mother. It wasn't out of any desire to change once and for all the metaphysical status quo, or because I wanted to open people's eyes to the reality of their lives, or even in order to try and blow a whistle on the Supreme Being. It was a far more selfish thing – wounded pride. Mother could have kept in touch, she let me go through all that grief while *she*, she was pottering around the shops in Crouch End. She could have fixed up some sort of gig with a séance or a medium, or even just written a letter or phoned. I would have understood. Well she wasn't going to push *my* buttons from beyond the grave. I was determined to blow the whistle on the whole set-up.

But the next day came and, standing on a tube platform contemplating the rim of a crushed styrofoam cup as if it contained some further relevation, I began to waver. I sat at my desk all morning in a daze, not that that matters. Then, at lunch time, I went and sat in a café in a daze.

When I got back to my desk after lunch the phone rang. It was Mother.

'I just called to see how you are.'

'I'm fine, Mother.'

'I called while you were out and spoke to some girl. Did she give you the message?'

'No, Mother.'

'I told her specifically to give you the message, to write it down. What's the matter with the people in your office?'

'Nothing, Mother. She probably forgot.'

Mother sighed. For her, neglected phone messages had always represented the very acme of Babylonian decadence. 'So what are you doing?'

'Working, Mother.'

'You're a little sulky today. What's the matter, didn't you sleep?'

'No, I didn't. I found yesterday all a bit much.'

'You'll adjust, kid. Come over tonight and meet Christos, he's a friend of mine – a Greek Cypriot – he runs a wholesale fruit business, but he writes in his spare time. You'll like him.'

'Yeah, I think I saw his photo at your place yesterday. Is he dead, Mother?'

'Of course he's dead. Be here by 8.00. I'm cooking. And bring some of your shirts, you can iron them here.' She hung up on me.

Ray, who works at the desk opposite, was looking at me strangely when I put down the receiver.

'Are you OK?' he said. 'It sounded like you were saying "Mother" on the phone just now.'

I felt tongue-tied and incoherent. How could I explain this away? 'No . . . no, ah . . . I wasn't saying "Mother", it was "Mudder", a guy called Mudder, he's an old friend of mine.'

Ray didn't look convinced. We'd worked with each other for quite a while and he knew most of what went on with me, but what could I say? I couldn't tell him who it *really* was. I'd never live down the ignominy of having a mother who phoned me at the office.

Ward 9

'Ha ha ha, ha-ha . . . Hoo, h', hoo, far, far and away, a mermaid sings in the silky sunlight.' An idiot cooed to himself on the park bench that stood at the crest of the hill. Below him the green-sward stretched down to the running track. In the middle distance the hospital squatted among the houses, a living ziggurat, thrusting out of a crumbling plain.

The idiot's hair had been chopped into a ragged tonsure. He wore a blue hooded anorak and bell-bottomed corduroy trousers, and rocked as he sang. As I passed by I looked into his face; it was a face like the bench he sat on, a sad, forlorn piece of municipal furniture – although the morning sun shone bright, this face was steadily being drizzled on.

This particular idiot lay outside my jurisdiction. He was, as it were, un-gazetted. I knew that by ignoring the opportunity to indulge in the sickly bellyburn of self-piteous caring, I was facing up to an occupational challenge. If I was to have any success in my new job I would need to keep myself emotionally inviolate, walled off. For, this morning, I was to begin an indefinite appointment as art therapist, attached to Ward 9. My destination was the squat fifteen-storey building that rose up ahead of me, out of the tangled confluence of Camden Town.

I bounced down the hill, the decrease in altitude matched pace for pace by the mounting density of the air. The freshness of the atmosphere on Parliament Hill gave way to the contaminated cotton wool of ground-floor, summer London. Already, at 8.45 a.m., the roads around Gospel Oak were solidly coagulated with metal while shirtsleeved drivers sat and blatted out fumes.

As I picked my way through the streets the hospital appeared and then disappeared. Its very vastness made its sight seem problematic. In one street the horizon would flukily exclude it in such a convincing way that it might never have existed, but when I rounded the corner there was its flank rearing up – the grey-blue haunch of some massive whale – turning away from me, sending up a terrace of concrete flats with a lazy flip of its giant tail.

I walked and walked and the hospital never seemed to get any closer. Its sloping sides were banded with mighty balconies, jutting concrete shelves the size of aircraft carrier flight decks. The front of the building was hidden behind a series of zigzagging walkways and ramps that rose in crisscross patterns from the lower ground to the third floor. At the hospital's feet and cuddled in the crook of its great wings-for-arms, were tumbles of auxiliary buildings: nurses' flatlets; parking fortlets; generator units two storeys high, housed in giant, venetian-blind-slatted boxes; and ghostly incinerators, their concrete walls and chimneys blackened with some awful stain.

I rounded the end of the street and found myself, quite suddenly, at the bottom of a ramp that led straight up to the main entrance. The two previous times I had been to the hospital it was a working wasps' nest in full diurnal swing. But now, their photoelectric cells disconnected, the main doors to the hospital were wedged open with orange milk crates. I picked my way through the long, low foyer, past the shop, at this hour still clad in its roll-over steel door, and in between miscellaneous islands of freestanding chairs, bolted together in multiples of two, seemingly at random. They were thinly upholstered in the same blue fabric as the floor covering. The room was lit by flickering strips of overhead neon, so that the whole effect was ghostly; the overwhelming impression was that this was a place of transit, an air terminal for the dying. It was impossible to differentiate the ill from the dossers who had leaked in from the streets and piled their old-clothes forms into the plastic chairs. All were reduced and diminished by the hospital's sterile bulk into untidy parasites. The occasional nurse, doctor or auxiliary walked by briskly. They were uniformed and correct, clearly members of some other, genetically distinct, grouping.

In the glassed-in corridor that led to the lifts there was an exhibition of paintings – not by the patients, but by some pale disciple of a forgotten landscape school. The etiolated blues and greens chosen to take the place of hills and plains were flattened to sheens behind glass, which reflected the dead architectural centre of the hospital: an atrium where a scree of cobblestones supported uncomfortable concrete tubs, which in turn sprouted spindly, spastic trees.

I shared the lift to the ninth floor with a silent young man in green, laced at hip and throat. His sandy, indented temples with their gently pulsing veins aroused in me an attack of itchy squeamishness – I had to touch what repelled me. I scratched the palms of my hands and longed to take off my shoes and scratch the soles of my feet. The itch spread over my body like a hive and still I couldn't take my eyes off that pulsing tube of blood, so close to both surface and bone.

At the ninth floor the sandy man straightened up, sighed, and disappeared off down a corridor with an entirely human shrug.

I'd been on to the ward before, albeit briefly, when Dr Busner had shown me round after the interview. What had struck me then and what struck me again now was the difference in smell between Ward 9 and the rest of the hospital. Elsewhere the air was a flat filtered brew; superficially odourless and machined, but latent with a remembered compound of dynasties of tea bags – squeezed between thumb and plastic spoon – merging into extended families of bleaching, disinfecting froths and great vanished tribes of plastic bags. But in Ward 9 the air had a real quality, it clamped itself over your face like a pad of cotton wool, soaked through with the sweet chloroform of utter sadness.

A short corridor led from the mouth of the lift to the central association area of the ward. This was a roughly oblong space with the glassed-off cabinet of the nurses' station on the short lift side; a dining area to the right looking out through a long strip of windows over the city; to the left were the doors to various offices and one-to-one treatment rooms; and straight ahead another short corridor led to the two dormitories.

Every attempt had been made to present Ward 9 as an ordinary sort of place where people were treated for mental illnesses.

There were bulletin boards positioned around the association area festooned with notices, small ads, flyers for theatrical performances by groups of hospital staff, clippings from newspapers, drawings and cartoons by the patients. Over in the dining area a few of the tables had rough clay sculptures blobbed on them, left there like psychotic turds. I assumed that they were the products of my predecessor's last art therapy session. Around the open part of the area there were scattered chairs, the short-legged, upholstered kind you only find in institutions. And everywhere the eye alighted – the dining area, the nurses' station, dotted in the open area – were ashtrays. Ashtrays on stands, cut-glass ashtrays, lopsided spiral clay ashtrays, ashtrays bearing the names of famous beers; all of them overflowing with butts.

There are two kinds of institution that stand alone on the issue of smoking. Whereas everywhere else you go you encounter barrages of signs enjoining you to desist, slashing your cigarette through with imperious red lines, in psychiatric wards and police stations the whole atmosphere positively cries out to you, 'Smoke! Smoke! We don't mind, we understand, we like smoking!' Ward 9 was no exception to this rule. Empty at this hour (the patients had no reason to get up, they didn't roll over in their beds at 8.00 sharp and think to themselves, 'Ooh! I must get up quickly and have my shot of thorazine . . . '), the whole ward still whirled and eddied with last night's acrid work.

I walked down the short corridor to the nurses' station. A young man sat behind the desk completely absorbed in a dog-eared paperback. He wore a black sweat shirt and black Levis; his sneakered feet, propped on the cluttered shelf of clipboards and Biros, pushed the rest of him back and up on two wheels of his swivel chair. As I stood and observed him, he rocked gently from side to side, his body unconsciously mirroring the short, tight arcs that his eyes made across the page.

I shuffled my feet a little on the linoleum to warn him that he was no longer alone. 'Good morning.'

He looked up from his book with a smile. 'Hi. What can I do you for?'

'I'm Misha Gurney, the new art therapist, I start on the ward today and Dr Busner asked me to come in early to get a feel for things.'

'Well, hello Misha Gurney, I'm Tom.' Tom swung his feet

off the ledge and proffered a hand. It was a slim, white hand, prominently bony at the wrist with long, tapering fingers. His handshake was light and dry but firm. His voice had the contrived mellowness of some Hollywood pilgrim paterfamilias. There was something unsettling in the contrast between this and his beautiful face: sandalwood skin and violet eyes. The body, under the stretchy black clothes, moved in an epicene, undulant way. 'Well, there's not a lot to see at this time. Zack isn't even in yet. He's probably just getting out of bed.' Tom rolled his lovely eyes back in their soft, scented sockets as if picturing the psychiatrist's matitudinal routine. 'How about some tea?'

'Yeah, great.'

'How do you take it?'

'Brown – no sugar.'

I followed Tom down the corridor that led to the staff offices and the consultation rooms. There was a small kitchenette off to one side. Tom hit the lights, which flickered once and then sprang into a hard, flat, neon glare. He squeaked around the lino in his sneakers. I examined the handwritten notices carefully taped to the kitchen cabinets. After a while I said, 'What do you do here, Tom?'

'Oh, I'm a patient.'

'I assume you're not on a section?'

He laughed. 'Oh, no. No, of course not, I'm a voluntary committal. A first-class volunteer, exemplary courage, first in line to be called for the mental health wars.' Again the light mocking irony, but not mad in any way, without the fateful snicker-snack of true schizo-talk.

'You don't seem too disturbed.'

'No, I'm not, that's why they let me go pretty much where I please and do pretty much what I want, as long as I live on the ward. You see, I'm a rare bird.' A downward twist of the corner of a sculpted mouth, 'The medication actually works for me. Zack doesn't really like it, but it's true. As long as I take it consistently I'm fine, but every time they've discharged me in the past, somehow I've managed to forget and then all hell breaks loose.'

'Meaning . . . ?'

'Oh, fits, delusions, hypermania, the usual sorts of things. I carry the Bible around with me and try and arrange spontaneous exegetical seminars in the street. You know, you've seen plenty of crazies, I'll bet.'

'But . . . but, you'll forgive me, but I'm not altogether convinced. If you're on any quantity of medication . . . '

'I know, I should be a little more slowed down, a little fuzzier around the edges, *un peu absent*. Like I say, I'm an exception, a one-off, an abiding proof of the efficacy of Hoffman La Roche's products. Zack doesn't like it at all.'

The kettle whistled and Tom poured the water into two styrofoam cups. We mucked around with plastic dipsticks and extracted the distended bags of tea, then wandered back to the association area. Tom led me over to the windows. The lower decks of the hospital poked out below us. Up here on the ninth floor, more than ever, one could appreciate the total shape of the building — a steeply sloping bullion bar, each ascending storey slightly smaller than the one below it. On the wide balcony beneath us figures were wafting about, clad in hospital clothing, green smocks and blue striped nightdresses, all bound on with tapes. The figures moved with infinite diffidence, as if wishing to offer no offence to the atmosphere. They trundled in slow eddies towards the edge of the balcony and stood rocking from heel to toe, or from side to side, and then moved back below us and out of sight again.

'Chronics,' said Tom, savouring the word as he slurped his tea. 'There's at least sixty of them down there. Quite a different ball game. Not a lot of use for your clay and sticky-backed paper down there. There's a fat ham of a man down there who went mad one day and drank some bleach. They replaced his oesophagus with a section cut from his intestine. On a quiet night you can hear him farting through his mouth. That's a strange sound, Misha.'

I remained silent, there was nothing to say. Behind me I could hear the ward beginning to wake up and start the day. There were footsteps and brisk salutations. An auxiliary came into the association area from the lift and began to mop the floor with studious inefficiency, pushing the zinc bucket around with a rubber foot. We stood and drank tea and looked out over the chronics' balcony to the Heath beyond, which rose up, mounded and green, with the sun shining on it, while the hospital remained in shadow. It was like some separate arcadia glimpsed down a long corridor. I fancied I could see the park bench I'd passed some forty minutes earlier and on it a blue speck: the tonsured idiot, still rocking, still free.

Zack Busner came hurrying in from the lift. He was a plump, fiftyish sort of man, with iron-grey hair brushed back in a widow's peak. He carried a bulging briefcase, the soft kind fastened with two straps. The straps were undone, because the case contained too many files, too many instruments, too many journals, too many books and a couple of unwrapped, fresh, cream-cheese bagels. Busner affected striped linen or poplin suits and open-necked shirts; his shoes were anomalous — black, steel-capped, policeman's shit kickers. He spotted me over by the window with Tom and, turning towards his office, gestured to me to follow him, with a quick, flicking kind of movement. I dropped my foam beaker into a bin, smiled at Tom and walked after the consultant.

'Well Misha, I see you've found a friend already.' Busner smiled at me quizzically and ushered me to the chair that faced his across the desk. We sat. His office was tiny, barely larger than a cubicle, and quite bare apart from a few textbooks and four artworks. Most psychiatrists try to humanise their offices with such pieces. They think that even the most awful rubbish somehow indicates that they have 'the finer feelings'. Busner's artworks were unusually dominant, four large clay bas-reliefs, one on each wall. These rectangular slabs of miniature upheaval, earth-coloured and unglazed, seemed to depict imaginary topographies.

'Yes, he's personable enough. What's the matter with him?'

'Actually, Tom's quite interesting.' Busner said this without a trace of irony and began fiddling around on the surface of his desk, as if looking for a tobacco pipe. 'He's subject to what I'd call a mimetic psychosis . . . '

'Meaning?'

'Meaning he literally mimics the symptoms of all sorts of other mental illnesses, at least those that have any kind of defined pathology: schizophrenia, chronic depression, hypermania, depressive psychosis. The thing about Tom's impersonations, or should I say the impersonations of his disease, is that they're bad performances. Tom carefully reiterates every recorded detail of aberrant behaviour, but with a singular lack of conviction; it's wooden and unconvincing. Your father would have found it fascinating to watch.'

'Well, I find it pretty fascinating myself, even if I don't have quite the same professional involvement. What phase is Tom in now?'

'You tell me.'

'Well, he seems to be playing the "Knowing Patient Introduces Naive Art Therapist to Hell of Ward" role.'

'And how well is he doing it?'

'Well, now you mention it, not too convincingly.'

Busner had abandoned his search for a pipe, if that's what it had been. He now turned and presented me with his outline set against the window. In profile I could see that he was in reality rather eroded, and that the impression of barely contained energy which he seemed determined to project was an illusion as well. Busner sat talking to me, rolling and then unrolling the brown tongue of a knitted tie he wore yanked around his neck. Overall, he reminded me of nothing so much as a giant frog.

Behind him light and then shadow moved across the face of the hospital at a jerky, unnatural speed. The clouds were whipping away overhead, out of sight. All I could see was their reflection on the hospital's rough, grey, barnacle-pitted skin.

The hospital was big. Truly big. With its winking lights, belching vents and tangled antennae, it slid away beneath the cloudscape. Its bulk was such that it suggested to the viewer the possibility of spaceships (or hospitals) larger still, which might engulf it, whole, through some docking port. The hospital was like this. I couldn't judge whether the rectangles I saw outlined on the protruding corner opposite Dr Busner's office were glass bricks or windows two storeys high. The street lay too far below to give me a sense of scale. I was left just with the hospital and the scudding shadows of the racing clouds.

Busner had given up his tie-rolling and taken up with an ashtray on his desk. This was crudely fashioned out of a spiralled snake of clay, varnished and painted with a bilious yellow glaze. Busner ran his fleshy digit around and around the rim as he said, 'I'd like you to stick close to me this morning, Misha. If you are to have any real impact on what we're trying to do here you need to be properly acquainted with the whole process of the ward: how we assess patients, how we book them in, how we decide on treatment. If you shadow me this morning, you can then get to know some of the patients informally this afternoon.'

'That sounds OK.'

'We've also got a ward meeting at noon which will give you an opportunity to get to know all your fellow workers and appreciate how they fit into the scheme of things.'

Busner set down the turd of clay on his desk with a clack and stood up. I stepped back to allow him to get round the desk and to the door. Despite being the senior consultant in the psychiatric department, Busner had about as much office space as a post-room boy. I followed him back down the short corridor to the association area. By now the sun had risen up behind the clouds and the bank of windows on the far side of the dining area shone brightly. Silhouetted against them was a slow line of patients, shuffling towards the nurses' station where they were picking up their morning medication.

The patients were like piles of empty clothes, held upright by some static charge. Behind the double sliding panes of glass which fronted the nurses' station sat two young people. One consulted a chart, the other selected pills and capsules from compartments in a moulded plastic tray. They then handed these over to the patient at the head of the queue, together with a paper beaker of water, which had a pointed base, rendering it unputdownable, like a best seller.

'Not ideal, but necessary.' Busner cupped his right hand as if to encapsulate the queue. 'We have to give medication. Why? Because without it we couldn't calm down our patients enough to actually talk to them and find out what the matter is. However, once we've medicated them they're often too displaced to be able to tell us anything useful. Catch-22.'

Busner cut through the queue to the dining area, muttering a few good mornings as he gently pushed aside his flock. We sat down at a table where a young woman in a frayed white coat was sipping a muddy Nescafé. Busner introduced us.

'Jane, this is Misha Gurney, Misha, Jane Bowen – Jane is the senior registrar here. Misha is joining us to manage art therapy – quite a coup, I think. His father, you know, was a friend of mine, a close contemporary.'

Jane Bowen extended her hand with an overarm gesture that told me she couldn't have cared less about me, or my antecedents, but because she thought of herself as an essentially open-minded and kind person she was going to show me a welcoming smile. I clasped her hand briefly and looked at her. She was slight, with one of those bodies that seemed to be all concavities – her cheeks were hollowed, her eyes scooped, her neck centrally cratered. Under her loose coat I sensed her body as an absence, her breasts as inversions. Her hair was tied back in one long plait, held by an ethnic leather clasp. Her top lip quested towards her styrofoam beaker. The unrolled, frayed ends of her stretchy pullover protruded beyond the frayed cuffs of her cotton coat. Her pockets were stuffed full. They overflowed with pens, thermometers, syringes, watches, stethoscopes, packets of tobacco and boxes of matches. The lapels of the coat were festooned with name badges, homemade badges, political badges and badges of cut-out cartoon characters: Roadrunner, Tweetypie, Bugs Bunny and Scooby Doo.

'Well, Misha, any ideas on how your participation in the ward's creative life will help to break the mould?' She gestured towards an adjacent table, where several misshapen clay vessels leant against one another like drunken Rotarians.

'Well, if the patients want to make clay ashtrays, let them make clay ashtrays.' I lit a cigarette and squinted at her through the smoke.

'Of course they could always try and solve The Riddle.'

I hadn't noticed as I sat down, but now I saw that she was shifting the four pieces of a portable version of The Riddle around on the melamine surface in front of her. Her fingers were bitten to the quick and beyond. Busner flushed and shifted uneasily in his chair.

'Erumph! Well . . . bankrupt stock and all that. We have rather a lot of The Riddle sets around the ward. I err . . . bought them up for a pittance, you know. At any rate, I still have some faith in them and the patients seem to like them.'

Busner had been responsible for designing, or 'posing', The Riddle in the early Seventies. It was one of those pop psychological devices that had had a brief vogue. Busner himself had been forging a modest career as a kind of media psychologist with a neat line in attacking the mores of conventional society. The Riddle tied in with this and with the work that Busner was doing at his revolutionary Concept House in Willesden. His involvement with the early development of the Quantity Theory also dated from that period.

Busner was a frequent trespasser on the telly screens of my childhood. Always interviewing, being interviewed, discussing an interview that had just been re-screened, or appearing in those discussion programmes where paunchy people sat on uncomfortable steel rack-type chairs in front of a woven back-drop. Busner's media activities had dropped away as he grew paunchier. He was now remembered, if at all, as the poser of The Riddle – and that chiefly because the short-lived popularity of this 'enquire-within tool' had spawned millions of square acrylic slabs of just the right size to get lost and turn up in idiosyncratic places around the house, along with spillikins, Lego blocks and hairpins. In fact it had become something of a catch-phrase to cry as you dug a tile out from between the carpet and the underlay, or from behind a radiator, 'I'm solving The Riddle!' Eventually The Riddle itself – what you were actually meant to do with the four square slabs in bright pastel shades, which you got with The Riddle set – was entirely forgotten.

'I'm sorry Zack, I didn't mean to sound caustic.' Jane Bowen placed a surprisingly tender hand on Busner's poplin sleeve.

'That's all right, I think I still deserve it, even after all these years. The funny thing is that I did believe in The Riddle. I suppose a cynic would say that anyone would believe in some-thing that brought in enough income to buy a four-bedroom house in Redington Road.'

'Even shrinks have to have somewhere to live,' said Jane Bowen. The two of them smiled wryly over this comment – a little more wryly than it strictly merited.

'Well, we're not helping anybody sitting here, are we?' said Busner. Once again this was a key motif. It had been his catch-phrase on all those discussion and interview programmes – always delivered with falsetto emphasis on the 'helping'. The catch-phrase, like The Riddle, outlived Busner's own popularity. I remember seeing him towards the very end of his TV sojourn, when he was reduced to going on one of those 'celebrity' game-shows where the celebrities sit in a rack of cubicles. Zack trotted out his obligatory line and the contestant dutifully pushed the button on the tape machine – as I recall, she ended up winning a suite of patio furniture. It was really quite a long way from the spirit of radical psychology. Now Busner was using the phrase again, clearly with a sense of irony – but somehow not altogether; there was also something else there, a strange kind of pride almost.

'I want you to shadow me while I do the ward round.' Busner guided me by placing his palm on my shoulder. We both nodded to Jane Bowen, who had forgotten us already and fallen into conversation with a nurse. Busner stashed his bursting briefcase behind the nurses' station, after extracting from it with difficulty a clipboard and some sheets of blank paper. We walked side by side down the short corridor that led to the entrance to the two wards. For some reason Busner and I were unwilling to precede one another, and as a result people coming in the other direction had to crush up against the walls to get around us. We were like a teenage couple – desperate to avoid any break in contact that might let in indifference.

The dormitories were laid out in a series of bays, four beds in each bay and four bays to the dormitory. Each bay was about the size of an average room, the beds laid out so as to provide the maximum surrounding space for each occupant to turn into their own private space. Some of the patients had stuck photographs and posters up on the walls with masking tape, some had placed knick-knacks on the shelves, and others had done nothing and lay on their beds, motionless, like ascetics or prisoners.

Busner kept up a commentary for my benefit as we stopped and consulted with each patient. The first one we came to was a pop-eyed man in his mid-thirties. He was wearing a decrepit Burton suit which was worn to a shine at knee and elbow. He was sitting on the easy chair by his bed and staring straight ahead. His shoulder-length hair was scraped down from a severe central parting. His eyes weren't just popping, they were half out of their sockets, resembling ping-pong balls with the pupils painted on to them like black spots.

'Clive is prone to bouts of mania, aren't you, Clive?'
'Good morning, Dr Busner.'
'How are you feeling, Clive?'
'Fine, thank you, Doctor.'
'Any problems with your medication? You'll be leaving us soon, won't you?'

'In answer to your first question, no. In answer to your second, yes.'

'Clive likes everything to be stated clearly, don't you, Clive?'

At the time I thought Busner was being sarcastic. In fact – as I realised later – this wasn't the case. If anything, Busner was being solicitous. He knew that Clive liked to expatiate on his attitudes and methods; Busner was providing him with the opportunity.

'You're staring very fixedly at the opposite wall, Clive, would you like to tell Misha why this is?'

I followed his line of sight; he was looking at a poster which showed two furry little kittens both dangling by their paws from the handle of a straw basket. The slogan underneath in curly script proclaimed, 'Faith isn't Faith until it's all you're hanging on to.'

'The kitten is powerful.' Clive smiled enigmatically and pointed with a dirt-rimmed nail, 'That kitten holds in its paws the balance, the egg of creation and more.' Having pronounced he lapsed back into a rigid silence. Busner and I left him.

Although there were only thirty or so patients on the ward they soon resolved themselves, not into names or individuals, but into distinct groups. Busner's catchment area for his ward was an L-shaped zone that extended from the hospital in one dog-leg into the very centre of the city. The hospital pulled in its sustenance from every conceivable level of society. But on Ward 9 insanity had proved a great leveller. A refugee sometimes seems to have no class. The English depend on class, to the extent that whenever two English people meet, they spend nano-seconds in high-speed calculation. Every nuance of accent, every detail of apparel, every implication of vocabulary, is analysed to produce the final formula. This in turn provides the coordinates that will locate the individual and determine the Attitude. The patients on Ward 9 had distanced themselves from this. They could not be gauged in such a fashion. Instead, I divided them up mentally into the following groups: thinnie-pukies, junkies, sads, schizes and maniacs. The first four groups were all represented about equally, whilst the fifth group was definitely in the ascendant; there were lots of maniacs on Ward 9 and by maniacs I mean not the culturally popular homicidal maniac, but his distant herbivorous cousin, hyper, rather than homicidal, and manic, rather than maniacal.

As Tom had already characterised himself earlier that morning, hypermanic types are lecturers; extramural, al fresco professors, who, like increasingly undulant or syncopated Wittgensteins, address the world at large on a patchwork syllabus made up of Kabbalah, astrology, tarot, numerology and Bible (specifically Revelations) study. They are sad-mad, they know they are ill, they have periods of conformity, but they are always somehow out of joint.

'Art therapy is very popular here, Misha.' Busner detained me in the vestibule between the two wards. 'We can't keep the patients sufficiently occupied, they have treatment sessions of various kinds in the mornings, but in the afternoons you'll be all they have to look forward to. Sometimes we can arrange an outing of some kind, or a friend or relative will be allowed to take them out on the Heath, but otherwise they're cooped up here in a fuddled daze.'

We went on into the women's dormitory. Here things seemed, at first, different. On the men's dormitory Busner and I had spoken with a few isolated individuals, backed off into their individual bays. But here the patients seemed to be associating with one another. They reclined on beds chatting, or sat round the formica-topped tables which formed a central reservation.

A skeleton with long, lush hair rocked on a bed in the bay to our right, an obscenely large catheter protruding out of her lolly-stick arm. Busner took me in under tow and introduced us.

'Hilary isn't that keen on eating – or at least she is sometimes, but she doesn't really like the nutritional side-effects of food. Hilary, this is Misha Gurney, he's our new art therapist.' Hilary stopped rocking and gave me a level smile from underneath neatly coiffed chestnut bangs.

'Hello. I'll look forward to this afternoon. I like to paint, I like watercolours. These are some of mine.' She gestured towards the wall at the head of the bed, where an area about a foot square was tiled with tiny watercolours, terribly painfully precise little paintings – all portraits, apparently of young women. Busner wandered off, but I remained and walked to the head of the bed, so that I could examine the pictures thoroughly. They had been executed with a fanatical attention to the detail of make-up and hair which made them almost grotesque. Hilary and I sat sideways to each other. With her neck canted around so that she could face me, Hilary's greaseproof-paper skin stretched, until I could see the twisted, knotted coils of tendon and artery that lay within.

'They're very good. Who are all these people?'

'They're my friends. I paint them from photographs.'

'Your pictures are very detailed. How do you manage it?'

'Oh, I have special pens and brushes. I'll show you later.'

I left Hilary and went over to where Busner was sitting at one of the tables in the central area of the dormitory.

'Has Hilary been telling you about her friends?'

'Yes . . . '

'Hilary doesn't have any friends, as such. She cuts pictures of models out of advertisements in magazines, then she paints over them. She's been in and out of this ward for the past three years. Every time she comes in she looks like she does now. She's so close to death we have to put her on a drip. She's usually completely demented; the amino acids have been leeched out of her brain. After she's been on the drip for a while we transfer her to a tight regime of supervised eating based on a punishment/reward system, and at the same time she undergoes an intensive course of psychotherapy with Jane Bowen. Jane is very much the expert on eating disorders. After six weeks to two months Hilary is back to a healthy weight and eating sensibly. She'll leave and we can predict her return usually to within the day – some four months later.'

'I thought a lot of anorexics and bulimics grew out of it?'

'To some extent, but there's always a hard core and at the moment it seems to be growing. These long-term anorexics are different, they're placid, resigned and apparently unconscious of any motivation. The temporaries tend to be wilful, obstinate and obviously powerfully neurotic. These hard-cores, like Hilary, could almost be psychologically blameless. Some of them even have fairly stable relationships. They're at a loss to explain what comes over them, it seems to be somehow external, imposed from elsewhere.'

I should have been paying attention to what Busner was saying, but I couldn't concentrate. For a start there was the strangeness of the situation – I'd only ever spent isolated periods of a few minutes on psychiatric wards before. I had known what to expect in broad terms, but it was the relentlessness of the ambience that was beginning to get to me. There was something cloacal about the atmosphere in the women's ward. None of the patients seemed to have bothered to dress, they sat here and there talking, wearing combinations of night and day clothes. There was a preponderance of brushed cotton. I sensed damp, and smelt oatmeal, porridge, canteen; indefinable, closed-in odours.

I could walk away from the tonsured idiot on the Heath, but inside Ward 9 I was trapped. And these people weren't pretending. They weren't closet neurotics or posing eccentrics, Bohemians. They were the real thing. Real loss of equilibrium, real confusion, real sadness, that wells up from inside like an unstaunchable flow of blood from a severed artery. I felt my gorge rising. I felt my forehead, it was sandpaper-dry. Busner was neglecting me and talking to a pneumatic nurse. The nurses on Ward 9 didn't wear a uniform as such, rather they affected various items of medical garb: tunics, coats and smocks, name-plates and watches pinned at the breast. This nurse had a man's Ingersoll attached by a safety-pin to her jacket lapel. She had blonde baby curls, bee-stung lips and the creamy, slightly spongy complexion that invariably goes with acrid coital sweats. I forced myself to listen to what they were saying, and fought down nausea with concentration.

'Take her out to the optician then, Mimi, if she has to go.'

'Oh, she does, Zack, she can barely see a yard in front of herself. She can't be expected to deal with reality if she can't see it.' The voluptuous Mimi was squidged on to the corner of the table. Behind her stood a short woman in her thirties with the hydrocephalic brow and oblique domed crop of an intelligent child. She stared at me with sightless eyes.

'Rachel shouldn't really be off the ward, considering the medication she's on.'

'But Zack, it's a walk down to the parade, ten minutes at most. Give her a break.'

'Oh, all right.'

'Come on then, Rachel, get your coat on.' Rachel bounced away into one of the bays. Mimi lifted herself off the edge of the table and winked at me in a languid way.

'Come on, Misha, we've got an admission for you to see. I'll leave you at the front desk. Anthony Valuam will pick you up and take you down to casualty.' We walked out of the women's dormitory and back to the association area. Tom, my friend from the earlier part of the morning, was back behind the nurses' station, reading his dog-eared Penguin. Busner despatched me to wait with him by giving me a gentle shove in the small of my back, then he crooked his finger at a scrofulous youth in a tattered sharkskin suit who sat smoking and disappeared with him towards his office. Tom put down his book and treated me to another little conspiratorial exchange.

'Has the good doctor given you a little tour?'

'We've been round the ward, yes.'

'Beginning to catch on yet?'

'What do you mean?'

'Well, who did you get introduced to? No, don't tell me. Let me guess. You talked to Clive and then you saw a lot of other male patients quite quickly until you ended up scrutinising Hilary's watercolours.'

'Err . . . yes.'

'And did Zack come out with his catch-phrase?'

'Yes, when we were talking to Jane Bowen.'

'Thought so. He's so predictable. That's one of the truly therapeutic aspects of this place, the unfailing regularity of Dr Busner. What are you doing now?'

'I'm meant to be going down to casualty to sit in on an admission with a Dr Valuam.'

'Tony, yeah. Well, he's my kind of a shrink, not like Dr B; more practical like, more chemical.'

A door opened to the right of the nurses' station which I hadn't noticed before. A very short man came out of it and with neat movements locked it behind him, using a key that was on an extremely large gaoler's bunch. He turned to face me. He was a funny little specimen. He had wispy fair hair teased ineffectually around his bare scalp. It wasn't as if he was going bald, it was more as if he'd never grown any hair to begin with. This impression was supported by the watery blue eyes, and the nose and chin which were soft and seemingly boneless. He wore a stiff blue synthetic suit of Seventies cut and vinyl shoes.

'You must be Misha Gurney. I'm Anthony Valuam.' His

handshake was twisted and rubberised, like holding a retort clamp in a laboratory, but his voice was absurdly mellow and basso. A voice-over rather than a real voice. His foetal face registered and then dismissed my surprise; he must have been used to it. Tom was stifling an obvious giggle behind his paper-back. Valuam ignored him and I followed suit. We walked off down the short corridor to the lift. Valuam launched into an introduction.

'It's very unusual to have an admission through casualty at this time of day. On this ward we deal almost exclusively with referrals, but we know this particular young man and there are very good reasons why he should be treated on Ward 9.'

'And they are . . . ?'

'I don't wish to be enigmatic, but you'll see.'

Valuam fell silent. We waited for the lift, which arrived and slid open and closed and then dropped us down through the hospital to casualty, which was situated in the first sub-basement. The lift stopped on every floor, to take on and drop passengers.

The architects, interior designers and colour consultants who had made the hospital were not insensitive to the difficulties posed by such a project, they had earnestly striven to make this vast, labyrinthine structure seem habitable and human in scale. To this end each floor had been given slightly different wall and floor coverings, slightly different-shaped neon strip-light covers, slightly different concrete cornicing, slightly different steel ventilation-unit housings and slightly different colourings: virology an emphatic pale blue, urology a teasing (but tasteful) green, surgery and cardiology a resilient pink and so on. At each floor the patients and their orderlies were also different colours. The faces and hands of the patients as they were transferred from ward to ward, on steel trolleys, in wheelchairs as heavy as siege engines, were stained with disease, as vividly as a pickled specimen injected with dye.

The orderlies were violently offhand; they manhandled the patients into the lifts like awkward, fifty-kilo bags of Spanish onions. Then they stood menacingly in the corners, lowering over their livid charges, their temples pulsing with insulting health. Occasionally a patient would be wheeled into the lift who was clearly the wrong colour for the direction we were headed in (this was evident as soon as the lift reached the next floor) and the orderly would back the chair or table out of the lift again, the faces of both porter and cargo registering careful weariness at the prospect of another purgatorial wait.

We reached the sub-basement. Valuam turned to the left outside of the lift and led me along the corridor. Down here the colour scheme was a muted beige. The persistent susurration of the air-conditioning was louder than on the ninth floor and was backed up by a deeper throb of generators. The industrial ambience was further underscored by the pieces of equipment which stood at intervals along the corridor, their steel rods, rubber wheels, plastic cylinders and dependant ganglia of electric wiring betrayed no utility.

The beige-tiled floor was scarred with dirty wheel tracks. We whipped past doors with cryptic signs on them: 'Hal-G Cupboard', 'Ex-Offex.Con', 'Broom Station'. The corridor now petered out into a series of partitioned walkways which Valuam picked his way through with complete assurance. We entered a wide area, although the ceiling here was no higher than in the corridor. On either side were soft-sided booths, curtained off with beige plastic sheeting. The beige lights overhead subsonically wittered. We passed stooped personnel – health miners who laboured here with heavy equipment to extract the diseased seam. They were directed by taller foremen, recognisable by their white coats, worn like flapping parodies. Valuam turned to the right, to the left, to the left again. In the unnatural light I felt terribly sensitive as we passed booths where figures lay humped in pain. I felt the tearing, cutting and mashing of tissue and bone like an electrified cotton-wool pad clamped across my mouth and nose.

At length Valuam reached the right booth. He swept aside the curtain. A youth of twenty or twenty-one cowered in a plastic scoop chair at the back of the oblong curtained area. On the left a fiercely preserved woman leant against the edge of the examination couch. On the right stood a wheeled aluminium table. Laid out on it were tissues, a kidney dish of tongue depressors, and a strip of disposable hypodermics wound out of a dispenser box.

Valuam pushed a sickly yellow sharps disposal bin to one side with his blue foot and pulled out another plastic chair. He stretched and shook hands with the woman, who murmured 'Anthony'. Valuam sat down facing the youth and untucked his clipboard from the crook of his arm. It was left for me to lean awkwardly in the opening, looming over the gathering like a malevolent interloper. I was conspicuously ignored.

'Good morning, Simon,' said Valuam. Simon drew a frond of wool out from the cuff of his pullover and let it ping inaudibly back into a tight spiral. Simon was wearing a very handsome pullover, made up of twenty or so irregular wool panels in shades of beige, grey and black. He pinged the thread again and fell to worrying a bloody stalk of cuticle that had detached itself from his gnawed paw.

'Simon and I felt it would be a good idea if he came to stay on the ward with you for a while, Anthony.' The woman uncrossed her ankles and hopped up on to the examination table. Her steely hair was sharply bobbed, one bang pointed at the youth who was her indigent son. She took a shiny clutch bag from under her arm, popped it open and withdrew a tube of mints which she aimed at me.

'Polo?'

'Err . . . thanks.' I took one. She smiled faintly and took one herself.

'How do you feel about that, Simon?' Valuam held his foetal face on one side, his basso voice sounding concerned.

'S'alright.' Simon was rotating the cuticle stalk with the tip of a finger. He was also starting to rock back and forth.

Valuam consulted the papers attached to his clipboard. 'Mmm . . . mm . . . ' He snuffled and ruffled the case notes while the steely-haired woman and I regarded one another peripherally. She really was pretty chic. At neck and wrist she was encircled with linked silver platelets cut into shapes; her clothes were made out of varieties of vicuna and rabbit; her stockings were so pure you could see the mulberry in them. I couldn't quite get the measure of why she was so blasé about Simon's voluntary committal. Genuine lack of caring? A defence mechanism? Something more sinister?

'You were discharged last October, Simon,' Valuam had found the right place, 'and went to the Galston Work Scheme. How did that go?'

'Oh, OK, I guess. I did some good things; worked on some

of my constructions. I enjoyed it.' Simon had given up on the cuticle, he looked up at Valuam and spoke with some animation. His face was quite green in hue and distorted by weeping infections. It was like watching a colour screen where the tube has started to pack up.

'But now you're in pretty bad shape again, aren't you?'

'Yeah, I guess. I'm fed up with living with the bitch.' Simon's mother winced. 'She puts me under pressure the whole time. Do this, do that. It's no wonder I start to freak out.'

'I see. And freaking out means stopping your medication and stopping going to the Galston and stopping your therapy and ending up looking like this.'

Simon had relapsed into torpor before Valuam had finished speaking. The cuticle had claimed his whole attention again. We were left regarding the top of his unruly head.

Valuam sighed. He ticked some boxes on the sheet uppermost on the clipboard and twisted sideways on his plastic chair to face the woman. 'Well, I suppose he'd better come in for a few weeks then.'

'I'm glad you see it that way, Anthony.' She eased herself of the examination couch with a whoosh of wool and silk and patted herself down. 'Well, goodbye then, Simon. I'll come and see you at the weekend.'

'Bye, Mum, take it easy.' Simon didn't look up, he'd found some antiseptic and fell to swabbing his bleeding finger with tight little arcs. His mother smiled absently at Valuam as if acknowledging his sartorial failure. I stood to one side and she nodded at me as she swished out of the cubicle and away.

Valuam got up and scraped the chair back against the wall. 'I have someone to see here, Misha, would you mind taking Simon up to the ward?'

'I'm, er, not sure I'll be able to find my way back.'

'Oh, that's OK, Simon knows the layout of the hospital far better than he knows his own mind.'

I wasn't sure whether I was meant to share in this sick irony – but looking at Valuam's miscarried countenance I could see that he wasn't joking. Simon seemed not to have noticed.

I followed the abstraction of Simon's pullover back through the twisting lanes of the casualty examination area. Even before we'd gained the corridor I found that I'd completely lost my bearings. Simon, however, didn't hesitate, he plunged on unswervingly, walking with long fluid strides. We travelled like a couple arguing; he would make gains on me of some twenty yards and then I'd have to put on a spurt to catch up with him. To begin with I feared that he was actually trying to lose me, but whenever there was a choice of directions and he was some way ahead he waited until I was close enough to see which way he went.

The nature of the corridors we bowled along was perceptibly changing. The machines that stood at intervals against the corridor walls were becoming more obviously utilitarian – parts were now painted black rather than chromed or rubberised – they had petrol engines rather than electric pumps. The walls themselves were changing, they were losing their therapeutic hue and reverting to concrete colour, as was the floor. Lights were becoming exposed, first the odd neon tube was naked and then all of them.

This part of the hospital was beyond the world of work, it was a secret underworld. From time to time we would pass workers clad in strange suits of protective clothing: wearing rubberised aprons, or plastic face masks, or Wellington boots, or leather shoulder pads. They looked at us inscrutably. It was clear that they were intent on their jobs; maintaining the whine, stoking the hum, directing the howl. It was also clear the Simon wasn't taking me back to the ward, he had business here. I caught him on a corner.

'Where are we going, Simon?'

'To see something, something worth seeing. I promise you won't be angry.'

'Can you tell me what it is?'

'No.' He wheeled away, calling over his shoulder, 'Come on, it's not much further.'

The corridor walls gave way to sections of masonry. Embedded in them were the filled-in remains of long-dead windows. I realised that we had reached the place where the new hospital had been grafted on to its predecessor. There were the marks of cast-iron railings, pressed and faint, like fossilised grass stems. More than ever I sensed the great weight of the hospital crouching overhead. A dankness entered the air; at intervals trickling pools of water seeped up on to the floor. Eventually

Simon stopped by a set of double doors, old doors belonging to the former hospital, the top halves glassed with many small panes. He pushed them apart on failing rails.

We were in some sort of conservatory. Round, twenty-five feet across, fifteen feet up the walls gave way to a dirty glass dome, which arched overhead, almost out of sight in the gloom. There was daylight here, filtering down weakly through the tarnished panes. Water dripped audibly. In the centre of the room stood a giant machine for doing things to people. This much was clear from the canted couch positioned halfway up its flank. Otherwise it resembled a giant microscope, the barrel obliquely filling the uncertain volume of the room, the lens pointing directly at the couch. The whole thing was festooned with hydraulic cabling. It had originally been painted a kitchen-cream colour but now it was corroded, atrophied.

Simon and I stood and looked.

'Good, isn't it.' His voice was full and resonant. He'd lost his sullen edge.

'Yes, very striking. What was it for?'

'Oh, I've no idea. I got left alone one night in casualty and just started wandering about, I found this. I don't think anyone's been here for years. Funny, really, because it's right in back of the MDR.'

'MDR?'

Simon beckoned me over to the grey-filmed window opposite the door we'd entered by. I circled the giant machine, stepping over the edge of the vast plate that riveted it to the floor. Bits had fallen off the machine – bolts, braces, other small components – but given the scale of the thing, they were large enough to bruise your shins if you knocked against them. Simon was vigorously rubbing the windowpane.

'Look, can you see?' There was no sense of sky, or the outside, but light came from somewhere. Outlining a squat blockhouse, clapboarded with massive concrete slabs. It was like some defence installation. 'That's the Mass Disaster Room. If there's ever a nuclear attack, or an earthquake, or something like that, that's where all the equipment is kept to deal with it.'

'Well, like what?'

'I don't know, no one will tell me. I only found out about it because I came across the door with the notice on it.'

We stood at the window for a while. The conservatory-like room, the giant machine, the blockhouse. All thinly lit by an invisible day. There was something eerie about the atmosphere. The eeriness that washes over when you step obliquely out of a populous area – from a crowded park into a little grey copse – and look behind you at the life that still goes on, children and dogs.

Back up in the ward Busner was hurrying about the place, gathering together all the staff members. A circle of chairs had been roughly arranged in the association area. Anthony Valuam and Jane Bowen were already seated and engaged in earnest discussion when we arrived. Valuam showed no curiosity about where we had been. Simon himself had reverted to sullen, disturbed type as soon as we arrived at the ninth floor. He disappeared into a shifting knot of movers and shakers and was gone from sight.

'Sit down, Misha, do sit down.' Busner flapped his poplin-bumped turkey-skin arms. I sat down next to Mimi, the voluptuous nurse, who had been and gone to the optician. The rest of the staff began to trickle into place, auxiliary as well as medical. There were canteen ladies here in nylon, elasticated hair covers, and psychiatric social workers with rolled-up newspaper supplements. They chatted to one another quite informally, swopping cigarettes and gesturing. The patients took no notice of this assembly – which to my mind more than anything else underlined their exclusion from the right-thinking world.

Busner called the meeting to order.

'Ahm! Hello everyone. We've a lot to get through today, so I'd like to get under way. We don't want to run over, the way we did last month. Before we come to the first item on the agenda I'd like to introduce to you all a new member of staff, Misha Gurney. Some of you will, no doubt, have heard of his father,' Busner's face purpled at the edges with sentimentality, 'who was a contemporary of mine and a dear friend. So it's an especial pleasure for me that Misha should be joining us on the ward as the new art therapist . . . '

'Wait till you hear what happened to the old art therapist . . . !' Before I had had time to wheel round in my chair and see who had whispered in my ear, Tom was gone, soft-shoe shuffling down the corridor.

From then on the meeting deteriorated into the usual trivial deliberations that – in my experience – seem to accompany all departmental meetings. There were discussions about the hours at which tea could be made, discussions about shift rostering, discussions about patients' visitors. My attention began to falter and then died away altogether. I was staring fixedly over the shoulder of a middle-aged woman who liaised with the ward on behalf of the local social services department. Through the two swing-doors, between her and the entrance to the dormitories, I could see Clive. He was staring at me fixedly, or so it seemed; his great globular eyes were incapable of anything but staring. He was rocking from side to side like a human metronome. If I narrowed my eyes it appeared as if his bizarre messianic hair-do was rhythmically pulsing out of the cheek of the middle-aged social worker. This trick hypnotised me.

Mimi jabbed me in the ribs. 'Misha, pay attention!'

Busner was saying something in my direction. 'Well Misha?' he said.

Mimi whispered, 'He's asking what you intend to do in the art therapy session this afternoon.'

I started guiltily. 'Um . . . well . . . err. I intend really to, ah, introduce myself to the patients with a series of demonstrations of different techniques and then invite them to show their own work so that we can discuss it.'

This seemed to satisfy Busner. He turned to Jane Bowen and whispered something in her ear, she smiled and nodded, tapping a yellow biro stem on the edge of her clipboard.

Soon after this the meeting broke up. I drew Mimi to one side.

'Thanks for that, you saved my hide there. I was miles away.'

'Yeah, absurd isn't it. Zack's like most benevolent dictators, he seems to think that by letting us all discuss a load of trivia we'll feel that we have an important decision-making role in ward policy.'

'How long have you been working here?'

'Oh, quite a while. Ever since I qualified, in fact. There's something about this ward. You might say that it and I were made for one another.' The middle-aged social worker came over to where we were standing, Mimi introduced us and then they went off together to discuss a patient. The social worker was blushing furiously. It wasn't until later that I realised she had thought I was staring at her throughout the ward meeting.

I took my sandwiches up on to the Heath for lunch and sat on the bench with the idiot. He went on ranting and rocking in a muted way, inhibited no doubt by my presence. I offered him a sandwich, which he accepted and then did hideous things to.

I looked over the city. The light pattern had been reversed as I was walking over from the hospital and now the vast ziggurat was bathed in bright light, while the bench where the idiot and I scrunged cheese through our teeth was in deep shadow. Tom had told me that he referred to the hospital, privately, as the Ministry of Love; and it was true that the sepulchral ship forging its way through the grid of streets had something of the future, the corporate about it, mixed in with the despotic past.

The wind whipped across the flight deck entrance to the hospital as I re-entered by the main gates. Well-heeled patients and visitors were being landed by taxis and mini-cabs, while their poorer fellows struggled against the updraft that roared off the hospital's oblique walls – air crewmen and women lacking enlarged ping-pong bats with which to semaphore.

On the ninth floor I met Jane Bowen. She was right outside the lift. Her hands fidgeted at her mouth as the doors rolled open.

'Well, Misha, where have you been?'

'I took my sandwiches up on the Heath. I like to get a little fresh air during the day.'

'Well don't make a habit of it.'

'Why's that?'

'Zack prefers it if all the staff eat in the canteen on the ward . . . '

'You can't be serious . . . !'

'Obviously it isn't imposed on anyone. You're free to do what you want. But Zack has good reasons for it and you need to witness lunch to understand them.'

The association area was thronged with patients, they eddied round the counter in the eating area – more of an enlarged serving hatch really – and then gravitated from there to the medication queue. Busner stood in the centre of it all, like some

Lord of Misrule. He'd donned a shortie white coat which rode up over his rounded hips. The coat pockets were stuffed to overflowing, and because of the way he was standing it looked as if he was wearing a codpiece. Busner waved his arms around his head and turned circles on his heels, his face contorted, with pain? With hilarity? It was impossible to say.

I approached him through swirls of the committed.

'Ah, Misha, I've tangled my spectacles cord up in my tie at the back. Can you see what's going on?' He turned his back on me and I fiddled with the two strands where they had become entwined. 'Ah, that's better.' He clamped the spectacles on to the red grooved bridge of his nose. 'Now I can see. We'd better sort out your materials for you.' He led me over to a wall cupboard at the far end of the dining area from the serving hatch and opened the ceiling-high doors. Inside there was a mess of materials and half-finished attempts at something or other. 'Gerry wasn't great on ordering the materials,' said Busner, stepping forward into the cupboard and crunching pieces of charcoal sticks beneath his heels, 'but everything is here that you could need. I should take it easy, let them come to you and show you what they're up to – try and build up some trust.'

Busner put a cloyingly affectionate arm around my shoulders, he didn't register my wince. We stood side by side, facing a shelf full of streaked tins of powder paint.

'Your father would have been proud of you, Misha. He would have understood what you're doing. You know, in a way I feel as if you're coming home to us here on the ward, that it's the right place for you, don't you agree?' I muttered something negative. 'I'm glad you feel the same way, come and see me when the session is over, tell me how it went.' He wheeled away from me and tracked a series of charcoal arcs across the lino. I was left alone – but not for long.

Tom materialised. At his shoulder was a thirtyish man of medium height and build, unremarkable in lumberjack shirt and denims, remarkable for his arms and his countenance: arms which struggled to escape his body and pushed forward long, muscular, mechanical arms. His face was stretched tight away and zoomed towards his flaring brown hair. The whole impression was one of contained speed.

'This is Jim,' said Tom, 'he can't bear to wait, he wants to get started right away.'

'Yeah. Hi. Jim.' He thrust a tool at me, I shook it, he retracted it. 'I really look forward to these sessions. I'd like to work on my thing all the time, but they won't let me.' I pulled the double doors open wider.

'Which one is it?'

'Here.' He pulled down a sort of sculpture, made from clay, from one of the higher shelves, his long arms cradling the irregular shape protectively. He turned and set it down on one of the rectangular melamine tables.

It was a large piece, perhaps some three and a half feet long and half that wide. Jim had used a base board and built on it with clay. The work had the kind of naive realism I associated with children's television programmes featuring animated figures moving around model villages. The work depicted a descending curve of elevated roadway which I immediately recognised as the Marylebone Flyover. Jim had neatly sculpted the point at which the two flyover lanes remerged with the Marylebone Road, there were tiny clay cars coming down off the flyover and one of them had knocked into a small Japanese fruiterer's van which was coming in from the Edgware Road. Two miniature clay figures were positioned in the road gesticulating. The whole thing cut off at the point where the Lisson Grove intersection would be to the east and where the flyover reaches its apex to the west.

'It's nearly finished,' said Jim. 'Today I'm going to paint and glaze it and then I'd like you to arrange for it to be fired.'

'Well, I can't see any problem with that. Tell me, what's the story behind this sculpture?'

'It's not a sculpture.' He sucked in air through teeth, the weary sigh of a child. 'It's an altarpiece.' He picked up the model flyover and went over to a table by the window with it. Tom giggled.

'Jim's got a messianic complex. He thinks that the Apocalypse isn't coming.'

'What does that mean?'

'It's a bit complicated. The Apocalypse will come when enough people have accepted that it isn't coming.'

'That just sounds stupid.'

43

'Well it isn't fucking stupid, it's you who are fucking stupid, Mister Squeaky, get it!' Tom's voice switched from light mockery to the hair-trigger aggression of the subnormal thug. It was a startling transformation, as if he'd been possessed by a weird demon. He stalked away and joined his friend. I dismissed the insult. Busner had told me about him; it was clear that this was another act.

Over the next half-hour or so, most of the other patients on the ward trickled into the association area and came over to where their peers were already at work, mixing powder paint, working clay with fingers, cutting and pasting pictures from magazines. I was astonished by their quiet industry as a group. There seemed hardly anyone on the ward who was genuinely disruptive. Two or three of the patients stood like metronomes around the working area, swaying and rocking, marking the beat of the others' labour.

Hilary sat at the window and worked on one of her tiny watercolours with hairline brushes. She had propped up the scrap of artboard on a little easel made from lolly sticks and she worked with deft strokes, each one pulling the mobile stand attached to the catheter in her arm, back and forth. The plastic bag that dangled from it contained a clear fluid and a particular sediment. As the stand moved back and forth this sediment puffed up in the bag, the motes occasionally catching and then gleaming in the afternoon sun that washed in through the huge windows.

Simon came over and asked me for scissors, glue and stiff paper. He took a half-finished collage from one of the cupboard shelves and sat down near me. It depicted the machine he'd taken me to see that morning, but recreated out of pictures of domestic appliances cut from colour magazines. I went over and stood by him for a moment. He smiled up at me, cracking the pusy rime at the corners of his mouth.

'Unfinished work, left it when I last went out . . . ' He bent his dirty carrot head to the task again.

I confined myself to handing out materials. I sensed that now was not the time to comment on the work that the patients were doing. When they began to trust me they would volunteer their own comments. There was a still atmosphere of concentration over the bent heads. I went and stood by the window, listening to the faint sounds of the hospital as it worked on through the afternoon. The distant thrum of generators, clack of feet, shingled slam of gates and trolleys. On the balcony below, two chronics in blue shifts struggled clumsily with one another, one of them bent back by the other against the parapet. I stared at their ill-coordinated aggression for a while, blankly, sightlessly. The 'O' I was looking at resolved itself into the stretched mouth of a geriatric. At the point where I snapped out of my reverie and realised I ought to do something an orderly appeared on the balcony and separated them, dragging the younger one away, out of sight beneath my feet.

Eventually I went and sat down at a table occupied only by a curly-haired man who had lain his head in the crook of his arm like a bored schoolboy. He was doing something with his other arm, but I couldn't see what. We sat opposite one another for ten minutes or so. Nothing happened. Around us the workers relit cigarettes and built up the fug.

'Psst . . . !' It was Tom. 'Come here.' He gestured to me to join him and Jim. I went over. They were working diligently on the altarpiece. Jim was doing the painting, it was Tom's job to wash the brushes and mix the colours. Jim had finished on the blue-brown surface of the road and was starting on the white lines. Tom was pirouetting lazily, a pathetic string lasso dangling in one hand, his voice modulated to a crazy Californian dude's whine; he had the part down pat. But wrong.

'That man there.' He pointed at the curly-haired man.

'Yes.'

'He's a real coup for Dr B.'

'How so?'

'Cocaine psychosis, authentic, full-blown. Used to be an accountant. Not just some scumball junkie. A real coup. Dr B diagnosed him, all the other units around here are real sore. Go and see what he's doing, it'll crack you up. And on your way back bring us another beaker of water, OK, fella.'

I did as I was told. Passing by Lionel, the drug addict, I bent down to pick up an invisible object and looked back to see what it was he was hiding in the crook of his arm. It was nothing. He was deftly picking up and ranging his own collection of invisible objects on the tiny patch of table. As I bent and looked he turned his face to me and smiled conspiratorially. His eyes stayed too long on my hand which was half closed, fingers shaping the indents and projections of my own invisible object. I hurriedly straightened and walked off down the short corridor to the staff kitchenette.

Halfway down on the left I noticed a door I hadn't seen before. It had a square of glass set into it at eye level, which cried out to be looked through. I stepped up to it. The scene I witnessed was rendered graphical, exemplary, by the wire-thread grid imprisoned in the glass. It was a silent scene played out in a brightly lit yellow room. A man in his early forties, who was somehow familiar, sat in one of the ubiquitous plastic chairs. He wore loose black clothes and his black hair was brushed back from high temples. He was sitting in profile. His legs were crossed and he was writing on a clipboard which he had balanced on his thigh. His lip and chin had the exposed, boiled look of a frequent shaver. The room was clearly given over to treatment. It had that unused corner-of-the-lobby feel of all such rooms. A reproduction of a reproduction hung on the wall, an empty wire magazine rack was adrift on the lino floor – the poor lino floor, its flesh scarified with cigarette burns. In the far corner of the room, diagonally opposite the man in black, a figure crouched, balled up face averted. I could tell by the lapel laden with badges, flapping in the emotional draft, that it was Jane Bowen.

The rest of the afternoon passed in silence and concentration. At 5.40 I gathered in the art materials and stacked all the patients' work in the cupboard in as orderly a fashion as I could manage. It took some time to tidy up the art materials properly. The patients for the most part stayed where they were, hunched over the tables, seemingly unwilling to leave. Tom and Jim muttered to one another by the window. They had the pantomime conspiratorial air of six year olds, still half convinced that if they didn't look they couldn't be seen.

I found Busner in his office. He sat staring out of his window at the lack of scale. On the far corner of the hospital a steel chimney which I hadn't noticed that morning belched out a solid column of white smoke. Busner noticed the direction of my gaze.

'A train going nowhere, eh, Misha?'

'Why do you say that?'

'Because it's true. We're a holding pen, a state-funded purgatory. People come in here and they wait. Nothing much else ever happens; they certainly don't get appreciably better. It's as if, once classified, they're pinned to some giant card. The same could be said of us as well, eh?' He shivered, as if he were witnessing a patient being pierced with a giant pin. 'But I'm forgetting myself, don't pay any attention, Misha, it's the end of a long day.'

'No, I'm interested in what you say. The patients here do seem to be different to those I've met at Halliwick or St Mary's.'

'Oh, you think so, do you? How's that?' Busner swivelled round to look at me over his glasses.

'Well, the art work they do. It's different ... it's ... how shall I put it ... rather contrived, as if they were acting out something. Like Tom's behaviour.'

'An involution?'

'That's it. It's a secondary reference. Their condition is itself a form of comment and the art work that they do is a further exegesis.'

'Interesting, interesting. I can't pretend that it isn't something we haven't noticed before. Your predecessor had very strong views about it. He was a psychologist, you know, very gifted, took on the art therapy job in order to develop functional relationships with the patients, freed as far as possible from the dialectics of orthodox treatment. A very intense young man. The direction the patients have taken with their work could well have something to do with his influence.'

Busner started stuffing his case with paper filling, as if it were a giant pitta bread. 'I'm off, Misha. I shall see you in the morning, bright and early, I trust. I think it would be a good idea if you really sorted out that materials cupboard tomorrow.'

'Yes, yes, of course.' I got up, scraping my chair backwards and left the office. In the corridor the long lights whickered and whinnied to themselves. The ward was quiet and deserted. But as I passed the door to one of the utility cupboards, it suddenly wheezed open and a hand emerged and tugged at my sleeve.

'Come in. Come on, don't be afraid.'

I stepped in through the narrow gap and the heavy door closed behind me. It was dark and the space I was in felt enclosed and stifling. There was an overpowering odour of starch and warm linen. I almost gagged. The darkness was complete. The hand that had grabbed my wrist approached my face. I could feel it hover over my features.

'It is you,' said the voice, 'don't say anything, it'll spoil it.' It was Mimi. I could smell the tang of her sweat; it cut right through the warm, cottony fug.

The hand lead mine to her breast which seemed vast in the darkness, I could feel the webbing of her bra and beneath it the raised bruise of her nipple. She pushed against me, her body was so soft and collapsed. Her flesh had the dewlap quality of a body that has had excess weight melted off it, leaving behind a subcutaneous sac. Her jeans were unzipped; she pulled at my trousers, a cool damp hand tugged on my penis and pressed it against her. We stood like that, her hand on me, mine on her. She led me forwards and hopped up on to what must have been a shelf or ledge, then she drew me, semi-erect, inside of her. My penis bent around the hard cleft of her jeans, the skin rasped against ridged seam and cold zipper. There was something frenzied rather than erotic about this tortured coupling. I clutched at her breast and tore away the two nylon layers. I plunged rigidly inside her. She squeaked and waves of sweat came off her and tanged in my nostrils. I ejaculated almost immediately and withdrew. There was a long moment while we panted together in the darkness. I could hear her rearranging her clothing. Then, 'till tomorrow,' a light touch on my brow. The door split the darkness from ceiling to floor, wheezed once and she was gone. After a while I straightened my clothing, left the linen cupboard and went home.

It wasn't until I stepped out of the tube station and started the ten-minute walk back to the house where I lived that I noticed the outdoor scent. The smell of the ward and the hospital had become for me the only smell. The cold privet of the damp road I trailed along was now alien and uncomfortable.

At home I boiled something in a bag and sat pushing rice pupae around the soiled plate. Friends called to ask about my first day in the new job. I left the answerphone on and heard their voices, distantly addressing my robotic self. Later, lying in bed, I looked around the walls hung with my various constructions, odd things I had made out of cloth that may have been collapsed bats, or umbrellas. The wooden and metal struts

filtered the sodium light which washed orange across the pillow.
I fell asleep.

I dreamt that the man I had seen in the treatment room, the
man taking notes in the chair while Jane Bowen crouched in
the corner, was doing some kind of presentation. I was in the
audience. We were sitting in a very small lecture theatre. It was
enclosed and dark, but the descending tiers of seats, some fifty
in all, were stone ledges set in grassy semi-circular banks.

The man in black stood in the centre of the circular stage and
manipulated a kind of holographic projector. It threw an image
of my head into the air, some four or five feet high. The image,
although clearly three-dimensional, was quite imperfect, billowy
and electrically cheesy. Gathered in the audience were all the
people I'd spoken with on the ward: Busner, Valuam, Mimi,
Jane Bowen, Tom, Simon, Jim and Hilary. Clive stood in the
aisle, rocking.

The man in black took a long pointer or baton and passed it
vertically through my holographic head. It was a cheap trick
because it was quite clear that the hologram wasn't a solid
object, but the audience annoyed me intensely by sychophanti-
cally applauding. I began to shout at them, saying that they
knew nothing about technology, or what it was capable of . . .

Morning. I had difficulty finding the hardened coils of my socks.
And when I did there was something hard and rectangular
tucked into the saline fold of one of them. It was a piece from
The Riddle. I had no idea how it had got there, but nonetheless I murmured automatically, mantrically, 'I'm solving The
Riddle . . . ' Suddenly the events I experienced on Ward 9 the
day before seemed quite bizarre. At the time I accepted them
unquestioningly, but now . . . Busner and his game, the concave
Bowen, the foetal Valuam, Simon's unfeeling mother, Tom with
the mimetic disease, the encounter with Mimi in the linen cupboard. Any one of these things would be sufficient to unsettle;
taken together . . .

I rallied myself. Any psychiatric ward is a test of the therapist's capacity; to embrace a fundamental contradiction, to
retain sympathy whilst maintaining detachment. The previous
day had been bizarre, because I had failed to maintain my
detachment . . . it was said that if you empathised too closely

with the insane you became insane yourself. Busner himself had had a period after the collapse of his Concept House project in the early Seventies when he had spent his time strumming electric basses in darkened recording studios, mouthing doggerel during radio interviews and undertaking other acts of revolutionary identification with those classified as insane. It was only fitting that I should start to fall victim to the same impulses under his aegis. Today I would have to watch myself.

I took the long route across the Heath and passed by my father's sculpture. I have no idea why he gave this specific one to the municipality. He had no particular love for this administration zone. And certainly no real concern with the aesthetic education of the masses. Not that the masses ever really come here. This is an unfenced preserve of the moneyed, they roam free here patrolled by dapper rangers in brown suits.

It is a large piece, depicting two shins cast in bronze. Each one some eight feet high and perhaps nine in circumference. There are no feet and no knees. No tendons are defined, there are no hairs picked out, or veins described. There is just the shape of the shins. It was typical of my father's work. All his working life he had striven to find the portions of the body which, when removed from the whole, became abstract. With the shins I think he had reached his zenith.

I walked on towards the hill from where I had viewed the hospital the previous morning. The idiot was tucked up in a dustbin liner underneath his bench residence, his face averted from the day. His chest was sheathed in a tatter of scraps, reminiscent of Simon's collage. I looked ahead. The hospital had today achieved another feat in distortion. Flatly lit, two-dimensional, depth eradicated, there was a strip of city, a strip of sky and interposed between these two the trapezoid of the sanitorium.

Sanity smells. How could I have forgotten it? No one can lose their reason under the pervasive influence of the nasal institution. It is too mundane. The doors of the lift rolled open and the pad clamped across my face. All was as the day before. Tom sat behind the nurses' station, and his violet eyes focused on mine as soon as I emerged in the short corridor that led from the lift.

'Colour-coded this morning, are we?' Tom's accent is a

strange mixture of clipped pre-war vowels and camp drawl. I looked down and noticed that I had pulled on a particularly bilious V-neck.

'Not intentionally.'

'Dahling, never is, never is.'

I left him and went over to the materials cupboard. Opening wide the two ceiling-high sets of double doors, I gathered up felt-tip pens and isolated them. Then I did the same with the crayons, the charcoal sticks, the pastels, the stained enamel trays of impacted watercolours, the few squiggled tubes of exhausted oils, the sheets of sugar paper, the rough paper, the rulers, and the encrusted brushes. Amongst the jumble were lumps of forgotten clay, grown primordial.

At length Tom came over. He had draped a stole of pink toilet paper around his shoulders and smoked a roll-up with quizzical attention. He stood akimbo and regarded me without speaking.

I started work on the works themselves. They were jumbled up, like the materials. The layered skin of some exercise in papier mâché had been torn by the rudely carved prong of a wooden boat. Crude daubs of powder paint on coloured sheets of rough paper had run into one another and finally impacted over the ubiquitous spiralled vessels. I prised all of these apart gingerly. I only discarded the hopelessly battered. On the rest I imposed order.

As I worked, the association area remained empty. Except for Tom, who paraded back and forth from the nurses' station to the great windows, to the serving hatch and back to my side, trailing his flushable fashion accessory and a second mantle of smoke. From time to time he paused and struck an attitude of such ridiculous campness that I was driven to stifled giggles. He came back just as I was reaching the higher shelves.

'I wouldn't . . . ' he said.

'Wouldn't what?'

'Touch the work up there.'

I dragged over a plastic chair and stepped up on to it. Now at eye level I could see that the works up here were the top of the range. Simon's collage, Hilary's miniatures, Jim's tableau and a couple of others I hadn't seen before. One was particularly striking. It was an abstract, constructed entirely out of pieces from The Riddle. The red acrylic squares had been glued together to form a box, open at the top, within which four more pieces had been set, up on edge, facing each other.

Standing on the plastic chair, eyes level with that top shelf, I had a momentary double-take. I whirled round and, too late, heard myself saying something stupid. 'Well, well, this seems to be where the top dogs put their stuff . . . '

Tom tugged at my trouser leg. I descended and he gathered me into a huddle in the corner of the great flat room, which was now washed with scummy light. My hand rested flacidly on the ventilation grill. Tom said, 'Get out of here Misha.'

'What do you mean?'

'Get out of here. This is a shit place, the people here are shit people. They're fucked up and weird, more weird than you can imagine. They're far more weird than mentally ill people. Mentally ill people are light entertainment compared to this lot.'

'What do you mean? Explain yourself.'

'Well, consider Simon, for one.'

'What about him?'

'You were there when Valuam assessed him?'

'Yes . . . '

'How many doctors have to examine a psychiatric patient before admission?'

'Two.'

'And . . . ?'

'Well, I suppose I thought that since Simon had plainly been in and out of the ward a great deal it was rather glossed over. Fair enough, really, if a little irregular.'

'Wrong. Simon's mother holds a teaching appointment with this ward . . . she regularly arranges to have her own son sectioned.'

'It does sound a little irregular.'

'Irregular! The whole thing is some weird fucking busman's holiday maan . . . ' Tom's arm tightened round my waist '. . . but that needn't upset our love Misha, we can screw together like Mec-ca-no . . . ' I pulled away from him '. . . Bitch!' And turned to see Jane Bowen, regarding me quizzically.

Later that morning, I started drawing up some group worksheets. These are an invention of my own. Large sheets that three or four people can work on at once. I would lay down a basic pattern of lines which the particular group could embroider on, using whatever materials they pleased, or ignore. I worked steadily, with concentration. Two patients who I didn't recognise were sitting at a table in the association area. They were striking some kind of a deal. From where I sat I couldn't hear a word they were saying. Every so often one of them, a little ferrety man wearing a yachting cap, leant out from the table to shoot me a stare. It occurred to me as not unlikely that the deal they were discussing with such attention to detail was, in fact, meaningless.

Eventually I heard a murmur of voices that suggested agreement. I turned to see them exchanging stacks of pieces from The Riddle. The acrylic squares had been threaded on to a cord or wire of some kind, through a hole pierced in the corner of each piece. The two men both had necklaces entirely constructed from the discarded elements of the pop psychological pastime.

The group worksheets took me all morning. No one paid any attention to me any more. I could see now that the atmosphere of the ward was as sodden as compost. It only took a matter of hours for any given individual to be enmeshed, and start to decay. I was yesterday's novelty.

Busner wasn't about. Valuam and I exchanged strained salutations, sometime in the empty mid-morning. He had a snappy little check number on today. His footsteps were even more like clockwork, more pathetically authoritative. I thought to myself, what exactly am I doing on this ward? I don't need the money. I'm not sure that I altogether believe that my particular skills can help the patients. Busner's cynicism had certainly had the effect of dampening whatever residual idealism I had had – I wonder if that was his intention?

Around noon a middle-aged patient called Judith had a partial fit in the short corridor that led from the association area to the women's ward. At first it seemed as if she was simply having a rather heated exchange of words – albeit with herself. But this escalated into hysteria. She vomited as well. Mimi and another nurse arrived very quickly, while I was still standing, poised between the inclination to pretend I hadn't noticed and the desire to show that I could cope. The nurses smoothed Judith's limbs, set her on her feet and led her away. The vomit and distress was somehow accounted for and absorbed.

I was conscious all morning of wanting to avoid Tom and Simon. I didn't really want to see Jim either. I ate lunch alone in the dining-room set aside for staff. I couldn't understand why I was meant to be there. None of the other staff from the ward were. Later on it transpired that it was someone's birthday and they had all gone for a drink in a pub across the road.

In the afternoon I got the patients who turned up to try and do something with the worksheets. Some of them were interested, some were immersed in their own projects. Clive turned out to be a surprisingly effective group leader. He dragooned three rather sheepish depressives into snaking wet trails of paint up and down the large gridded sheet. Their regular actions formed swirl after swirl. He stood back and surveyed them at work like some sort of gaffer. Looking at Clive, his jaw working, rocking as ever, I remembered that he was meant to have been discharged today. I wondered why he was still on the ward, but his pop-eyes, his shiny elbow pads, dissuaded me from asking.

Neither Tom nor Jim appeared for the afternoon session. The model flyover stayed on its shelf. Simon cut and pasted his collage. He had lost interest in me as well. He had reverted to the exaggerated, scab-picking parody of surly adolescence. I wondered where Mimi was, with the faint, sickly lust of an adolescent. I wondered if she had thought me a wimp, or chicken, for not helping out with Judith.

The afternoon ended and I was headed for the lift. This time it was the door to the cleaning cupboard that swung open an invitation. Her buttocks pulsed and scrunched against a plastic sack of soda crystals. Once again it was sickeningly brief. But this time before she left she made me eat two small, green, candied pills.

'What are these?' I said.

'Parstelin – it's a compound preparation of the MAO inhibitor tranylcypromine and trifluoperazine. It's not recommended for children.'

'Why should I take them?'

'To understand, dummy. After all, since you aren't mad, they won't have any effect on you, will they?' Her voice was offhand, light, mocking. It was no big deal.

'S'pose not.' I dryly swallowed them.

'Don't eat any cheese, or drink Chianti. You might have a bad reaction if you do.' She slid out through the gap in the door. One breast, delineated by soiled nylon, and again by ridged cotton, was outlined against the doorjamb for a moment, and then gone.

The rest of the week passed on the ward. I carried on with the worksheets and seemed to be making some progress. Increasing numbers of patients came to the afternoon art therapy sessions and stayed to try their hand. I started to get on well with the quieter patients. This was a mixed blessing. On more than one occasion Hilary held me prisoner for over an hour with talk of her friends, and the mechanics of her exact rendition of them as watercolour images. Likewise Lionel, the mysteriously psychotic accountant, was intent on sitting down with me on Thursday afternoon, a companionable arm about my shoulders, and together we leafed through glossy sales brochures for office equipment. Each article was a revelation to him; one he viewed purely aesthetically. 'Look at this one,' he said, gesturing at a modular workstation done in mushroom, 'lovely, isn't it?' It was all I could do to mumble assent.

As for Bowen and Valuam they murmured at me cordially and passed by. There was no apparent reason for contact and Busner remained absent. I suspected that his juniors were prejudiced against me because of my father and all the sentimental crap Busner mouthed when I arrived on the ward, but I didn't particularly care. And at lunch I talked to auxiliaries or nurses.

Every night Mimi rendezvoused with me in another cupboard. I never knew which one it would be but somehow she always knew where to catch me just when I was about to finish clearing away the art materials and leave the ward for the night. Our couplings remained brief and stylised. She resisted my unspoken pressure towards some intimacy with offers of more green pills, which I took, hoping they might bring us together. On Friday she gave me four more after I had taken my normal two and told me to administer them myself over the weekend.

On Saturday night I went to see a film with a friend. We

normally met up every month or so and at least half our time was, naturally enough, taken up with relaying a cursory outline of what we had been doing in the intervening period. On this occasion I was more circumspect than usual. I had the suspicion that what had been happening to me on the ward, especially my relationship with Mimi, was something that I shouldn't talk about to outsiders. It wasn't that it was wrong exactly – it was rather that the experience so clearly didn't apply.

I was also very conscious of the green pills that lay in the soft mess of lint at the bottom of my pockets. My finger sought them out as we talked, and to the probing digit they felt preposterously large and tactile, the way objects in the mouth feel to the tongue.

We were sitting in the cinema. I was idly watching the film, when I felt for the first time what must have been an effect of the drug. It was remarkably similar to the sensation I had had on the ward, when I was standing up on the chair looking for the first time at the patients' artworks on the top shelf of the materials cupboard. It was a feeling of detachment, but not from the external world; this was an internal detachment, a membraneous tearing away, inside of me.

After the film we went to get something to eat in a kebab joint. As we entered the eatery through an arch, band-sawn out of chipboard, I felt the rending inside me, again. For some reason I found myself unable to discuss the film. Abstracted, I started to casually shred the flesh from my splayed baby chicken with my hands. I had amassed quite a pile before my friend reacted with concerned disgust. I shrugged the episode off.

At the end of the evening I said goodbye to my friend and returned to my house. Sitting in the yellow light from the road, coiling and uncoiling my sock, I resolved, quietly and with no emotional fuss, never to see him again.

It's funny. It's funny – but after that it became easy to dismantle the emotional and spiritual framework of my life. Relatives, friends, ex-lovers; it became apparent that their relationships with me had always been as contingent as I had suspected. It only took an instance of irregularity, one, or at most two phone calls unreturned by me, an engagement not attended, for whole swathes of human contact to lie down, to fall into short stooks.

ᐟ After a few weeks on Ward 9, and a generous handful of mutant M&Ms, everything began to resolve itself into the patterns I had always dimly thought I apprehended. The violet swirls, purple beams and glowing coils that lie within the world of the pressed eyelid – the distressed retina. I seemed to have acquired an air-cushioned soul. I felt no resistance to doing things that would have plagued my conscience in the past, at least that is what I felt. I had no precise examples of these things other than taking Parstelin itself. My liaisons with Mimi? But they were just knee-jerk experiences.

Why have I isolated myself like this? My only human contact now comes within working hours and mostly with the patients on the ward. I have no idea. I can make no claim to being depressed or alienated. Indeed I seem to have suffered from less disaffection in my life than most of my contemporaries, perhaps because of my father's death. Yet I felt more at home on the ward than I ever felt . . . at home.

The patients have thrown themselves into the worksheets with a vengeance. There was something about the size and complexity of the job that really appealed to them. The method also gave them the opportunity to blend together all their different styles. When they were working quietly on the sheets in the late afternoon one could almost be in a normal working situation. All their idiosyncrasies and psychic tics seemed smoothed out by their absorption. Clive no longer rocked at all. Hilary, having integrated her miniatures into Simon's new swirl of encrusted mâché, was content to work on backgrounds. Her bag-on-a-stand swished around her, a fixed point which delineated the circumference of her enterprise.

There was one thing missing in all of this: Busner. Despite the fact that I now seemed to get on with all and sundry on the ward; despite the fact that I felt accepted; despite the fact that when the lift door rolled back and I found myself at the head of the familiar, short corridor that led to the association area, I no longer felt the atmosphere as oppressive; on the contrary it was cozy, from beneath the covers. Despite all this there was Busner's profound absence. An absence towards which I felt a surprising ambivalence.

Busner is the Hierophant. He oversees the auguries, decocts potions, presides over rituals that piddle the everyday into a teastrainer reality. And he is a reminder of everything I wish to bury with my childhood. A world of complacency, of theory in the face of real distress. My father and Busner would sit together for hours at the head of the dining-room table and set the world to rights. Their conversation – I realised later – loaded with the slop of banality and sentimentality that was the direct result of their own sense of failure. Their wives would repair to another room and there do things that *had* to be done, while they carried on and on, eliding their adolescence still further into middle age. The awful oatmeal carpets of my childhood and the shame of having been a part of it all. When I think of Busner now he is a ghastly throwback, threatening to drag me into a conspiracy to evade reality.

Where is he? Valuam told me over bourbons and tea that he was in Helsinki, reading a paper to a conference. Valuam dunked his biscuits and sucked on them noisily, which is something I wouldn't have expected from this little scrap of anal retention. We talked a little about my art therapy work, but really he had no time for it and pointed instead to the success he was having with a new anti-depressant. 'Seemingly intractable states, verging on total withdrawal, now with noticeable effect.' He was referring to Lionel, who now no longer sat by the windows staring blankly down on to the chronics' balcony, but instead paced the men's ward like a caged lion, desperate to get back into business. Where was Busner? I didn't believe Valuam; I kept expecting the door to the utilities cupboard to swing open and to find crouching there, sweaty pills in pudgy palm, the discredited guru, waiting with affectionate arm to jerk me off, for old times' sake.

Monday morning, again. The sun cannot penetrate a low sodden bank of cloud and the light wells from behind it, oozing up from the ground through a thick spongy pile of ground mist as I foot my way across the sward. The air around me distorts to form rooms and corridors, and rooms within them and sliding partitions which I never come up against. The ward has come out to meet me today; I feel its shape around me, its scuffed skirting boards at my ankles, as I move towards the idiot's bench.

He is lying under it, caulked in free newspapers. Pathetic small ads show intaglioed across his neck. In the confined space he rolls over and clonks his shin against the bench leg. His face is exposed for a moment against the greasy collar of his anorak. His eyes have swollen up and exploded in a series of burst ramparts and lesions of diseased flesh. I feel my oily tea slop up from my stomach, the nausea is as clear and pure as pain. I vomit with precision and vomit again until my nausea has no function and I can look once more.

It's not clear what has happened to the idiot. Has he drunk some bleach? Some oven cleaner? Or is it a disease of a rarefied kind, a human myxomatosis designed to eliminate the crap from the fringe of society, to stop the piss-heads copulating and producing more of their degenerate kind? Whichever. The fact is that it's evident that he hasn't been dead for long – his corpse is still moving into rigor. He has died in the night and I am the first to happen along. It is my responsibility to alert the authorities. And now I feel the presence of the Parstelin in my blood stream. It replaces the sense of nausea as – for the first time – a positive rather than a negative attribute. The drug provides me with another fuzzy frame of reference, within which the idiot's death is no responsibility of mine. Someone else will report it, someone else will find him. I glissade down the hillside on my fluffy Lilo. The arguments from my conscience are remote, like memories of a television debate between contesting pompous pundits, witnessed several years ago . . .

A long morning in the hospital. On the ward there is an uncharacteristic, brisk efficiency. Valuam trots hither and thither with a clipboard compiling what look like inventories. For some reason he is dressed casually today, or at least in superficially casual clothes. It was always obvious that he would iron his jeans and check shirts, and also that he would wear sleeveless grey pullovers. Not for the first time it occurs to me that there is a strange symmetry between the sartorial sense of the psychiatric staff and that of their patients. Valuam with his strict dress which looks hopelessly contrived, Bowen with her bag lady chic, Busner with his escaping underwear. All of them match up with the patients in their charge . . .

I am working on something of my own which I hope will provide some inspiration for the patients. It's a worksheet, about six feet square, on which I have done several representations of the hospital. Each one has been executed using a different technique: pen and wash, gouache, oils, charcoals, pencils, clay. This morning I spend time cutting the stencil for a silk-screen print.

Patients, *en route* for therapy sessions, or dropping out of the medication line, pause by the tables I've pushed together in the dining area and ask me about the work. An auxiliary, a middle-aged Philippino woman, stops her swirling, watery work with tousled mop and zinc bucket on the ward floor to discourse at length on swollen ankles, injustice and the vagaries of public transport. I listen and work distractedly; the image of the dead idiot imposes itself on me startlingly. It slides in front of my eyes from time to time with an audible click: the ridge of greasy, nylon quilted collar, the scrubby, scrawny neck, the long face, the exploded eyes . . .

At noon then. Jane Bowen comes and sits near me, salutes me but does not converse. She rolls one of her withered cigarettes and stares out of the window abstractedly, drawing heavily. Her hair is scraped back tightly from the violet, inverted bruises of her temples. She gazes towards the hill where the idiot lies. I have an impulse to tell her about it, which I repress. The weather outside the hospital is playing tricks again; long, high bands of cirrus cloud are filtering the wan sunlight into vertical bars, which cut across the area that lies between the hospital and the Heath, creating shadows of diminishing perspective, like the exposed working on an artist's sketch.

Eventually I get up and go and stand beside her. I am conscious of her body retreating from me inside the starched front of her white coat, leaving behind a white buckler. We both look out of the window in silence. My gaze drops from the idiot's bier-bench (I cannot see any evidence of discovery, service vehicles, or whatever) to the chronics' balcony below, the open area projecting out from Ward 8.

As once before, two cretins are embracing in a painful muted struggle. Their gowns flap in the wind, they strain against one another, locked in a clumsy bear-hug. Then one moves with surprising speed and agility, changing his hold so that he grips the other from behind, pinning his arms – and at the same time leaning backwards over the rail that runs above the concrete wall bounding the balcony. The two faces tip up towards Jane

Bowen and I, white splashes that resolve themselves into ...
Mark, Busner's son, who was at school with me, who had a
breakdown at university and attempted suicide. He is pinioned
by the handsome, black-haired man who I saw in the treatment
room with Jane Bowen. The man's face is glazed over with
brutish imbecility. I feel another jolt of nausea, stagger and place
my hand against the pane for support. Jane Bowen looks at me
pityingly and gestures with her fag.

'Your predecessor, Misha, our ex-art therapist. Who just happens, purely by coincidence, to be my brother, Gerry.'

'That's Mark with him, Busner's son!'

'Yes, Zack felt it would be a good idea to have them farmed
out to Ward 8 for a little while. He thought you might find it a
tad shocking to encounter them as patients.' She turned to face
me and said quite calmly, in a flat kind of a voice, 'Get out of
here Misha. Get out of here now.'

She wasn't issuing advice on a career move. This was a fire
alarm. I acted on it quickly, but hesitated on my way across the
wide expanse of industrial-wear floor covering, skittering on one
leg like a cartoon character speeding around a corner that turns
into a vase. Abruptly I realise that the Parstelin has completely
altered my sense of my own body. I am acutely aware of the
connection between each impulse, each message and the nerve-
ending it comes from. My whole physical orientation has shifted,
but remains whole.

This apprehension occupies me as I run to the lift. Patients
'O' at me hysterically, but there is silence, or rather a descending wail that has nothing to do with speech and everything
to do with what children hear when they press the flaps of
cartilage over their ears, in and out, very fast. Sheuuooo-
sheeeuuooo.

'A, hehehahahoohoohoohoo!' Clive does the twist by the
coiled hosepipe in an anonymous bay, off the short corridor I
run down on my way to the lift.

'Misha, a word please,' Valuam comes out from his office,
trouser material high on each thigh, scrunched up in marmoset
hands. His peeled face tilts toward me, fungus poking out from
the door. Another door swings open five yards further on and a
hand emerges to pluck at my sleeve, a round, dimpled hand on
the end of that dripping sundae body. I run past it and in my

mind the flashback of thrust seems hard and mechanical; my penis a rubberised claw torn from a laboratory retort and thrust into the side of a putrefying animal. I must take the stairs.

Four flights down I stop running. They're going to let me leave the hospital. A drug is just a drug. I was bloody stupid to take it at all, to fuck with Mimi, but if I stop it now my head will clear in a couple of days and I'll be back to normal. I won't have this strange sense that I am someone else, someone who is compelled to be reasonable.

There is no cause for alarm. I certainly cannot question the quintessential character of the stairwell. There is no denying its objective status. Thick bars of unpainted concrete punched through with four-inch bolts. The handrail a fire-engine red bar, as thick as an acroprop. Parstelin is a drug – I realise – that makes you acutely aware of things-in-themselves. Their standing into existence is no longer nauseous, but splendidly replete. That said, I gag a little and cough up a whitey dollop, somewhere between sputum and vomit, which plops into the drift of fluff wedged at the back of the stair I stand on.

Among the scraps of silver paper, safety-pins and nameless bits of detritus, a part of me. The fugue is broken by a whoosh of dead air that gusts up the well from below. Someone else has entered the staircase, pushed hard on a pneumatic door, maybe three flights down. The windows on the stairway are cut at oblique angles into the outer wall of the hospital. It is clear from the view, which affords me no sight of the huge bulk that contains me, that the staircase runs down the outer edge of the ziggurat's sloping wall.

I pick my way down, pausing from time to time to cock an ear and listen for sounds of pursuit, but there are none. It is plain to me now that I have been suffering from a delusion, that the ward has overtaken me in part. I never denied that I was highly strung. I need some bed rest and the opportunity to read the papers. The lower I get the freer I feel. I know I haven't really escaped from anything – and yet there's the temptation to laugh and skip, to strike some attitudes.

I calculate that I am still two floors above ground level when the staircase blocks off its own windows. Light is now supplied by yellow discs that shine on the walls. The yellow light disorientates me. It must have done. I can genuinely no longer tell whether I am above or below ground level. The doors that lead off the staircase are blank oblongs. I panic and push at one, it wheezes under my palm and I tumble out into a corridor.

It is immediately clear that the stairway has diverged significantly in its path, that it hasn't followed the lift shaft and deposited me in one of the open areas that form a natural reception concourse for each floor. Instead, it has thrown me off to one side, into the hinterland of the hospital, added to which I'm not on the mezzanine floor, I'm on the lower ground floor. I recognise where I am. I'm somewhere along the route Simon took me on my first day. I'm on the way to see the giant obsolete machine. I am in the same wetly shining concrete corridor. In either direction the naked neon tubes dash away; even they are hurrying off from this crushing place.

Which way? Whoever entered the stairwell while I was coming down is now on their way up. I can hear the cold slap of feet ascending and this hastens my decision. I turn to the left and start off down the corridor, trusting to my intuition to find my way to casualty and out of the hospital. As I walk I am aware that I'm positioned chemically at the eye of the storm. I no longer feel muzzy; I know that my body is saturated with Parstelin, but I've swum into a bubble of clarity. Nevertheless, I still don't seem able to gain a definitive view of Busner and his ward. What has been happening? Those patients – with their madness – as stylised as a ballet. Were they the logical result of Busner's philosophy? Were theirs the performances of madmen-as-idealists? Or just idealists? Their symptoms . . . was it true that they genuinely caricatured the recorded pathologies, all of them, not just Tom, or was my perception of them a function of the Parstelin?

These speculations give me heart. I feel my old self. I pause and look in a stainless steel panel screwed to a door. My reflection, dimpled here and there by the metal, looks back at me, amused, diffident. I feel cosy with my self-observation and immensely reassured by this moment of ordinary, unthinking vanity.

But where am I? No nearer casualty. The corridor has not swapped its concrete floor for tiling, there is no paint on the walls. I have turned the wrong way. Twenty feet ahead I can see the two swing-doors that lead to the conservatory. What the hell. I'll pop in and have a look; it will be the last time I come near the hospital for a while. The doors whicker apart on their rusty rails and as I turn and pull them shut behind me they cut out the steady undertow of thrum that powers the hospital. The light in the high-domed room is the same as before and the obscure machine with its cream bakelite surfaces projects up above me, inviolate.

Tom and Jim step out from behind its flanged base, they move quite unaffectedly into my sight, as if expecting no particular reaction. I am very frightened.

'Misha, where are you going?' says Tom. Jim is casting his eyes about with rapid jerks of his head. He keeps flexing and rolling his arms back and forth, opening the palm forwards to disclose plastic mouth tubes – the kind used to stop people who are fitting from biting their tongues off – which he has adapted to some manual exercise routine.

'I'm going off for the rest of the day, Tom, I came here by accident. I was looking for casualty.'

Tom listens to me, nodding, and then gestures for me to join him and Jim. The three of us then, squat down between the outstretched paws of the great instrument, which are bolted heavily to the floor. We are like Africans under some fat-trunked tree, timelessly talking, until Jim drops his adapted muscle expanders on to the cracked tiles of the floor with a clatter.

'I'm glad you listened to my advice, Misha. You're leaving, aren't you?'

'Just for a couple of days. I . . . I need a rest. The atmosphere on the ward is quite overwhelming.'

'Yes, it can be, can't it. That's why Jim and I like to come down here and play with the machine, it's peaceful down here, quiet. Do you think I'm mad, Misha?'

'What about me, am I mad too?' Jim chimes in as well. I find myself embarrassed, which is absurd. To be frightened seems right, but to be embarrassed as well, that's ridiculous.

'Does the question embarrass you?' Tom is rolling a cigarette with deft fingers. He flicks over the lip of paper and raises it to his budding, sensual mouth.

'I hadn't thought about it in those terms.'

'Oh, oh, I see, you are a disciple of good Dr Zee, so we're

just behaving in a way which others choose to describe as mad. We're simply non-conformists.'

'I think you're simplifying his position a little.'

'Of course, of course. Are you mad, Misha?' Jim snickers and rakes the tiles with long, cracked nails.

I can't answer. My eyes cast up to the ceiling some twenty feet away. The conservatory is roofed with a glass cupola, the inside of which seems dirtied as if by soot. Beneath this a complete circle of dirty dormer windows lets in the grey light. From the very centre hangs a flex – which dangles a cluster of naked bulbs just above the highest shoulder of the machine.

After a while, Tom reaches out from where he squats and touches me lightly on the arm. 'I'm sorry Misha, come on, let's climb.'

'Yeah, lets.' Jim is on his feet in one bound, a foot already on the kidney-shaped step, which is set two feet up into the base of the machine. In turn we haul ourselves up. Tom comes last. The machine is designed to be climbed; we ascend to a horizontal platform about seven feet up. This is girded with massive gimbals, the purpose of which is to tilt the platform under the main barrel of the contraption. What the machine ever did to the patients who were lain out on the platform is obscure. Perhaps it projected something through them: radiation; ultrasound; a light beam, or even something solid ... The barrel itself has been de-cored; all that's left is a hank of plaited black wires, spilling from its mouth.

The three of us then, sit in a row on the platform, passing back and forth the wet end of tobacco. The curved well of dead light that falls on to us and the heavy machinery we sit on conspire to effect timelessness. Jews about to be shot or gassed are caught against the straight rod and round wheel of a railway engine. Crash survivors crawl from buckled aluminium sections rammed into the compost earth of the rainforest. We sit and smoke and I hear the 'peep-peep' of a small bird, outside the hospital, sounding like a doctor's pager. It completes the dead finality of my situation. My neck, rigid with absorbed tension, mushy with tranquillisers, feels as if it is welling up over my head to form a fleshly cowl.

The texture of things parodies itself. The creamy hardness of the machine's surfaces, the dusty clink of the tiled floor, the smelly abrasion of the arm of Tom's sweater. Even surfaces refuse to be straight with me. Tom's profile is rippably perfect, a slash of purity. Jim's bulbous nose and styled, collar-length hair make him absurd, an impression heightened by his simian arms which rest on the platform like the prongs of an idling forklift truck. But he reassures me now. They both reassure me. I put an arm around each of them and they snuggle into me, adults being children, being parents. They are my comrades, my blood brothers.

'Go now, Misha.' Tom pulls away and pushes me gently, indicating that I should get down from the platform. I climb down heavily. My limbs have the dripping, melting feeling that I know indicates the absorption of more Parstelin. But I don't know why; I haven't taken any. On the floor I turn, not towards the doors, but away from them, and circle the machine. Jim and Tom watch me but say nothing. I pick my way over twisted lianas of defunct cabling, once pinioned to the floor but now adrift. Behind the machine, directly opposite the door to the corridor, the door that faces the Mass Disaster Room is open.

Outside there is a scrap of land, room-sized, open to the air that voyages fifteen storeys down to find it and its tangled side-swipe of nameless shrubs. There, set lopsidedly on the irregular rubbled surface, stands one of the rectangular melamine-topped tables from the dining area on the ward. I can see a fold of belly, a dollop of jowl, a white hand fidgeting with an acrylic rectangle, the failing end of a mohair tie. Dr Busner is trying to solve The Riddle.

'Ah, there you are, Misha. Come out, come out, don't hover like that.' Busner sits, flanked by Valuam and Bowen. On the table in front of them are ranged objects that clearly relate to me: a pot of green pills, Jim's bas-relief which had so impressed me, a note I had sent to Mimi in an idle moment. I move across the little yard and sit by Valuam, who surprises me by smiling warmly. Flash of recognition: the slashed profile. If the features were undrowned? Valuam and Tom are brothers.

'We are all family here, Misha.'

'What's that?'

'We are all family . . . I see that something is coming home to you, as you have come home to us. It hardly matters whether we are doctors or patients, does it, Misha? The important thing is to be at home.' Busner rises and starts to pace the area. The massive walls of the hospital are joined irregularly to the squat citadel that houses the Mass Disaster Room. Busner describes a trapezoid on the uneven surface, sketching out with his feet the elevation of the hospital.

'You see, what we have here is a situation that calls for mutual aid. My son, Jane and Anthony's siblings, Simon, Jim, Clive, Harriet, indeed all of the patients on the ward, could be said to be casualties of a war that we ourselves have waged. That's why we felt it was our duty to care for them in a special kind of environment. You, of course, noticed the curious involution of the pathology that they exhibit, Misha, and that was right – you passed the first step. They are not mad in any accepted sense, rather they are meta-mad. Their madness is a conscious parody of the relation in which the psyche stands to itself . . . but you know this. Unfortunately, you didn't do so well on the other tests . . . ' Busner tipped out some of the Parstelin from the pot on to the table. 'You took these, Misha, and you fucked Mimi in just about every available cupboard on the ward. This is not the behaviour of a responsible therapist. You had a choice, Misha. On Ward 9 you could have been therapist or patient; it seems that you have decided to become a patient.'

Busner stopped pacing and sat down again at the table. I sat, trapped in sweet gorge. What he said made sense. I did not resent it. Jane Bowen picked her nails with the edge of a Riddle counter. The same bird paged Nature. The four of us sat in the peculiar space, in silence. One thing confused me.

'But Dr Busner . . . Zack, my parents, my father. They had nothing to do with any therapeutic application of psychology, they were both artists. Surely I don't qualify for the ward?'

'Later on, Misha, later on . . . Your father became a sculptor in his thirties. Before that he studied with Alkan. He would have made an excellent analyst, but perhaps he didn't want you to pay the price.'

The doors behind me clacked in a down draft. The interview was clearly over.

'Would you take Misha back up to the ward, Anthony. We can foregather and handle the paperwork after lunch.'

Yes, lunch, I felt quite hungry. But I didn't like it down here.

The Quantity Theory of Insanity

There was something moribund about this patch of ground, cemented with white splashes that streaked the high walls and starred the crusted earth. I wanted to get back upstairs – I want to get back upstairs – ha! Perhaps that's the effect of the chloropromasine, a kind of continual time lag between thought and self-consciousness – I want to get back upstairs . . . and lie on my bed. I need a cigarette.

Understanding the Ur-Bororo

When I first met Janner at Reigate in the early Seventies, he'd been an unprepossessing character. He was a driven young man whose wimpy physical appearance all too accurately complemented his obsessive nature. His body looked as if it had been constructed out of pipecleaners dunked repeatedly in flesh-coloured wax. All his features were eroded and soft except for his nose, which was the droplet of wax that hardens as it runs down the shaft of the candle. There was also something fungoid about Janner, it was somehow indefinable, but I always suspected that underneath his clothes Janner had athlete's foot — all over his entire body.

You mustn't misunderstand me, in a manner of speaking Janner and I were best friends. Actually, that is a little strong, it was rather that it was us against the rest — Janner and I versus the entire faculty and the entire student body combined.

I suppose I now realise that my feelings are not Janner's responsibility and they never were. He just had the misfortune to come along at that point in my life where I was open to the idea of mystery. Janner took the part of Prospero; I gnashed and yowled — and somewhere on the island lurked the beautiful, the tantalising, the Ur-Bororo.

Not everyone has the opportunity to experience a real mystery in their lives. I at least did, even if the disillusionment that has followed the resolution of my mystery sometimes seems worse than the shuttered ignorance I might otherwise have enjoyed. This then is the story of a rite of passage. A coming of age that took ten years to arrive. And although it was my maturity that was at issue, it is Janner who is the central character of this story.

I can believe that in a more stimulating environment, somewhere where intellectual qualities are admired and social peculiarities sought after, Janner would have been a tremendous success. He was an excellent conversationalist, witty and informed. And if there was something rather repulsive about the way catarrh gurgled and huffled up and down his windpipe when he was speaking, it was more than compensated for by his animation, his excitement, and his capacity for getting completely involved with ideas.

Janner and I weren't appreciated by the rest of the student body at Reigate. We thought them immature and pathetic, with their *passé*, hippy hair and consuming passion for incredibly long guitar solos. I dare say they thought nothing of us at all. We were peripheral.

You guessed it; I was jealous. I didn't want to be sectioned off with waxy Janner. I wanted to be mingling my honeyed locks with similar honeyed locks to the sound of those stringed bagpipes. I wanted to provide an ideal arterial road for crabs, but I wasn't allowed to play. It was the students in the arts faculties who were at the centre of most of the cliques. If, like me, you were reading geography and physical education, you were ruled out of court – especially if you didn't look right, or talk right. Without these essential qualifications I was marginalised. At school my ability to do the four hundred metres hurdles comfortably under fifty seconds had made me a hero; at Reigate it was derided.

Ostracised by the cliques that mattered I found Janner, and I've lived to regret it. If only I'd poached my brain with psychotropics! Today I could be living a peaceful life, haggling with a recalcitrant DHSS official in rural Wales, or beating a damp strip of carpet hung over a sagging clothesline outside some inner-city squat. Janner cheated me out of this, his extreme example bred my moderation. At nineteen I could have gone either way.

I cemented my friendship with Janner during long walks in what passed for countryside around Reigate. Even at that time this part of Surrey was just the odds and ends that had been forgotten in the clashes between adjacent municipalities. The irregular strips of grey and brown farmland, the purposeless concrete aprons stippled with weeds and the low, humped downs covered with sooty, stained scrub. We traversed them all and as we walked he talked.

Janner was an anthropology student. Now, of course, he is The Anthropologist, but in those days he was simply one student among several, five to be precise. Quite why Reigate had a department of anthropology was a mystery to most of the faculty and certainly to the students. Hardly anyone knew about the Lurie Foundation, who had endowed it, and − even I didn't know until years later − why.

During the time Janner and I were at Reigate (you could hardly say 'up' at Reigate) the department was run by Dr Marston. He was a striking-looking man. To say he had a prognathous jaw would have been a gross understatement. His jaw shot out in a dead flat line from his neck and went on travelling for quite a while. Looking at the rest of his face the most obvious explanation was that his chin was desperately trying to escape his formidably beetling brows. These rolled down over his eyes like great lowering storm clouds. Add to this two steady black eyes, tiny little teeth, a keel for a nose, and a mouth trying to hide behind a fringe of savagely cut black beard, and you had someone whose skull looked as if it had been assembled in an attempt to perpetrate a nineteenth-century hoax.

To see Dr Marston and Janner talking to one another was to feel that one was witnessing the meeting between two different species that had just discovered a mutual language. Not that I saw them together that often; Dr Marston had no time for me, and Janner, after his first year, was excused from regular attendance at the college and allowed to get on with his own research.

I think it would be fair to say (and please remember that this is a turn of phrase resolved solely for the use of the extremely opinionated and the hopelessly diffident) that during that year I received a fairly comprehensive anthropological education at second hand. Janner had very little interest in what I was studying. At best he used my scant geographical knowledge as a sort of card index, and when he was discoursing on the habits and customs of this or that isolated people he would consult my internal map of the world. For most of the time we were together I listened and Janner talked.

Janner talked of the pioneers in his field. He was in awe of the colossal stature of the first men and women who had aspired to objectivity in relation to the study of humankind. He talked to me of their theories and hypotheses, their intrigues and battles, their collections of objects and artefacts, and came back again and again, as we strode round and round the brown hills, to their fieldwork.

For Janner all life was a prelude to fieldwork. Reigate was only an antechamber to the real world. A world in which Janner wanted to submerge himself completely – in order to become a pure observer. He was unmoved by the relatavistic, structuralist and post-structuralist theories of anthropology with their painful concern with the effect of the observer on the observed. Janner had no doubts; as soon as he got into the field he would effectively disappear, becoming like a battery of sensitive recording devices hidden in a tree. His whole life was leading up to this pure period of observation. Janner wanted to be the ultimate voyeur. He wanted to sit on a kitchen chair in the corner of the world and watch while societies played with themselves.

When Janner wasn't telling me about infibulation among the Tuareg or Shan propitiation ceremonies, he was sharing with me the fruits of his concerted observation of Reigate society. Janner was intrigued by Reigate. He saw it as a unique society at a crucial point in its development.

Walking with him, up by the county hospital, or down in the network of lanes that formed the old town, I would squirm with embarrassment as Janner stopped passersby; milkmen, clerks and housewives. Janner encouraged them to talk about themselves, their lives, and what they were doing, just like that; impromptu, with no explanation. Needless to say they invariably obliged, and usually fulsomely.

As we passed cinema queues or discos on our interminable walks, or stopped off at cafés to eat bacon sandwiches, Janner would shape and form what he observed into a delicate tableau of practice, ritual and belief. Reigate was for him a 'society' and as such was as worthy of respect as any other society. It was not for him to judge the relative values of killing a bandicoot versus taking a girl on the back of your Yamaha 250 up the A23 at a hundred miles an hour; both were equally valid rites of passage.

After his first year at Reigate Janner moved out of his digs at Mrs Beasley's on Station Road, and into a shed on the edge of the North Downs. It was his intention to get started as soon as possible on the business of living authentically – in harmony with his chosen object of field study – for by now Janner had fallen under the spell of the Ur-Bororo.

If it was unusual to study anthropology at Reigate, rather than some other branch of the humanities, it was even more unusual for an undergraduate student to nurse dreams of going to another continent for postgraduate field study. Dr Marston was well used to packing his charges off to Prestatyn to study the decline of Methodist Valley communities, or to Yorkshire to study the decline of moorland Unitarian communities, or to the Orkneys to study the decline of offshore gull-eating communities. Reigate was, if not exactly famous, at least moderately well known for its tradition of doing work on stagnating subsocietal groups. Dr Marston's own doctorate had been entitled 'Ritual Tiffin and Teatime Taboo: Declining Practices Among Retired Indian Army Colonels in Cheltenham'.

But that being said, Dr Marston himself had had a brief period of field study abroad. This was among the Ur-Bororo of the Paquatyl region of the Amazon. It was Marston who first fired Janner with enthusiasm for this hitherto undistinguished tribe of Indians. I have no idea what he told Janner, certainly it must have contained an element of truth, but Janner told me a severely restricted version. If one listened to Janner on the subject one soon found out that his information about the Ur-Bororo consisted almost entirely of negative statements. What was known was hearsay and very little *was* known; what little hearsay was known was hopelessly out of date – and so forth. I didn't trouble to challenge Janner over this, by now he was beyond my reach. He had retired to his hut on the Downs, was seldom seen at the college, and dissuaded me, politely but firmly, from calling on him.

I did go a couple of times to see him. In a way I suppose I wanted to plead with him not to abandon me. For Janner, with his pipe-stem torso sheathed in the stringy tube of a sleeveless, Fair Isle sweater, and with his eyes wetly gleaming behind round

73

lenses, was more than a friend as far as I was concerned. I couldn't admit it to myself but I was a little bit in love with him. He told me that his hut was a faithful reconstruction of an Ur-Bororo traditional dwelling. I didn't believe him for a second; anyone looking at the hut could see that it had been ordered out of the back of *Exchange & Mart*. Its creosoted clapboard sides, its macadamised roofing, its one little leaded window, the way the floor wasn't level with the ground. All of these facts betrayed its prefabricated nature. Inside the hut we drank tea out of crude clay vessels. Once again Janner assured me that these were of traditional Ur-Bororo manufacture, but I couldn't really see the point of the statement. By now I could see just by looking at him that he was lost to me. He no longer needed me as a passive intermediary between his mind and the world he studied. He had found his destiny.

I left the hut without pleading at all and cycled back to Reigate. I had accepted that from now on I would be alone. But it's difficult to get that Wertherish in Reigate, certainly not when you're lodging in a clipped crescent of double-glazed, dormered windows. My depression soon ate itself. Without Janner to talk to I was forced back among my fellow students. I made some other friends; I even had a girlfriend. It wasn't that I forgot about Janner, that would have been impossible, it was just that I tried to construct a life for myself to which he wouldn't be relevant. I succeeded in this, but it had its own consequences.

During the next ten years very little happened to me. Sure, I left Reigate and went to teach at a school in Sanderstead. I met, fell in love with, and speedily married the geography and PE teacher at a neighbouring school. We became owner-occupiers and a child arrived, who was small, well made and finished; and dreamy and introverted to the point of imbecility. We had friends and opinions, both in moderation. It was a full life, seemingly without severe problems. I had grown through my modest and unturbulent adolescence into a modest and unturbulent adult. I even gained a certain celebrity for my phlegm at the school where I taught, because I could face down aggressive pupils with indifference. Some of my colleagues became convinced that within me lurked quite violent impulses. This, I'm afraid, was far from the truth. The reality was that I felt padded, as if all the gaps in my view of the world had been neatly filled with some kind of cavity life insulation. I felt ludicrously contained and static. I saw events unroll around me. I felt, I emoted, but the volume control was always on. Somewhere along the line someone had clapped a mute on my head and I hadn't any idea who, or why.

During this whole period I heard nothing of Janner. I knew he had graduated from Reigate with unprecedented first-class honours and, with Dr Marston's blessing and a none too generous grant from the SSRC, had gone abroad to visit his precious tribe. But beyond that, nothing. The only evidence I had of Janner's existence during that ten-year period was finding by chance, while looking absent-mindedly through a stack of World Music records, an album Janner had acted as 'consultant producer' for. It was entitled *Some Chants from Failed Cultures*. I bought it immediately and rushed home.

If I had hoped for some kind of enlightenment, or to recapture the rapture of our scrubland walks together I was to be disappointed. The album was gloomy and perverse. The producers had visited diverse groups of indigenes around the world, remarkable only for their persistence in chanting to no avail. Here were the Ketchem of Belize with their muttering eructation 'Fall Out of the Water – Fish'. The I-Arana of Guinea, disillusioned cargo cultists who moaned gently, 'Get Me Room Service', and many others too tedious and depressing to mention.

The gist of all these failed chants I gathered from the sleeve notes, written by Janner. The chants themselves were badly recorded and incomprehensible. After two or three plays the needle on our record player started to score twists of vinyl out of the bottom of the grooves – and that was the end of that. Janner's sleeve notes, as far as I was concerned, were unilluminating and discursive. They told me nothing concrete about his involvement with the project and gave me no clue as to where he might be now. When I tried to find out more through the record company I drew another blank. Ha-Cha-Cha Records had gone into receivership.

I may not have found the friend of my adolescence, but the record had gravely unsettled me. I had assumed that Janner was by now safely ensconced in some provincial university's anthropology department, his tremendous enthusiasm and drive winding down through the dreary cycle of teaching. But the record and its sleeve notes presented an alternative picture, a picture of a different Janner and a more unsettled career. The evening that I brought the record home I sat in the living-room for hours, using the time while my wife was at her class, to try and fathom Janner's fate, with only the flimsy record sleeve to go on.

My son James didn't help. He'd picked up a couple of the failed chants and as I put him to bed that night he said, in passable Uraic, 'Lo! The crops are withering.' Somehow, even among the cartoon stickers and the bright bendy limbs of bendy toys, this didn't sound as incongruous as it perhaps should have.

Then, nothing. For another two years no word or sign of Janner. I didn't pursue him, but I did go to the trouble of finding out about the Lurie Foundation, the body which I knew had part-funded Janner's research into the Ur-Bororo. The secretary of the foundation was unforthcoming. He wrote me a letter stating the aims of the foundation in the barest outline: 'To contribute to the understanding of the Ur-Bororo, a bursary will be provided for one post-graduate student every twenty years. Following his fieldwork the student will be required to lodge a paper of not less than 30,000 words with the Lurie Archive at the British Library.' The letter was signed by Dr Marston. I spoke to a librarian at the British Library, but she told me that all the documents relating to the Lurie Foundation were held in a closed stack. I had reached a dead end.

Janner had represented for me a set of possibilities that were unfulfilled. Even after twelve years these wider horizons continued to advance beyond my measured tread. Occasionally, sitting in the staff-room during a vacant period, I would suddenly find myself crying. I felt the tears, damp on my cheek, and into my stomach came a bubble of sweet sentimentality. But my hands gripped the edges of the *Education Supplement* too tightly, held it too stiffly in front of my face. All around me the talk was of interest rates. From time to time a corduroy trouser leg loomed into view.

Then one day in late summer, just after the school sports day, I was walking down the hill towards Purley when something caught my eye in the window of a launderette. An etiolated, waxy-looking individual was having an altercation with a rotund, middle-aged woman. Voices were raised and it was clear that they were on the verge of coming to blows. I heard the woman say quite distinctly, 'Coming in here and sitting staring at other people's laundry, you ought to be ashamed of yourself. Haven't you got any laundry of your own to look at, you filthy pervert?' She raised her hand to strike the man. As he turned to ward off the blow I saw his profile. It was Janner.

I stepped inside the launderette. Janner had evaded the first blow and was backing off to avoid a second. I touched him on the shoulder and said in my best disciplinary manner, 'Would you step outside for a minute please, sir?' The Protectress of Gussets was immediately convinced that here were the Proper Authorities. She surrendered her temporary deputy's badge with good grace. Janner stepped outside.

And continued a conversation with me as if it had been subject only to an hour's, rather than a decade's interruption.

'I'm living down here in Purley [a gurgle of catarrh] in a funny sort of a place. I've only been back from abroad for a couple of months. I was just observing this business of observing laundry. I'm convinced that the spinning circle of laundry has some of the properties of the mandala.'

We were by now heading down the hill at a brisk trot. Janner went on and on and on at length, trying to fit Purley laundering practices into a complex and highly unconvincing portrait of South London suburban society. He had lost none of his vigour. Any attempts I made to break into his monologue he interpreted as a desire to know still more. We fetched up by the station. Janner was still talking, still gesticulating.

'You see, Wingate Crescent represents a kind of epicentre; in order to reach the High Street you have to describe a circle. The positioning of the four launderettes – Washmatic, Blue Ribbon, Purley Way and Allnite – is also circular.' He stopped as if he had reached some kind of self-evident conclusion. I broke in.

'Where have you been, Janner? Have you been in the Amazon all this time? I found a record you'd written the sleeve notes for. Have you been collecting more failed chants? Are you married? I am. Are you going to give me any facts, or only more theories?' Janner was gobsmacked. When we'd been at Reigate I'd hardly ever answered back. My interjections had been designed purely to oil the machinery of his discourse. He became evasive.

'Um . . . well, just resting up. Yes, I have been away. Pretty boring really, just some fieldwork, due to publish a paper. I'm doing some teaching at Croydon for the moment. Living here in Purley. That's it, really.' He stopped in the centre of the pavement and pointed his hardened drip of a nose at the ground, I could hear the discreet burble of mucus in his thorax. A train from Victoria clattered across the points at Purley Junction. I could sense that Janner was about to slip away from me again.

'I did a bit of research of my own, Janner. I read up what I could about this tribe, the Ur-Bororo. Seems that some kind of foundation exists for anthropologists who are prepared to do fieldwork on them. The man who set it up, Lurie, was an eccentric amateur. He gifted his field notes to the British Library, but only on the condition that they remain unread. The only exceptions being those anthropologists who are prepared to go and carry on Lurie's fieldwork. Apparently, the number of recipients of Lurie Foundation grants were also to be severely restricted. Since Lurie set it up in the Thirties there have only been two – Marston and yourself.'

A double-decker bus pulled away from the stop across the road. For a moment it seemed poised in mid-acceleration, like some preposterous space rocket too heavy to lift itself from the earth, and then it surged off up the hill, rattling and roaring, a cloud of sticky diesel fumes, heavier and more tangible than the earth itself, spreading out behind. Janner spat yellow mucus into the gutter. In the late afternoon light his mouth was puckered with disapproval like an anus.

'I suppose you want to know all about it, then?'

'That's right, Janner. I've thought about you a lot during these past ten years. I always knew you'd do something remarkable, and now I want to know what it is – or was.'

He agreed to come to my house for dinner the following evening and I left him, standing in the High Street. To me he seemed suspiciously inconspicuous. His nondescript clothes, his everyman mien. It was as if he had been specially trained to infiltrate Purley. I bought my ticket and headed for the barrier. When I turned to look back at him he had reverted entirely to type. Standing, back against a duct, he was apparently reading the evening paper. But I could tell that he was carefully observing the commuters who thronged the station concourse.

The following evening Janner arrived punctually at 7.30 for dinner. He brought a bottle of wine with him and greeted my wife with the words, 'I expect you're quite a toughie being married to this one.' Words which were met with approval. He took off his gaberdine raincoat, sat down, and started to play with James. Janner was a big hit. If you had asked me beforehand I wouldn't have said that Janner was the kind of man who would have any rapport with small children, but as it was he was such a success that James asked him to read a bedtime story.

While Janner was upstairs my wife said to me, 'I like your friend. You've never told me about him before.' Dinner was even more of a success. Janner had developed a facility for companionable small talk which amazed me. He displayed a lively interest in all the minutiae of our lives: James, our jobs, our garden, our mortgage, our activities with local voluntary groups. All of it was grist to the mill of his curiosity and yet he never appeared to be condescending or merely inquisitive for the sake of gathering more anthropological data.

After dinner my wife went out. She had an evening class at the local CFE. Janner and I settled down in the living-room, passing the bottle of Piat d'Or back and forth to one another in an increasingly languid fashion.

'You were never like this when we were Reigate,' I said at length. 'Then all your pronouncements were weighty and wordy. How have you managed to become such an adept small-talker?'

'I learnt to small talk from the Ur-Bororo.' And with that strange introduction Janner launched into his story. He spoke as brilliantly as he ever had, without pausing, as if he had prepared a lecture to be delivered to a solo audience. It was, of course, what I had been dying to hear. All day I had feared that he wouldn't come and that I would have to spend weeks searching the launderettes of South London in order to find him again. Even if he did come, I was worried that he would tell me nothing. That he would remain an enigma and walk out of my life, perhaps this time for good.

'The Ur-Bororo are a tribe, or interlinked group of extended families, living in the Parasquitos region of the Amazon basin. In several respects they closely resemble the indigenous Amerindian tribes of the Brazilian rainforest: they are hunter-gatherers. They subsist on a diet of manioc supplemented with animal protein and miscellaneous vegetables. They are semi-nomadic – following a fixed circuit that leads them through their territory on a yearly cycle. Their social system is closely defined by the inter-relation of individuals to family, totemic family and the tribe as a whole. Social interaction is defined by a keen awareness of the incest taboo. Their spiritual beliefs can be characterised as animistic, although as we shall see this view stands up to only the slightest examination. Perhaps the only superficial character-istics that mark them out from neighbouring tribal groups are the extreme crudity of their manufacture. Ur-Bororo pottery, woodcarving and shelter construction must be unrivalled in their meanness and lack of decoration – this is what strikes the out-sider immediately. That and the fact that the Ur-Bororo are racially distinct . . . '

'Racially distinct?'

'Shh . . . ' Janner held up his hand for silence.

In the brief hiatus before he began to speak again I heard the low warble of the doves in the garden, and, looking across the railway line that ran at the bottom of the garden, I could make out the crenellations and chimneys of the row of semis opposite, drawing in the darkness, like some suburban jungle.

'It is said of any people that language defines their reality. It is only through a subtle appreciation of language that one can enter into the collective consciousness of a tribal grouping, let alone explore the delicate and subtle relationships between that consciousness, the individual consciousness and the noumenal world. Language among the Amerindian tribes of the Amazon is typically supplemented by interleaved semiological systems that, again, represent the coexstensive nature of kinship ties and the natural order. Typically among a tribe such as the Iguatil, body and facial tattooing, cicatrisation, decoration of ceramics, lip plugs and breech clouts will all contribute to the overall body of language.

'What is notable about the Ur-Bororo is that they exhibit none of these semiological systems. They aren't tattooed or cica-trised and they dress in a uniform fashion.'

'Dress?'

'Shhh . . . ! Lurie penetrated to the reality of the Ur-Bororo and was horrified by what he found. He locked his secret away. Marston lived among the Ur-Bororo for only a few months and ended up suspicious but still deceived by them. It was left for me to uncover the secret springs and cogs that drive the Ur-Bororo's world view; it was left for me to reveal them.'

Janner paused, seemingly for effect. He took a pull on his glass of Piat d'Or and drew out a pack of Embassy Regal. He lit one up and looked around for an ashtray. I passed him a small bowl, the kind you get free when you buy duck pâté at Sainsburys. This he examined with some interest, turning it this way and that in the yellow light of the standard lamp, before resuming his tale.

'The basic language of the Ur-Bororo is fairly simple and easy to learn, for a European. Neither its syntax nor its vocabulary is remarkable. It refers to the world which it is intended to describe with simple literal-mindedness. The juxtaposition of subject-object-predicate, in its clear-cut consistency, would seem to reflect a cosmology marked by the same conceptual dualism as our own. This is deceptive. I learnt the basic language of the Ur-Bororo within a couple of months of living with them. As we moved around the rainforest the elders of the tribe took it in turns to tutor me. They would point at objects, mimic actions and so forth. When I had become proficient in this workaday communication they began to refer to more complex ideas and concepts.

'I may add at this stage that their attitude towards me during this period was singular. They were not particularly amazed by me – although to my certain knowledge I was only the third European they had ever met – nor were they overly suspicious. It wasn't until months later that I was able to adequately characterise their manner: they were bland.

'To begin with, the conceptual language of the Ur-Bororo seemed quite unproblematic. It described a world of animistic deities who needed to be propitiated, kinship rituals that needed to be performed, and so forth. The remarkable thing was that in the life of Ur-Bororo society there was no evidence whatsoever of either propitiation or performance. I would hear some of the older men discussing the vital importance of handling the next batch of initiates: sending the adolescent boys to live in an isolated longhouse in the jungle and arranging for their circumcision. They would talk as if this were imminent, and then nothing would happen.

'The reasons for this became evident as I began to accurately decipher their conceptual language: the Ur-Bororo are a boring tribe.' Janner paused again.

A boring tribe? What could that mean?

'When I say that the Ur-Bororo are a boring tribe, this statement is not intended to be pejorative, or worse still, ironic.' Janner pushed himself forward in his chair, screwed up his eyes, and clenched his hands around the edges of the coffee table. 'The Ur-Bororo are objectively boring. They also view themselves as boring. Despite the superficially intriguing nature of the tribe, their obscure racial provenance, their fostering of the illusion of similarity to other Amazonian tribes, and the tiered structure of their language, the more time I spent with the Ur-Bororo, the more relentlessly banal they became.

'The Ur-Bororo believe that they were created by the Sky God, that this deity fashioned their forefathers and foremothers out of primordial muck. It wasn't what the Sky God should have been doing, it should have been doing some finishing work on the heavens and the stars. Creating the Ur-Bororo was what might be called a divine displacement activity. Unlike a great number of isolated tribal groups, the Ur-Bororo do not view themselves as being in any way the "typical" or "essential" human beings. Many such tribes refer to themselves as "The People" or "The Human Beings" and to all others as barbarians, half-animals and so forth. "Ur-Bororo" is a convenient translation of the name neighbouring tribes use for them, which simply means "here before the Bororo". The Ur-Bororo actually refer to themselves with typically irritating self-deprecation as "The People Who You Wouldn't Like to be Cornered by at a Party". They view other tribal peoples as leading infinitely more alluring lives than themselves, and often speak, not without a trace of hurt feelings, of the many parties and other social events to which they are never invited.

'I spoke earlier of a "deeper" conceptual language, spoken by the Ur-Bororo. This is not strictly accurate. The Ur-Bororo have a level of nuance that they can impart to all their conceptual beliefs and this more or less corresponds to the various levels of inflection they can place on their everyday language. To put it another way: the Ur-Bororo speak often of various religious beliefs and accepted cosmological situations but always with the implication that they are at best sceptical. Mostly the "nuance" implies that they are indifferent.

'By extension every word in the Ur-Bororo language has a number of different inflections to express kinds of boredom, or emotional states associated with boredom, such as apathy, ennui, lassitude, enervation, depression, indifference, tedium, and so on. Lurie made the mistake of interpreting the Ur-Bororo language as if "Boring" were the root word. As a result he identified no less than two thousand subjects and predicates corresponding in meaning to the English word. Such as boring hunting, boring gathering, boring fishing, boring sexual inter-course, boring religious ceremony and so on. He was right in one sense — namely that the Ur-Bororo regard most of what they do as a waste of time. In fact the expression that roughly corresponds to "now" in Ur-Bororo is "waste of time".'

Janner paused again and contemplated the empty glass he held in his hand.

'Do you want a cup of coffee?' I said.

'Oh, er . . . Yeah, OK.'

'It's only instant, I'm afraid.'

'That's all right.'

Out in the kitchen I looked around at the familiar objects while I waited for the kettle to boil. The dishwasher that had been our pride and joy when we were first married, the joke cruets shaped like Grecian statues which I'd bought in Brixton Market, James's childish daubs stuck to the fridge with insulating tape. I felt as if I had been looking at these things every day for a thousand days and that nothing had changed. And indeed this was true. Never before had the familiar seemed so . . . familiar. I returned to the living-room, shaken by my epiphany.

We sat back in our chairs and the next few moments passed in companionable silence as we used our teaspoons to break up the undissolved chunks of brown goo in our coffee mugs. Eventually Janner began to speak again.

'I had lived among the Ur-Bororo for nine months. I hunted with the men and I gathered with the women. At first I lived with the adolescent boys in their longhouse, but then I built a hut of my own and moved into it. I felt that I had gained about as much of an insight into Ur-Bororo society as I wanted. I had grown thin and sported a long beard. The Ur-Bororo had ceased to approach me with banal conversational sallies about the weather, which never changed anyway, and began to regard me with total indifference. They were well aware of what it was I was doing among them and they regarded the practice of anthropology with indifference as well. They have a saying in Ur-Bororo that can be roughly translated as, "Wherever you go in the world you occupy the same volume of space".

'As each new day broke over the forest canopy I felt the force of this aphorism. Despite the singular character of the Ur-Bororo I felt that on balance I might as well have never left Reigate.

'I had written up my notes and knew that if I returned to England I would be in a position to complete my doctoral thesis, but I felt a strange sense of inertia. Actually, there was nothing strange about it at all, I simply felt a sense of inertia. There was something wrong with the forest. It felt senescent. Cascades of lianas coated with fungus fell fifty, seventy, a hundred feet, down from the vegetable vaults and buttresses. The complicated twists and petrified coils reminded me of nothing so much as an ancient cardigan, lightly frosted with flecks of scalp and snot, as its wearer nods on and on into the fog of old age.

'The Ur-Bororo profess to believe that a spirit inhabits every tree, bush and animal – all living things have a spirit. The sense in which they believe this is ambiguous; it isn't a positive, assertive belief. Rather, they are content to let the hypothesis stand until it is proved otherwise. These spirits – like the Ur-Bororo themselves – are in a constant state of blank reverie. They are turned in upon the moment, belly-up to the very fact of life.

'It may have been my imagination, or the effect of having been for so long away from society, but I too began to feel the presence of the rainforest as one of transcendent being. The great, damp, dappled room was unfinished and unmade. Somewhere the spirits lay about, bloated on sofas, sleeping off a carbohydrate binge. All days merged into one long Tuesday afternoon. I knew I should leave the Ur-Bororo, but just when I had finally made up my mind to go, something happened. I fell in love.

'It was the time in the Ur-Bororo's yearly cycle when the tribe decamped *en masse*. The object of their excursion was to catch the lazy fish. These listless and enervated creatures live exclusively beneath a series of waterfalls, situated on the tributary of the Amazon which forms the northern boundary of the Ur-Bororos' territory.

'The tribe moved off in the dawn half-light. As we walked, the sun came up. The jungle gave way to a scrubland, over which rags of mist blew. It was a primordial scene, disturbed only by the incessant, strident chatter of the Ur-Bororo. It was a fact that never ceased to astonish me, that despite their professed utter boredom, the Ur-Bororo continued to have the urge to bore one another still further.

'On this particular morning – just as they had every other morning during the time I had spent among them – they were all telling one another the dreams they had had the night before. They all chose to regard their dreams as singular and unique. This provided them with the rationale for constant repetition. In truth, you have never heard anything more crushingly obvious than an Ur-Bororo dream anecdote. They went on and on, repeating the same patterns and the same caricatures of reality. It was like a kind of surreal nursery wallpaper. "And then I turned into a fish," one would say. "That's funny," would come the utterly predictable reply, "I changed into a fish in my dream as well, and today we're going fishing." And so on. Strict correspondence between dream and reality, that was the Ur-Bororo's idea of profundity and as a consequence they placed only the most irritating interpretations on their dreams. As far as I was aware the Ur-Bororo had no particular view about the status of the unconscious – they certainly didn't attach any mystical significance to it. On the whole the impression their dreams gave was of a kind of psychic clearing house where all the detritus of the waking world could be packaged away into neat coincidences.

'While I listened to this drivel I gnawed the inside of my cheek with irritation:

'"I dreamt I was in a forest."

'"A rainforest?"

'"Sort of. I was walking along with some other people in single file. You know what I mean?"

'"Were they the kind of people you wouldn't like to be cornered by at a party?"

'"Definitely, it was us. Then I started turning into ... " (What would it be this time? A bird, a lizard, a moth, a yam ... no, it was ...) "... a twig! Isn't that amazing?"

'"Amazing."

'Yeah, amazing. I was so absorbed by my mounting irritation that I simply hadn't noticed the person who was walking in front of me along the forest path. But, coming out into a clearing for a moment, a clear shaft of bright light penetrated the forest canopy and struck the path. Suddenly I saw a young girl, bathed in bright light, her lissom figure edged with gold. She turned to face me. She was wearing the traditional Ur-Bororo garment — a long shapeless grey shift. She glanced for a moment into my eyes; hers were filmed over with immobility, her hand picked and fidgeted at the hem of her shift. She made a little *moue*, brushed a fly off her top lip and said, "I dreamt last night that I was hairball."

'At that precise moment I fell in love. The girl's name was Jane. She was the daughter of one of the tribal elders, although that was of hardly any real significance. You must understand that by this time I was pretty well conditioned by the Ur-Bororo's aesthetic values and to me Jane appeared to be, if not exactly beautiful, at least very appealing, in a homely, comfortable sort of a way. She was in many ways a typical Ur-Bororo, of medium height, with a rather pasty complexion and mousey hair. Her features were rather lumpy, but roughly symmetrical, and her mouth was tantalising, downturned by an infuriatingly erotic expression of sullen indifference.

'Our courtship started immediately. There are no particular guidelines for courtship in Ur-Bororo society. In fact the whole Ur-Bororo attitude to sex, gender and sexuality is muddied and ambiguous. At least formally, pre-marital sex, homosexuality and infidelity are frowned on, but in practice the Ur-Bororo's sexual drive is so circumscribed that no one really minds what anyone else gets up to. The general reaction is simply mild amazement that you have the energy for it.

'All day the kingfishers dived in and out of the glistening brown stream. And the Ur-Bororo stood about in the shallows, perfectly motionless for minutes on end, scrutinising the water.

From time to time one of them would bend down and with infinite languor pull out a fish. I soon grew bored and wandered off with Jane into the undergrowth. We strolled along side by side, neither speaking nor touching. The midday sun was high overhead, but its rays barely penetrated the forest canopy two hundred feet above us.

'Gradually, the strangeness of the situation began to impinge on my idle consciousness and I started to look around at the forest, as if for the first time. I had paid attention to the natural world only insofar as it had a bearing on the life of the Ur-Bororo, but now I found myself taking the alien scene in in an aesthetic sense, with the eyes of a lover. And a pretty dull and unexciting scene it was too. You didn't have to be a botanist to see that this area of the rainforest was exceptionally lacking in variegation as far as flora and fauna were concerned. The dun-coloured trunks of the tall trees lifted off into the sky like so many irregular lamp standards, while the immediate foreground was occupied by rank upon rank of rhododendron-type shrubs, none of which seemed to be in flower. It was a scene of unrivalled monotony – the Amazonian equivalent of an enormous municipal park.

'I knew that Jane and I were straying towards the traditional boundary of the Ur-Bororo lands, but neither of us was unduly concerned. Although the neighbouring tribe, the Yanumani, were notorious as headhunters and cannibals, their attempts to engage the young Ur-Bororo men in ritual warfare had been met in the past with such apathy on the part of the Ur-Bororo that they had long since given up trying. There was neither the sense of danger nor the beauty of nature to augment my sense of erotic frisson and after an hour or so's walk it entirely died away. I wondered what I was doing walking in the middle of nowhere with this rather sulky, drably dressed young woman. Then I saw the fag packet.

'It was an old Silk Cut packet, crushed flat and muddy, the inked lettering faded but still sharply legible, especially in this alien context. But I didn't have long to marvel at its incongruous presence, I could already hear the distant whine of chainsaws. I turned to Jane.

'"White men?"

'"Yes, they're extending the Pan-American Highway through

here. The estimated completion date is June 1985." She tugged and picked at her hem.

'"But aren't you frightened? Aren't you concerned? The coming of the road will destroy your entire culture, it may even destroy you."

'"Big deal."

'We turned round and started back to the river. That night as Jane and I lay together, her leaden form cutting off my circulation and gradually crushing the life out of my arm, I made a decision . . . '

There was the sound of the front door closing my and wife came into the room. She was carrying her bicycle lamps and wearing an orange cagoule.

'What, still talking? Has James been calling, darling?'

'No, not a peep out of him all evening.'

'Good, that means he hasn't done it. I'll get him up now and then put him down for the night.' She turned to Janner, 'James is going through a bed-wetting stage.'

'Really?' said Janner. 'You know, I wet the bed right up until I went to Reigate.' And they were off again. Janner seemed to sense no incongruity at all in moving directly from relating the high drama of his sojourn with the Ur-Bororo, to discussing the virtues of rubber sheets with my wife. I squeaked back in the vinyl of my armchair and waited for them to wind one another down. I had to hear the rest of Janner's story, I wouldn't let him go until he had finished. If necessary I would force him to stay until morning.

'Well, you must come again. You two seem to have such a lot to catch up on.'

'We do, but next time you must come over to our place. My wife doesn't know many people in Purley and she's trying to get out of the house a bit more now that she's had the baby.'

I sat upright with a jerk. What was that Janner had said? Wife? Baby? My wife had said goodnight and reminded me to lock up. She was padding quietly up the stairs.

'Your wife, Janner, is it . . . ?'

'Jane, yes. Now if you keep quiet I'll tell you the rest of the story.

'I courted Jane for three weeks. This involved little more than sitting around with her parents, making small talk. The

Ur-Bororo have an almost inexhaustible appetite for small talk. Like the English they preface almost all conversations with a lengthy discussion of the weather, although in their monotonous climate there is far less to talk about. So little in fact, that they are reduced to mulling over the minutiae of temperature, humidity and precipitation. Jane's parents were affable enough characters. They seemed to have no objection to our marriage, as long as we were seen to observe the customary formalities and rituals. I was packed off to receive instruction from the shaman.

'The shaman was uncharacteristically interesting for an Ur-Bororo. I suppose it was something to do with his profession. His shed was set slightly apart from those of the rest of the tribe. (You remember the shed I lived in when we were at Reigate. It was almost an exact replica of an Ur-Bororo dwelling shed, except of course that the Amazonian ones have rather rougher clapboarding and no window, only a square opening.)

'"Come in my dear boy, do come in," he said. "So you're going to marry young Jane and take her away from us are you?" I nodded my assent.

'"Well, I expect as an anthropologist that you know a little of our beliefs, don't you? How we were created inadvertently by the Sky God. How we live our lives. How we practise circumcision and infibulation as cleansing rituals. How our young men undergo rigorous rites of passage and how our initiation rites last for weeks and involve the ingestion of toxic quantities of psychotropic roots; you know all this, don't you?"

'"Well, in outline, yes, but I can't say that I've ever seen any of you ever do any of these things at all."

'"No. Quite right, jolly good, jolly good. That's the ticket, you seem to have a good head on your shoulders. Of course we don't actually do any of these things."

'"But why? Surely you're frightened of all the gods and spirits?"

'"Well, we don't really believe in them in quite that way you know. We believe in their validity as er . . . examples, metaphors if you will, of the way that things are, but we don't actually believe in tree spirits, good Lord no!"

'The shaman chuckled for quite a while at the thought such excessive religious zeal, and then offered me a cup of coya. Coya

89

is a lukewarm drink made from the powdered root of the coya tree, it looks alarmingly like instant coffee, but the taste is a lot blander. I couldn't be bothered to argue with this absurd figure. Unlike other tribes who have shamen, the status of the shaman in Ur-Bororo society is ambiguous and somewhat irrelevant. The shaman often sketched out the form of some of the rigorous rituals the Ur-Bororo nominally believe in, but hardly anyone even bothered to attend these mock performances. On the whole he was regarded with a kind of amused disdain. Although it was still thought important to have pale versions of the ceremonies performed for births, marriages and deaths.

'I saw the shaman a couple more times before our marriage. He went through the tired motions of instructing me in the Ur-Bororo faith and also retailed me a lot of useless advice on how to make marriage work. Stuff about counting to ten when I got angry, giving Jane the opportunity to state her case when we had a disagreement, and all this kind of twaddle, the sort of thing you'd expect from an advice column in a fourth-rate women's magazine.

'The ceremony itself was held to be a great success. Twenty or thirty of us gathered outside the shaman's shed and Jane and I joined hands while we all listened to him irritate us by wittering inanities in a high fluting voice. I can quite honestly say that I've never seen a drabber social occasion than that Ur-Bororo wedding ceremony. All of us in our grey tunics, standing in the gloomy clearing being comprehensively bored.

'After the actual ceremony, the guests disported themselves around the clearing, talking nineteen to the dozen. Jane led me among them and introduced me to aunts, cousins and friends. All of whom I knew too well already. The aunts pinched my cheek and made fatuous comments. There was much ingestion of rather watery manioc beer, which was followed, inevitably, by the kind of turgid flatulence which passes for high spirits among the Ur-Bororo.

'Jane has a brother, David, and the Ur-Bororo knew that I intended to take both of them back to England with me after the wedding, but they showed little surprise or emotion about it. They also knew that I was convinced that their society was doomed to extinction, but this too failed to exercise them. They had no particular feelings about the coming of civilisation and

I found it impossible to rouse them out of their torpor. To be honest, I had long since given up trying.

'Our departure was an unemotional experience. There were slight hugs, pecks on the cheek and handclasps all round. Jane seemed mildly piqued. As our canoe slid off down river, one of the younger men cried out, "Come back soon, if you can stand the pace!" And then we were gone. In two days we were at the town of Mentzos where we boarded a launch that took us to the mouth of the Amazon. Two days after that we were in Buenos Aires and a day later we arrived in Purley, where we have remained ever since.'

'And that's it? That's the story?'

'Yes. Like I said, I live in Purley now and I do a little teaching at Croydon Polytechnic. If you like to put it this way: I'm cured of my obsession with the Ur-Bororo.'

'But what about the Lurie Foundation? Don't you have to publish your work? Won't it be popularised in the Sunday supplements?'

'No, no, there's no necessity for that. All Lurie wanted was for some other poor idiot to suffer the unbelievable tedium he experienced when staying with the Ur-Bororo in the Thirties.'

'And what about Jane and David? You can't tell me that you've managed to integrate them into English society with no difficulty at all. You said that the Ur-Bororo are racially distinct, what does that mean?'

'Yes that's true, and I suppose in a way intriguing; the Ur-Bororo don't really have any defining characteristics as a people. They aren't Mongoloid or Negro or Caucasian or anything for that matter. But their appearance as a people is so unremarkable that one – how can I put it – doesn't feel inclined to remark upon it. As for Jane, I'm very much in love with her. I must confess that although we can't be said to have a great rapport, I still find her maddeningly erotic; it's something about her complete inertia when she's in bed, it makes me feel so . . . so like a man. We have a child now, Derek, and he's all that you could want. And David still lives with us. Why don't you and your wife come over next week and meet them, you'll be able to see how well they've assimilated.'

After Janner had gone I sat staring at the twin elements of the electric fire. It was high summer and they were cold and lifeless and covered with a fine furring of dust which I knew would singe with a metallic smell when winter came. Funny how no one ever thinks of dusting the elements of electric fires. Perhaps there was room on the market for some kind of special-ised product.

Exactly a week later my wife and I stood outside 47 Fernwood Crescent. The house was lit up in a cheery sort of way, the curtains were pulled back from the windows and inside every-thing looked spic and span. Number 47 was a more or less typical Purley residence, semi-detached with a corrugated car port to the side of the house in lieu of the garage. Like the other residents of Fernwood Crescent Janner had taken the trouble to paint the exterior woodwork and drainpipes in an individual colour, in his case bright green. The bell ding-donged under my finger and the green door swung open.

'You must be Jane?'

'That's right, come in. I've heard such a lot about you.'

What I first noticed about her was her accent, remarkably flat and colourless – it was pure South London, right down to the slightly nasal character. I can't say that I paid any attention at all to what she looked like; in this respect Janner's description of her was entirely accurate. She was like someone that you pass in a crowd, a face that you momentarily focus on and then forget for ever. As for her brother David, who got up from the sofa to greet us, there was an obvious family resemblance.

We hung up our coats and sat down in a rough semi-circle around the redundant fireplace, and exchanged the conver-sational inanities which signify 'getting-to-know-one-another'. After a while Janner came in. 'Sorry, I didn't hear you arrive. I've just been in the garden doing a little pottering. Would any-one like a drink?' He took orders and repaired to the kitchen. By the time he returned I was deeply embroiled with David in a discussion of the relative merits of the Dewey decimal system, as against other methods of cataloguing. Janner caught the tail-end of something we were saying. 'I see David's caught you already,' he laughed. 'He won't let up now, he's a demon for classification since he started work at the library. Why, he's even colour-coded the spice jars in the kitchen.' We all laughed at this.

What Janner said was true. David wouldn't let go of me all evening. He was an irritating conversationalist who had the habit of not only repeating everything that you said, but also ending your sentences for you, so that a typical exchange went something like this:

'Yes, we try and maintain a microfiche ... '

'Catalogue at the school for the older students – maintain a microfiche catalogue for the older students, hmn ... '

I would have felt like hitting David if it wasn't for the fact that he was so affable and ingratiating. Dinner was unremarkable. We had some kind of casseroled meat with vegetables, but I couldn't say what kind of meat it was.

David's pressing interest in taxonomy cast a deep sense of enervation over me. I nearly slumped down on my chair during the dessert course and once or twice the vinyl did give off a squawk. My wife and Jane were deep in conversation about the Local Education Authority and Janner had disappeared upstairs to change the baby's nappy. I excused myself from David and tiptoed after him.

I found him in a little room under the eaves which had been tricked out as a nursery. He was deftly manipulating the Wet Ones, as a man born to it. The baby was a nondescript little thing with putty-coloured skin and a whorl of indeterminate mousey hair on its little scalp.

'Takes after its mother,' said Janner grasping two tiny feet in his one bony hand. 'Can't say I'm sorry. Wouldn't wish my face on any child.'

'Janner, what are you going to do?'

'Do? Do about what?'

'About Jane, about David, about the Ur-Bororo.'

'Why, nothing, nothing at all.' He fastened the sticky-backed tapes and plunked the baby back in its cot. It stared up at us with blank, unfocused, incurious eyes.

'But Janner, you're a scientist, you have a duty to tell. Is it the Lurie Foundation, have they got some kind of a hold on you?'

'Nothing of the sort. Of course I could publish if I wanted to, but for some reason the whole subject of the Ur-Bororo leaves me cold, I just can't get worked up about it. I don't think the world would be any the wiser for my insights.'

Soon afterwards we took our leave. All the way home my wife talked about Jane. They seemed to have really hit it off together. I was silent, entirely preoccupied by my thoughts about Janner and the Ur-Bororo.

Our two families became quite close during that autumn. I should say that we saw each other at least once a fortnight, sometimes more. I even grew to appreciate David. There was something admirable about his dogged adherence to the most simple categories he could latch on to. As for Janner, I raised the subject of the Ur-Bororo with him several more times but he was completely unconcerned. He was in the process of becoming quite a minor celebrity – the sort of pop academic the general public takes up from time to time and turns into a television personality. His book linking the observation of swirling laundry to traditional Buddhist meditation surprisingly had become a hit and he was in the process of negotiating serialisation with the colour supplements.

As for me, I went on teaching, playing volleyball and asking recalcitrant pupils the names of power stations. The lagging which had for a brief period been removed from my mind came back – together with new, improved, cavity-wall insulation.

The Quantity Theory of Insanity

Denver, Colorado

A depressing day here at the special interdisciplinary conference.
I suppose that as the author of the theory that has generated so
much academic activity I should feel a certain proprietorial glee
at the sight of hundreds of psychologists, sociologists, social
scientists and other less mainstream academics running hither
and thither, talking, disputing, gesturing, debating and confer-
ring. Instead I feel only depressed and alienated from the great
industry of thought I myself have engineered. And added to that
I think the low quality of the celluloid they've used for the
name badges betrays the fact that the department simply hasn't
allocated a big enough budget.

I spent the morning in the main auditorium of the university
giving my address to the assembled conferees. Dagglebert,
against my expressed wishes, had put together some kind of
video display or slide show to accompany my introductory lecture, 'Some Aspects of the Quantity Theory of Insanity'. Sadly,
even though Dagglebert has irrepressible faith in visual aids, he
has absolutely no spatial awareness whatsoever. I kept looking
up and realising that flow charts were running over my face,
and at one stage I looked down to discover that my stomach was
neatly encompassed by a Venn diagram section tagged 'Manic
Depressives in Coventry 1977–79'.

Despite these and other drawbacks, it went well. Several hundred hirsute men and women sat on the edge of their seats for

a full three hours while I went over the principal aspects of the theory. If the truth be told I could have gargled and they would have been just as attentive. I've now reached that rarefied position in academia where I have the cachet of a lecturing Miles Davis. I could have allowed Dagglebert to project slides for three hours and then sauntered on for five minutes of disjointed and facile muttering – and still I would have been vigorously applauded.

As it was I declined to cash in on the credulousness of my audience. For once I would attempt the truth. I would take a serious stab at stopping the feverish growth of an industry I myself was responsible for helping to create. I would demystify the Quantity Theory myth, and in the process take a few clay idols down with me.

Accordingly, I dealt with the subject personally as well as historically. As with all great theories I felt that it was especially important for an academic audience to understand the personal dimension, the essential *humanity* of the origin of such an idea. But it didn't work. Once one has a certain kind of academic status, any statement that you make, if it is couched in the language of your discipline, no matter how critical, how searching, is seen only as an embellishment, another layer of crystalline accretion to the stalactite. To break it off at the root, one's language would have to be brutal, uncompromising, emotional, non-technical.

So I began by telling them of the grey cold afternoon in suburban Birmingham, when, labouring to complete the index to an American college press's edition of my doctoral thesis, 'Some Social Aspects of Academic Grant Application in 1970's Britain', I was visited in one pure thought bite with the main constituents of the theory as we know it today.

At least that would be one way of looking at the experience. Seen from another angle the Quantity Theory was merely the logical conclusion of years of frustrated thinking, the butter that eventually formed after the long rhythm of churning. I have often had occasion to observe – and indeed Stacking has recently and belatedly stated the observation as a tentative syndrome which he expresses: $(Á \rightarrow Å)$. Where $Å = $ *a subsequent state of affairs* – that events are reconstructed more than they are ever constructed.

*

Once you have published, grown old and then died, the events surrounding the original theoretical discovery with which you have been associated take on an impossible causal direction and momentum. One which certainly wasn't apparent at the time. Scientists are particularly prone to this syndrome. For example, take Gödel and his Incompleteness. Once he had made the proposition, everything in his life had necessarily led up to that moment, that piece of work. Thus, when the infant Gödel cried in his cot, the particular twist of phlegm striations, wafted in his gullet by his bawling, implied that no logical symbolic system can construct full grounds for its own proof. Poor Gödel, his breakdowns, his anorexia, all of them inextricably bound up with his fifteen minutes of academic fame. Why?

Well, put simply, when aberrant events occur they become subject to the same principle – at the level of human, social observation – as particles do to instrumental observation at the sub-atomic level. The effect of observation has a direct impact on the nature of the event, altering its coordinates as it were, although not in any simple dimension. I mean, if an aberrant event occurs it doesn't then occur in another place or time because of the attention it subsequently attracts. It doesn't retro-actively take up that other position or time, or even *rate of occurrence* before it has in fact taken place. That would be absurd.

Rather all of these: the effect of observation on aberrant events tends to be the reversal of their causality, their causal direction. However, there is no reversal of necessity as far as the occurrence of P is concerned – and I think this is something that has been ignored.

So when I 'thought up' the Quantity Theory of Insanity, I was in fact being caused to think it up by the subsequent fact of the general reaction that occurred: public commotion, academic furore, even a front-page paragraph in the quality press. Let me make this clearer by means of an example: with murders, to take a commonplace aberrant event, this syndrome is so obvious that it hardly arouses any comment. X commits a murder, or he *apparently* commits a murder. Perhaps it was a very unfortunate accident? Maybe he was arguing with Y and pushed her rather too vigorously and she tripped on the lino and dashed her brains out on the edge of the gas cooker, just like that. Furthermore, perhaps X, crazed with grief, went mad, cut up Y and buried her in the garden. Subsequently caught, X was then *retrospectively* branded 'psychopathic', by anyone and everyone who had any connection with him. 'Oooh, yairs,' says a neighbour, 'the way he rattled those empty milk bottles together when he put them out on the front step, there was something demonic about it.' X, once upstanding, loyal, prone, perhaps, to the same slight eccentricities as anyone – G, for example, although let us not bandy capitals – has been ruined, now and in the past, by the observation factor.

None of this, you can now appreciate (and perhaps always have) is by way of digression. If we are to talk meaningfully of my life, and of the part that I played in the origination of Quantity Theory, we must be able to account for observational factors – and then be able to ignore them. Ironically, given the tendency to subordinate the individual consciousness to some creative zeitgeist, I turn out to be the best possible Quantity Theory historian. After all, I was there. Which is more than can be said for Musselborough, Nantwich and the rest of those twerps.

Well, then. My own early life was fraught with neurotic illness. The debacle surrounding my analysis by Alkan is well known to the public, so there's no point in trying to hide it. The received understanding about my background, my early life, my schooling, and indeed my undergraduate studies with Müeller, is that they were all spectacularly mundane. My circumstances and character – if you listen to these biographers – had the absolute banality of a Hitler. They were so ordinary, that reading the facts on paper one could only conclude that they had been recorded as the prelude to some cautionary tale.

In this respect the 'official version' is wholly correct. Mine was a childhood of Terylene sheets, bunion plasters and Sunday afternoon excursions to witness the construction of Heathrow Airport. My parents were quiet people, who conspired together gently to live in a world where no one shitted, ejaculated, or killed one another violently. This upbringing left me morbidly incapable of dealing with the real world. I was appalled by my own body. The obsession I developed in my teens with the theoretical aspects of psychology was a logical path to take, it offered me a liberation from the nauseating, cloacal confines of my own skin.

I had no sense of being singled out as unique, or blessed. I had no suspicion that I might be the *ubermensch*. Quite the reverse. It was painfully clear to me that I was destined to become like my father, constantly striving to stave off chaos through rigorous application to detail. My father was an actuary, but he never regarded the calculations he made all day as relating to real risks, or real people. Indeed, when asked by people what he did for a living he would invariably say that he was a mathematician.

You can see, therefore, that meeting Alkan was a godsend; his impact on me was enormous. He really had his breakdown for me insofar as it actually propelled me further into the awful mundanity I was prey to, so far and so fast that I could not help but emerge. Without Alkan's influence I might have remained eking out my feeble studies over decades.

A bleak flatland day, that's how I remember it. At the time I had received the first of many postgraduate grants. This one was to enable me to do some work on phrenological and physiognomic theories of the nineteenth century. I was particularly taken by the work of Gruton, an English near-contemporary and sometime collaborator with Fleiss. Gruton maintained (and it was his only real gift to posterity) that the visible nose represented only ⅛ of the 'real' nose. The nose we see rising above the surface of our faces was, according to Gruton, literally the tip of the psychological iceberg of hereditary predisposition. The 'shape' of the real, internal nose is the true indicator of character, proclivities and so forth.

In the 1880s Gruton developed a system of measuring the internal nose using very bright spotlights inserted into ears, eyes and indeed the nose itself. The patient's head was shaved and when the light was switched on, the shadow area defined on the scalp was traced on to paper. Using a complex topological equation Gruton would then cross-reference all the different projections to produce what he called a 'nasoscope'. This then was an accurate representation of the shape of the internal nose.

The morning I met Alkan I was crossing the campus on my way back from the library to my bed-sitting-room. I had a sheaf of nasoscopes, which I'd received that morning by rail from the archivist at the Gruton Clinic, tucked under my arm.

I must explain at this juncture that at this time Alkan was nearing the height of his celebrity. Predictably, I eschewed attending his seminars which he held regularly in the squat, twenty-two-storey psychology faculty building. These were clearly for sychopants and groupies – besides which Alkan himself, although he had trained first as a medical doctor and then as a psychiatrist, was nonetheless sympathetic to the psychotherapeutic movement. I, on the other hand, made empirical testability the benchmark of all theory and could not abide the woolly fantasising that seemed to dominate couch-pushing.

Alkan was an imposing figure. In appearance somewhat like Le Corbusier, but much taller and thinner. Entirely bald, he affected a manner of almost complete naturalness, which was difficult to fault. Undoubtedly it was this that had given him his tremendous reputation as a clinician. When Alkan said, 'How are you?' the question had total nuance: he really wanted to know how you were, although at the same time he was asking the question purely for the sake of social form. Yet he managed simultaneously to acknowledge both of these conflicting messages and still reformulated the question so that it incorporated them and yet was devoid of all assumptions. Furthermore none of the above seemed to be *implied*.

Alkan, then. Striding across the concrete agora at Chelmsford, his form complementing the anthropomorphic brutalism of the campus architecture. Shoulders twisted – arbitrarily, like the sprigs of steel that protrude from reinforced concrete. And I, wholly anonymous, at that time consciously cultivating a social apathy and lack of character which was beginning to border on the pathological. We collided in the very centre of the agora, because I was not looking at where I was going. The impact knocked the loose bundle of nasoscopes from under my arm and they fell about us, lapping the paving slabs. The two of us then ducked and dove, until they were all gathered up again, smiling all the while.

Before handing them back to me Alkan paused and examined one of the nasoscopes. I was impressed, he clearly knew what it was. He was following its shape to see if it conformed with the 'character equation' Gruton had inked in below.

'Fascinating, a nasoscope. I haven't seen one for years. I did some work on Gruton once . . . '

'Oh, er . . . Oh. I didn't know, at least I haven't read it.' I felt absolutely at a loss. I was meant to have the license to hate the playboy Alkan and here he was professing detailed knowledge of the obscure corner of the field to which I had staked my own claim.

'No reason why you should have. It was never published.' He fell to examining the plasticised sheet again. As he scanned the meticulously shaded areas that formed the character map, he pursed his lips and blew through them, making an odd whiffling noise. This was just one of Alkan's numerous idiosyncrasies which I later made my own.

'D'you see there.' He pointed at a long, lacy blob, not dissimilar to the north island of New Zealand. 'Gruton would have said that that indicated *heimic* tendencies.'

'Sorry?'

'*Heimic* tendencies. Gruton believed that masturbation could not only cause moral degeneration in terms of the individual psyche, he also thought that it could influence people politically. He developed a whole vocabulary of terms to describe these different forms of degeneration, one of which was *heimic*. If you care to come to my rooms I'll show you a little dictionary of these terms that Gruton put together and had printed at his own expense.'

Alkan's rooms were in the Monoplex, the tower built in 1952 for the Festival of Britain, which dominated the Chelmsford campus. A weird, cantilevered construction shaped like a cigar, it zoomed up into the flat Essex sky. The lift, as ever, was out of order and Alkan attacked the staircase with great gusto. I remember that he seemed entirely unaffected by the climb when I staggered into a seat in his rooms some five minutes later, a hundred and fifty feet higher up.

We spent the rest of that morning together. Alkan was an amazing teacher and as we looked at his cache of Gruton papers and then moved on to broader subjects he amazed me by the way he illuminated grey area after grey area. His dialectical method was bizarre to say the least. It took the form of antithesis succeeding antithesis. Alkan would guide the student into acknowledging that he found a theory, or even a body of fact, untenable but that he could not supply an alternative; and then he would admit that he couldn't either. His favourite expression was 'I don't know'. Area after area of the most complex thought was illuminated for me by those 'I don't knows'.

At that time Alkan was still practising as an analyst and it was his contention that no educative relationship could proceed without a simultaneous therapeutic relationship. Alkan's student/analysands were a raucous bunch. Zack Busner, Simon Gurney, Adam Sikorski, Phillip Hurst and the other Adam, Adam Harley. Now of course these are virtually household names, but at that time they were like any other group of young bloods – doing their doctoral work, affecting a particular dress style and swaggering about the campus as if they owned it.

Alkan's bloods delighted in playing elaborate psychological tricks on one another – the aim of which was to convince the victim that he was psychotic. They went to great lengths to perpetrate these. Spiking each others' breakfast cereals with peyote, constructing elaborate *trompe l'oeil* effects – false landscapes glued to the outside of the window – and insinuating bugging equipment into rooms so that they could then 'unconsciously' voice their comrades' private ejaculations. These high jinks were looked down on benignly by Alkan, who viewed them as the necessary flexing of the muscles of the psyche. As for other members of the faculty, academics and students alike viewed Alkan's bloods with undisguised suspicion, bordering on loathing.

I was totally disarmed by the interest that Alkan had taken in my Gruton work. He seemed genuinely impressed by the research that I had done – and he put my lack of conviction easily on a par with his own. I would say that that morning in his eyrie-office I was as near to knowing the *real* Alkan as I ever would be. His subsequent behaviour ran back into his early work after he was dead and formed a composite view of a man who was much more than the sum of his parts – and I suppose there is a certain justice in the judgement of posterity – he had, after all, incorporated parts of other people as well as his own.

Nonetheless, I was genuinely astonished when I realised the next month that Alkan, had, without in any way consulting or warning me, arranged to take over the role of my supervisor Dr Katell. The first I knew of this was a handwritten list on a noticeboard which stated quite clearly that I was due to see Dr Alkan for my monthly meeting. I hurried along to see Dr Katell. He was sitting in his blond wood office by the rectangular lily pond. The place stank of furniture polish, a bright bunch of dahlias stood squeaking in a cut-glass vase.

'My dear boy . . . ' he said, squeaking forward his little ovoid body on the synthetic leather seat of his synthetic leather armchair. I made my goodbyes and left.

When I appeared for my first supervisory session Alkan was all smiles. He took the bundle of manuscript and nasoscopes out from under my arm and ushered me to a seat.

'My dear boy,' he said, hunching his lanky body in the leather sling that stretched between the two stainless steel handlebars which constituted the arms of his chair. 'My dear boy. You realise of course that as your thesis supervisor I feel it my duty, my obligation, to undertake an analysis with you . . . '

We started at once. Alkan's analytic method, which still has some practitioners to this day, despite the impact of Quantity Theory, was commonly termed 'Implication'. Its full title came from Alkan's 1956 paper of the same name, 'Implied Techniques of Psychotherapy'. Put simply (and to my mind it was a ludicrously simple idea), instead of the analyst listening to the patient and then providing an interpretation, of whatever kind, Alkan would say what he *thought* the analysand would say. The analysand was then obliged to furnish the interpretation he thought Alkan would make. Alternatively, Alkan would give an interpretation and the analysand was required to give an account that adequately matched it.

The theory that lay behind this practice was that the psyche contained a 'refractive membrane'. An interior, reflective barrier which automatically mirrored any stimuli. Naturally the only way to 'trick' the reflective membrane was to present it with information that was incapable of 'reflection'. Information that assumed the reflection from the off. I suppose the remarkable thing about Alkan's method — and indeed its subsequent practitioners — is that all their published case histories bear a startling resemblance to those of entirely conventional methods. In other words, the implication technique made no difference whatsoever to either the actual content of an analysis, or the ultimate course.

I lived in digs in Colchester during the final two years I spent under Alkan's supervision. My doctoral thesis grew by leaps and bounds, until I was unable to pay for the typist. As far as Alkan was concerned, Implication gave me the confidence I needed to reach my full, neurotic potential. If I had been withdrawn before, I now became posivitely hermitic. I never saw my fellow post-graduates, except for the monthly post-graduate meetings.

Alkan implied, time after time, that I was a colourless, deliberately bland individual whose whole psyche was bent to the task of deflecting whatever stimuli the world had to give me. My studies, my personal habits, even my appearance, were merely extensions of my primary defensive nature. He was right. I hated to socialise; I had no sense of fun at all. I deliberately affected the utmost anonymity. I was obsessively neat, but devoid of any redeeming idiosyncrasies. My room at Mrs Harris's was the same the day I left as it was the day I arrived. The bedside lamp stood on the same paper doily, the gas fire whiffled, the puppies sported on the wall, the plastic-backed brush and comb set was correctly aligned. Mrs Harris was a stolid, taciturn woman and that suited me just fine. I would sit silently at the breakfast table and she would lay impossible mounds of food in front of me. I would eat the food and suffer accordingly. It is the great success of a certain strain of English puritan to have almost completely internalised the mortification they feel it necessary to inflict, both on themselves and others.

And so the most banal of things were effortlessly metamorphosed into experiences over a period of some months. There was no real progress until the day Alkan disappeared. Arriving early (as was dictated by the psychopathology that Alkan had himself implied for me) for the monthly meeting of Alkan's analysand/students I found the group prematurely assembled. They ignored me as I slid awkwardly into a tip-up chair and desk combination at the back of the classroom. Adam Harley was speaking.

'There's no sign of him anywhere, no note, no indication of where he might be . . . '

'Run through it all again, Adam, from the beginning. There may be something you've neglected,' Sikorski broke in.

'All right. Here it is. I arrived for my session with Alkan at about 9.30 this morning. I knocked on the door to his rooms and he shouted "Come in". I entered. He wasn't in the main room so I assumed he was in the bathroom. I sat down and waited, after about five minutes I became a little restless and began to wander about. I took some books out of the bookcase, leafed through them and put them back. I was trying to create just enough noise to remind Alkan that I was there without being intrusive. Eventually I became curious, the door to the bathroom was ajar, I pushed it open ... the bathroom was empty, there was no one there.'

'And you're absolutely sure that you heard him call to you.'

'Certain. Unless it was one of you with a tape recorder.'

There was general laughter at this point. I took the opportunity to slip out of the prefabricated classroom. I had a hunch.

Across the receding chessboard of flagstones whipped by the wind, I skittered from side to side. The crux, as it were, of my early experience lay in this decision, this leap into the unknown; this act of what could only be called initiative. It could be argued (and indeed has been, see Stenning: 'Fluid Participles, Choice and Change'), that I was merely responding to an appropriate transference, in the appropriate infantile/neurotic manner.

Today, if I remember that day at all, it is summed up for me by one of my last, powerfully retentive fugues. The sharp, East Anglian gusts cut into me. I looked around and was visited with a powerful urge to rearrange the disordered buildings that made up the campus, many of them at unsatisfactory angles to one another. The steps that spirally ascended the core of the Monoplex shone bright beams of certainty at me. I took them four at a time, pausing to pant on landings every three flights where black vinyl benches reflected the chromium struts of the ascending bannister.

I lingered outside Alkan's door until a lapine huddle of research chemists had waddled past and round the bend of the corridor. For a brief moment their incisors overbit the twenty miles of Essex countryside, which was visible from the twentieth floor. Then I entered. In the bathroom, by the subsiding warm coils of Alkan's recently worn clothing I found a clue. A card for a cab service. The office address was on Dean Street in Soho, London.

Soho at that time was a quiet backwater where vice was conducted with a minimum of effort. The aspidistra of English prostitution was kept flying down pissy alleys. And the occasional influx of kids from the suburbs, or men from the ships, flushed the network of drinking clubs and knocking shops clean for another fortnight.

Vice still had the same scale as the architecture, it was only three or four storeys high. Homosexuals, jazz musicians and journalists formed companionable gaggles. Things that people did were still risqué before they became sordid.

I put up at the Majestic Hotel in Muswell Hill, a pink, pebble-dashed edifice. Originally it must have been intended for an Edwardian extended family, but it had become home to riff-raff from all over the world: salesmen, confidence tricksters, actors and graduate students. I ventured by juddering bus down into the West End on a daily basis. The cab company the card in Alkan's bathroom referred to was easily found. It was a cubbyhole tenanted by an Italian speaker in a flat tweed cap. He made no sign of remembering a tall, thin man, somewhat like Le Corbusier. Indeed, it could have been a resistance to the Modernist movement as a whole that made him so abusive towards me when I pressed him for information.

I took to wandering hither and thither, aimlessly crossing and recrossing my steps. I was convinced that Alkan was in the West End of London and that he wanted to be found. I saw his behaviour as purposive. I gave no thought to the fact that my grant had run out, that I was due to appear before the supervisory panel in a matter of weeks, and that my leviathan of a thesis lay beached on the nylon counterpane of my foldaway bed in Chelmsford.

One of the main disadvantages of an impoverished, nomadic metropolitan existence is that in winter you cannot have privacy without either purchasing it, or gaining access to it in a lockable toilet cubicle. I desperately needed privacy, for, during my years of retreat from the world, I had developed certain private habits, certain rituals combining magical twists of thought with bodily functions that I had to perform on a four-hourly basis. Lacking the wherewithal for a hotel (we were formally expelled from the Majestic every morning at 9.00 and not allowed back in until 5.30), I took to the conveniences, becoming adept at selecting the toilets where I would have the most genuine peace and quiet. This was a difficult and absorbing task. So many of the public toilets and even those in large hotels and restaurants were frequented by homosexuals. I had no argument with these people, either moral or psychological (and I may point out at this juncture that Quantity Theory as a *whole* maintains no defined perspective), but the push, shove and then rasp of flesh, cloth and metal fastener against ill-secured prefabricated panels and grouted gulleys tended to interrupt my rituals.

So, I elevated my search for the ideal cubicle – warm, discrete, well lit – to an exact science. Unnoticed by me, this search was beginning to usurp the primary quest. It is ironic, therefore, that unknowingly, unintentionally, I began to find evidence of the great psychologist where I myself sought refuge.

I could avoid the actual congress of homosexuals quite easily. However, without abandoning my private study altogether I could not hope to avoid the evidence of their activities: crude but believable advertisements, scrawled in Biro or neatly lettered; seemingly hacked with an axe, or delicately carved with a pen-knife; they drew the reader's attention inexorably to penile size:

I'm 45 and my wife gives me no satisfaction coz shes too slack. If you have a 9" cock, or better, meet me here after 6 any wensday. I will take on any number of lusty boys.

and:

Boys under 21 with 6" or more meet me here. You do it to me I'll do it to you.

And the direct, if disturbing:

Give me big dix.

There was one of these water-closet communicants who was more readily recognisable and more prolific than the rest – I began to see his entreaties in a lot of my favourite haunts, and to come across them occasionally when I broached new territory. This person was distinguishable by his rounded, laboured writing in red Biro, which reminded me of the hand of an adolescent schoolgirl – especially the characteristic of drawing small circles in place of the point over the 'i'. Furthermore, his graffiti were always written neatly on the wall directly above or below the point where the toilet paper dispenser was mounted. They were also very carefully executed. With some of the best examples I could actually see where the artist had used a ruler to get his script to line up just so. As for content, alas that was wearisomely predictable:

Meet me here on Friday or Saturday evening if you are better than 7″. I have a 9″ cock which I like to have kissed and sucked till I come in someone's mouth. I like young boys of around 16, but also more experienced men.

This I noted down in my leather-bound journal from the wall of an unpretentious, unfrequented, spotlessly clean, underground municipal convenience in Pimlico. I had no idea why I had taken to recording such things. I had been in London only a fortnight or so; I had no fixed view about the status of my quest for Alkan. On the whole I was inclined to view it as spectacularly important. I had, after all, given up my forthcoming exam in order to find him. My analysis with him was incomplete, I had no family or friends to support me. On the other hand I could just as easily feel dismissive and indifferent about the quest for Alkan. Who needed the daft old coot anyway? Nonetheless I did immediately notice the connection between the advertisement above and this:

I like to suck young boys cocks and to have mine sucked as well. I've only 5″, but it's hard all the time. If you're 16 or under meet me here on Tuesday at 9.00.

neatly scripted beneath the Smallbone of Devizes ceramic, interleaved sheet-holder clamped to the distempered wall of the warm and capacious gents at the Wallace Collection. And this:

Fun time every evening here or at the xxxx [illegible] club. All experienced men better than 8″ meet me for sucking frolics. I am 27 and I have 9 good inches which you can nip and lick.

incongruously proclaimed from a bare space of rendering, framed with grout, left available, as if on purpose, by the absence of a tile in the checkerboard that skirted the commode in the denizens of the Reform Club.

If I idly noted down this smut cycle it was not for any reason but boredom. It wasn't until later, days later, that, glancing on passing, in the canted, cracked, oval mirror that capitulated on top of the dead bureau in my L-shaped wind-tunnel at the Majestic, I saw the hidden significance of these three bites. I saw it as a sequence solely of numbers, integers, detached from the penises-in-themselves, thus:

7, 9, 16, 5, 16, 9, 8, 27, 9

This in itself obviously represented an intentional sequence. The very fact of the way relation between primes and roots was organised, implied a capricious mind intent on toying with a willing enquirer. I immediately felt the presence of Alkan in that simple sequence. I knew that I was in no real position to analyse the sequence as it stood – and that infuriated me . . . I knew that if the sequence was to prove meaningful it must have a progression.

My cottaging became more intense. I spent virtually all my days in toilets. The one day I had to abandon my quest and attend the National Assistance Board, I managed to contrive to wait for some hours in the toilet. When I emerged my number was called, an example, I feel, of perfect timing.

Eventually I began to find little outpourings, here and there, which were unmistakably more elements of Alkan's coded message. Each set of figures was couched in the same form, written in the same hand and situated within the toilet cubicle in the same place. After a fortnight I had an impressive set of integers of the form:

16, 3, 19, 19, 5, 17, 27, 9, 8, 13, 33, 11, 4, 9, 9,
14, 16, 27, 7, 9, 16, 5, 16, 9, 8, 27, 9 . . .

but running to some four handwritten sides. I submitted this sequence to rigorous analysis. On the face of it there seemed no reason to think that the sequence had been devised in the order in which I discovered it. So I cut it up into individual strips which I arranged and rearranged and rearranged, for hour after hour after hour, until a lattice work of discarded strips of exercise paper overlaid the bilious pastel lozenges which snicker-snacked across the wind-tunnel at the Majestic.

I found that I could extract quite elegant sets of equations from the sequence whichever way I arranged it, some of which were quite tantalisingly pregnant. But although I could satisfactorily resolve them they remained mere abstractions devoid of real values, real content. From the shape of some of these equations I could deduce that Alkan was working on some kind of methodology for statistical inference, but just as clearly other sets seemed to indicate that his thoughts were running towards decision trees which reflected the organic structure of long-term clinical trials. But statistical studies of what? Clinical trials of what?

I lapsed into torpor. There seemed no solution. I felt more than ever abandoned, washed up, beyond the pale of society. With no way of retreat from the tidal line of mental wrack, back down the beach and into the sea.

Late one evening, a fellow Majestic resident, Mr Rabindirath, came in to challenge me to a game of Cluedo. We played in a desultory fashion for half an hour or so. Rabindirath was an infuriating opponent because he kept incorporating members of his own family into the game as if they were fictional suspects.

Next to his cheaply suited thigh, on the Terylene counterpane of my bed, lay a well-thumbed *A–Z*. Open at pages 61a & b, the West End. I idly translated the coordinates into numerical values . . . Covent Garden, the coordinates were I, 16. Translating the I into a numerical value according to its position in the alphabet gave 9. 9, 16 – it was a fragment of the sequence! My head began to spin. Rabindirath barked angrily as I swept the Cluedo board off the cork-topped bathroom stool and began to labour feverishly over the *A–Z*.

By morning I had worked it all out. All the sequence was a set of coordinates which mapped a journey across central London. A journey which at every juncture prefigured my own. Clearly Alkan was tailing me from the front; damnably clever. He had started by tailing my simple and monotonous circuit and once I had become obsessed by following him he had led me on. Now I looked at the route laid out on the map it was quite clear that I had been mapping out a basic geometric configuration. I had simply to extrapolate the next set of coordinates in order to confront the errant psychologist.

By ten that morning I was waiting for him in the public toilet under the central reservation on High Holborn. It was a snug place, well warmed, with an attendant on duty all the time. Not the sort of toilet anyone would tend to linger in, nowhere to really hide yourself away. I waited and collected different versions of disgust from the insurance salesmen and civil servants who marched through, dumped their steamy load and strode out shaking their legs and heads.

I became uneasy. If something didn't happen soon I would be running the risk of harassment or even arrest. Then from the solid row of cubicles which framed a corridor at the far end of the tiled submarine came a cough, and then a flush, and then a door wheezed ajar . . . nothing . . . no one emerged . . . I footed down to the end and gingerly pushed open the door. Alkan was turning to face me. He was wearing a grey flannel suit and a belted Gannex mac, he carried a briefcase and was in the middle of tucking an umbrella under his free arm. He looked terribly shocked to see me. The first thing he said was, 'What the bloody hell are you doing here?'

It turned out that the whole thing was an utter fluke, an example of the most preposterous chance, an amazing coincidence; or, laden synchronicity, evidence of fate, karma, the godhead. Alkan thought chance. I was inclined to agree with him. For he had nothing to say to me, absolutely nothing, but a kind of chewed-up, pop-eyed obsession with a set of conspiracies being fomented against him by Communist psychiatrists. Alkan had gone completely mad, psychotic, subject to delusions. His abrupt flight from Chelmsford had come in the midst of an extended paranoid interlude. He was a useless husk. After sitting with him over tea for a while, I gave him the rest of my money. It was the only way I could convince him that my presence in the toilet was not due to my involvement with the conspiracy of conspiracies. My last sight of Alkan was of him sitting at the coated table, hands tightly clasped, eyes eroding from the stream of edginess that poured out of his brain. I looked into those eyes for too long while I ate my toast. By the time I'd finished, all my faith in Alkan was quite burned away.

I went back to the Majestic and picked up my things. Then I left London. I wasn't to go back again for another seven years.

I applied for and was accepted to work as a research psychologist for Mr Euan MacLintock, the Chairman and Managing Director of Morton-Maclintock, the giant cattle-feed manufacturers. MacLintock was an old-fashioned Scottish dilettante, his particular obsession was psychology. He had few pretensions to originality himself, but was determined to test out some of his theories and, as a consequence, throughout his long and barren life funded one research project after another.

MacLintock had come up the hard way. He was born in the direst of Highland poverty, and had worked hard all his life, mostly as an itinerant cattleman. Long years of watching the animals graze and defecate accounted for his uncanny rapport with the bovine. And no doubt this also accounted for the phenomenal success of the cattle-feed he manufactured when he started his own business.

Somehow MacLintock had found time to educate himself. He had the reckless and unstructured mind of the autodidact. In some areas (for example, South American Volcanoes, heights thereof) he was an exhaustive expert; whereas in others (the History of Western Thought) he was notably deficient. The occasional beams of light that the world would shine into MacLintock's cave of ignorance used to drive him insane with anger. I well remember the day he reduced a solid mahogany sideboard to kindling upon being informed by me that even in space you could not 'see' gravity.

It would be wrong of me to give you the impression that MacLintock was a kindly man. He was incredibly mean, moody and occasionally violent. After the frozen, incestuous arrogance of Chelmsford academia I found his company a positive tonic. Just learning to get through a day with MacLintock without sparking a row was a valuable lesson in self-assertion.

Morton-MacLintock's head office was near Dundee, but MacLintock lived in a vast mouldering Victorian hunting lodge an hour's drive north. I was provided with an apartment at the lodge and was expected to reside there unless my work called me to some far-flung portion of the M-M empire.

MacLintock's real obsession was with the relationship

between bovine and human social forms. This was appropriate enough for a manufacturer of cattle-feed (and other farinaceous products aimed at the bipedal market). The full and frightening extent of his eccentricity only became clear to me over a period of two years or so. During that time I laboured diligently to compile a series of studies, monographs and even articles (which I naively believed I might get published). All of which aimed to draw out the underlying similarities between humans and cows and to suggest ways in which the two species could be brought closer together.

I think that in retrospect this scholastic enterprise doesn't sound as stupid as it did at the time. It is only in the past decade that the rights of animals have started to be seriously addressed as a concern of moral philosophy. The animal has shifted from the wings to the centre stage of our collective will-to-relate. Environmentalism, conservation, the developing world, the issue of canine waste products; increasingly our relationship to one another cannot be adequately defined without reference to the bestial dimension. In this context my work for Euan MacLintock now appears as breaking new ground.

To say that I came out of my shell altogether during this period would be an exaggeration. But I did realise that my days at Chelmsford had been effectively wasted. I had allowed myself to become marginalised. I had relinquished control of my own destiny. I had thought at the time that I was ensuring the objectivity that would be necessary for formulating a new large-scale theory of the psychopathology of societies as a whole. But really I had been teetering towards institutionalisation.

Wandering the MacLintock estate, moodily kicking failed, wet divots into the expectant faces of short Highland cattle I developed a new resolve to go back into the fray. I realised that to make any lasting contribution, to be listened to, I would have to manifest myself in some way. I would have to unite my own personality with my theories.

So, of an evening, while MacLintock fulminated and stalked, I parried with my pirated idiosyncrasies. We would sit either side of the baronial fireplace, wherein a few slats from a broken orange box feebly glowed. He, nibbling charcoal biscuit after biscuit, only to discard each sample, half-eaten, into a sodden heaplet on the lino, while I would suckle ballpoint pens, stare up at the creosoted rafters and make either whiffling or ululating noises, depending on the phase of the moon.

To MacLintock's credit he never paid much attention to the generation of this personal myth. He was possessed of a delightful self-obsession that guarded him against being interested in anyone else. A short man with absurd mutton-chop sideburns, he always wore a business suit. His notable efficiency, punctiliousness and businesslike manner – while inspiring devotion and respect at Head Office, at the plant and at the experimental testing station on Eugh – at home came across as a wearing emptiness of human feeling.

The great lodge was empty but for him, me and an aged houskeeper, Mrs Hogg, a woman so wedded to Calvinist fatalism that she would happily watch a pullet burst into flame, rather than adjust the oven setting. Bizarrely lit by vari-tilted spotlights of some cheap variety, the great hall would occasionally be enlivened of an evening as Mrs Hogg progressed towards us down a promenade of joined carpet offcuts. Her squashed profile was thrown into shocking, shadowed relief against the stippled wall, the angles, for a moment, cheating the fact that her nose actually did touch her chin. She would deposit a chipboard tray on the fender, gesture towards the Tupperware cups of tea and the fresh mound of burnt biscuits and then depart, rolling back over the causeway and into the darkness.

Eventually MacLintock became dissatisfied with my work. He had had very precise objectives which he believed my work should fulfil:

1. The creation of an ideal community in which men and cattle would live together on equal terms. This was to be jointly funded by MacLintock and the Scottish Development Office.

2. The publication of a popular work which would make MacLintock's theories accessible to a mass audience (he was also quite keen on the idea of a television documentary).

He couldn't blame me solely for the failure to realise the first of these objectives, although I suppose my work didn't altogether help to convince the relevant bureaucrats. On the other hand he certainly did blame me for the collapse of the second objective. Blame, I felt, was unjustified. I had consulted with him on a regular basis during the writing of *Men and Cows: Towards the Society of the Future?* And he had passed each chapter as it came. Nonetheless he became nasty when the book failed to find a mainstream publisher. Eventually it was brought out by one of the small, alternative publishers that were beginning to operate, but it was instantaneously remaindered. MacLintock wandered the lodge for days, skipping from carpet tile to carpet tile, buoyed up by fury. Every so often he would swivel on his heel and deliver a tirade of abuse at me. At last, sickening of his tirade, I packed my bag and departed.

The last thing I saw as I squelched down the drive, away from the lodge, was Mrs Hogg. She was standing in the paddock behind the house, leaning on the fence, apparently adopting a conversational tone with a giant Herefordshire bull.

That wasn't the last I heard of Euan MacLintock, or of the work I had done for him. About eight years later, when the controversy that blew up around Quantity Theory was reaching its height, Harding, one of my staunchest critics, found a copy of *Men and Cows*. He brandished this, as it were, in the face of my reputation. Naturally the attempted discrediting backfired against him nastily, the general public took to the book, seeing it as satire. I believe a twelfth edition is about to appear.

As for MacLintock he went on without the Scottish Development Office and founded his utopia in an isolated glen on Eugh. There was never any information as to whether the experiment met with success. But after a shepherd heard unnatural cries in the vicinity of the commune the constabulary were called in. MacLintock was subsequently charged with murder. No doubt the story is apocryphal, but it was widely rumoured at the time that the insane (note please the entirely plausible reclassification from 'eccentric' to 'mad') bovine comestibles magnate was found naked with a group of rabid cattle. MacLintock and the cows were eating strips and straggles of flesh and sinew; all that remained of the last of MacLintock's fellow human communalists.

And so to Birmingham, at that time unpromising soil for the psycho-social plant to grow in. Fortunately this was a period when if you had an idea that was even halfway towards being coherent, there was at least the possibility of getting some kind of funding. Added to that, I discovered on my return from the wastes of cow and man that I had obtained a 'reputation'. A reputation, however, that existed entirely by proxy. None of my doing, but rather the fact of Alkan's breakdown. Busner, Gurney, Sikorski, Hurst and Adam Harley. All of them were beginning to make little names for themselves. And there was a rumour that there was some 'purpose' to their work, that Alkan had vouchsafed some 'secret', or inaugurated a 'quest' of some kind before he went mad.

As a member of this select band I was accorded a good deal of respect. I had no difficulty at all in gaining a modest grant to do some research towards a book on aspects of grant application. The form of this project took me away from the precincts of Aston (to which I was nominally attached) and into the ambit of the Institute of Job Reductivism, at that time being run by John (later Sir John) Green, who went on to become Director of the Institute of Directors.

Things were informal at the institute, there was a kind of seminar-cum-coffee morning on Wednesdays and Fridays. Research fellows were encouraged to come in and chat about their work with one another and even present short papers. Here was a socialised setting which I at last found congenial. The roseate glow of synthetic coals; bourbons passed round on a blue plastic plate; the plash of tea into cup – and over it all the companionable hubbub coming from the people who sat in the groups of oatmeal-upholstered chairs.

Most of the fellows were engaged in straightforward reductivist studies. There were papers being written on – among other things – recruiting personnel to the personnel recruitment industry, writing in-house magazines for corporate communications companies, auditing procedures to be adopted for accountants, and assessing life cover rates for actuaries. The resident Marxist was engaged on a complex analysis of the division of domestic cleaning labour among people who worked in the domestic cleaning industry. I fitted in rather well with these people, they accepted me as being like themselves and this was a tremendous relief to me.

For about five years I lead a quiet but productive life. After a while I transferred to the institute, although I continued to take an undergraduate course at Aston under the aegis of the sociology faculty. I finished my thesis on grant application and started making some preliminary notes towards tackling the whole question of job reductivism from a theoretical perspective. I suppose with the benefit of hindsight I can see clearly what was going on here, but believe me, at the time I was oblivious. I had no thoughts of disturbing the pattern of life that I had cautiously built up for myself. I had acquired some slight professional standing; I had rented a flat – granted, it was furnished and I hardly spent any time there, but nonetheless these trappings of what is laughably called 'social acceptability' had begun to matter to me. After all, even the most conceited bore is often considered a social asset, if he has clean hands and a clean suit. All in all, for a virtual indigent, I had come a long way.

Into this Midlands arcadia fell a letter from Zack Busner:

Dear Harold,

It is possible that this isn't a letter you wouldn't want to receive, but I will have to accept that at the outset. You may not remember me, but I was a contemporary of yours at Chelmsford and also one of Alkan's analysand/students. I can barely remember you but, be that as it may, your work has come to my attention and I am in need of assistance – urgently in need of assistance, at my Concept House in Willesden. I cannot adequately describe the work involved in a letter, nor can I do justice to the new framework within which we are 'practising'. Perhaps you would be good enough to come and see me and we can discuss it?

Busner was the student/analysand of Alkan's I had most disliked. He had been a rounded ham of a young man, irrepressibly jolly, and, of the five, the most given to practical jokes. It was he, I recalled, who had had all Adam Harley's suits adjusted overnight to fit a midget. He had wandered around the campus at Chelmsford clapping people around the shoulders and greeting them effusively with a phoney hail-fellow-well-met manner, which set my teeth on edge. However, no one, least of all me, had failed to notice that despite his endless appetite for high jinks, or perhaps because of it, Busner was becoming a formidable researcher. I knew that his doctoral thesis had received very favourable attention. And that, a medical doctor by training, he had gone on to qualify as a psychiatrist and take up work as a respected clinician.

I went down to London. Busner had helpfully sent me a tube map with a cross on it marking Willesden Junction. The Concept House was on Chapter Road, one of those long north-west London avenues that in winter are flanked by receding rows of what appear to be the amputated, arthritic, decomposing limbs of giants. Snow had been falling all day and Chapter Road was a dirty bath mat of cold, grey flakes. It was dark as I plodded along, cursing the slippery PVC soles of the shoes I'd just bought. Ahead of me in the centre of the road two children of about five or six walked hand in hand.

The whole atmosphere depressed me. The feeling it gave me, walking down that endless road, was of being in a dirty, cold room, a room where no one had bothered to vacuum between the tattered edge of the beige carpet and the scuffed, chipped paintwork of the skirting board for a very long time. I wished that I had driven there instead of leaving my car at Tolworth services and hitching the rest of the way.

The Concept House was no different to any of the other large Edwardian residences which lined the road. If anything it looked a little more like a home and a little less like an institution than the rest. The garden was littered with discarded children's toys, and in an upstairs window I could see the back of finger-paintings which had been stuck to the windows with masking tape. Busner himself opened the door to me; had he not been wearing an aggressively loud jumper with 'Zack' appliquéd across its breast in red cartoon lettering I don't think I would have recognised him.

Busner's cheeks had sunk, his face was thin and hollow. The rest of him was just as plump as ever, but he had the countenance of a driven ascetic. His eyes glowed with an ill-suppressed fanaticism. In that instant I nearly turned on my heel and abandoned the interview. I had been prepared for Busner the Buffoon, but Busner the Revolutionary was something I hadn't bargained for.

We goggled at one another. Then quick as a flash he had drawn me into the vestibule, persuaded me to abandon my sodden mac and dripping briefcase and led me on, into a large, warm kitchen where he proceeded to make me a cup of cocoa, talking all the while.

'I hadn't imagined you as such a dapper little thing, my dear. Your suit is marvellous.' In truth the cheap compressed nap of the material was beginning to bunch into an elephant's hide of wrinkles under the onslaught of quick drying. 'Really, I wouldn't have recognised you if I hadn't known you were coming. I was expecting the timorous little beastie we had at Chelmsford.'

With amazing rapidity Busner outlined for me the philosophy of the Concept House, what he was trying to do and how he needed my help. In essence the house was an autonomous community of therapists and patients, except that instead of these rôles being concretely divided among the residents, all were free to take on either mantle at any time.

Over our cocoa Busner set out for me his vision of the Concept House and of the future of psychotherapy. Disgusted by his experience of hospital psychology – and the narrow drive to reduce mental illness to a chemical formula – Busner had rebelled:

'I sat up for night after night, reading Nietschze, Schopenhauer, Dostoevsky and Sartre. I began to systematically doubt the principles on which I had based my career to date. I deconstructed the entire world that I had been inhabiting for the past thirty years.

'It was dawning on me that the whole way in which people have hitherto viewed mental illness has been philosophically suspect. The division between doctor and patient has corresponded to an unwarranted epistemological assumption. Here at the Concept House we are dedicated to redefining this key relationship.

'We're really finding out the extent to which all the categories of psychopathology are just that: dry, empty categories, devoid of real content, representing only the taxonomic, psychic fascism of a gang of twisted old men.'

It was a long speech and Busner spoke eloquently, punctuating his remarks by moving oven gloves around on his chest. I think, in retrospect, they must have been adhering to his woolly by strips of Velcro that I couldn't see, but at the time I was tremendously impressed by the trick.

Busner went on to explain that within the Concept House everything was ordered democratically. At the house meetings, which were held every morning, rotas and agendas were drawn up and jobs distributed. The house was Busner's own, or rather Busner's parents'. He had persuaded them to donate it to what he styled his 'League for Psychic Liberation'. In the weeks that followed I occasionally saw the older Busners wandering around the upper storeys of the house like fitful ghosts, sheepishly reading the *Sunday Telegraph Magazine* in reproduction Queen Anne armchairs, while feverish psychotics, charged with some unearthly energy, toyed with their ornaments.

Having set out his theories, and explained the philosophy of this novel institution to which he had given birth, Busner picked up the drained cocoa mugs and put them on the draining board. He turned to me with a quizzical expression.

'You're wondering why I wrote to you, aren't you?'

'Well, yes. I suppose I am.'

'After all, we were never exactly *sympatico*, were we?'

'Yes, yes. I think I'd agree with you there.'

'Well, here it is. The fact is that I'm attracting a good deal of publicity with what I'm trying to do here. Some of it is distinctly favourable, but that fact only seems to persuade those who are seeking to discredit me to redouble their efforts. I know that you have never programatically defined yourself as belonging to any avant-garde movement. But on the other hand I know that you have allied yourself with some pretty weird courses of study during your career, isn't that so?

'What I want you to do here is what you do best: research. There is one way that I can really kick over the hornet's nest of the psychiatric and psychotherapeutic establishment and get them all buzzing furiously. And that is to prove not that my methods of helping people who suffer from so-called 'mental illnesses' are more effective than conventional ones, but that they are more cost effective; that would really upset people. If I could prove that Concept Houses the length and breadth of the country would reduce public expenditure, I might well become unstoppable.'

'And me?'

'I want you to construct and manage the trials and to collate the results, to be published in the form of an article co-authored by the two of us in the *BJE**.'

And so it was. I became a member of the Concept House team and abandoned my suits and shiny shoes in favour of uncomfortable overalls which rode up my cleft and shoes that appeared half-baked. Why? Well, because whatever the extent of Busner's rampant egoism, whatever the dubious nature of his ideas, there was a sense of human warmth at the Concept House that I found lacking, either at Aston or at the Institute of Job Reductivism. I craved some of that warmth. You have to remember that since the age of seventeen, I had lived an almost exclusively institutionalised life. Nonetheless, ever prudent, I didn't give up my academic positions, I merely secured a leave of absence to work on Busner's study. Of course there were mutterings about what I was getting involved with, but I paid them no mind.

The trial I evolved for Busner was complex in the extreme. There were two aspects to the problem: how much diagnosed mental patients spent themselves and what was spent on them. It was to be a double-blind trial, which operated itself in the context of a double-blind. There were to be three trial groups: the inmates of the Concept House, a group of patients diagnosed as afflicted with major psychoses at Friern Barnet, and fourteen Beth Din approved butchers living in the Temple Fortune area. That the latter group was chosen was to bedevil the validity of our results for years to come. I would like to state here, once and for all, that the fact was that the people who applied for the trial, and who fulfilled the necessary criteria, all happened to be kosher butchers domiciled in that area. Of course in retrospect this fact was undoubtedly one of the secret springs, the 'subtle connections' which I had begun to make unconsciously, and which led eventually to the full-blown Quantity Theory.

The trial was conducted over a period of six months in four distinct 'trial periods'. The results were monitored by me purely in the form of computer data. I never had any direct access to either the mechanics of the trial itself, or even to the intermediate collection of data. Naturally a double-double-blind trial involves

---

* *British Journal of Ephemera*

not only the technician who is directly monitoring the trial to be unaware of whether he is administering a placebo or not, but also the overall administrator of the trial – be he psychologist or statistician – to be unaware of whether he really is administering a trial, or just carefully collating and analysing figures, totals and percentages, completely at random. Thus, two of the groups of data that Zack Busner fed through to me comprised respectively: the number of snail trails he had counted, smearing across the fissured concrete apron, wreathed in bindweed, that lay in the dead centre of the waste ground behind the Concept House; and, a random selection of handicapping weights from the pages of a back number of the *Sporting Life*.

On the other two occasions the data was, of course, 'real' – although in a very restricted sense. The two real trials contained an obvious reversal. In one, the mental patients were given an economic placebo and the Concept House inhabitants, money. In the other this was reversed. The butchers were given, arbitrarily, either money or virtually useless discount vouchers for household cleaning products. Thus, the overall form of the trial could be depicted by a schematic diagram:

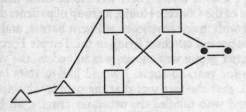

To my mind this expressed with absolute clarity the limiting conditions necessary for a cost-benefit analysis of sanity variables. Of course the informed reader will have already detected the lineaments of Quantity Theory in the structure of the trial diagram. My purpose here is expressly to avoid the crude attempts that are made to retrospectively manufacture the genesis of an idea. The problems I have been most interested in that arose from the Concept House trial were purely methodological. For instance, Olsen's 1978 paper in the *BJE* in which he presented the results of his own trials. Olsen took three groups of recently diagnosed and sectioned mental patients. One group was given in equal thirds, lithium, chlorapromasine and a tri-cyclic anti-depressant. The second group was given a placebo and the third group was given nothing; instead Olsen had the patients in this group mercilessly beaten to a bloody pulp.

If any of the patients in the three groups manifested any signs of severe deterioration in their overall condition they were administered ECT. However, the substance of Olsen's trial and indeed the validity or otherwise of his results are of little interest to me. Rather it was Olsen's argument that my error in the double negative implied by the double-double-blind trial that exercised me greatly. Fortunately I was saved from having to answer the accusation by the revelation that Olsen had himself participated in administering beatings to the control group in his experiment. Such a violation of the blind status of the trial naturally discredited him entirely.

The trials took six months to complete and during that time I was accepted into the Concept House community. This, as you will hear in due course, was altogether a mixed blessing. Busner and his therapists had long since ceased to make any practical distinction between themselves and their patients. So another involution of the trial sequence was that at the end of it no one could be really sure who had been giving what to whom. The trial money and placebo money were given out at random times when I was sure not to be in the vicinity. Occasionally I would catch a glimpse of a man, skull-capped and be-locked, his apron suspiciously stained and clutching a handful of glossy paper slips. But I discounted these peripheral visions, putting them down to the generally heightened psychic atmosphere of the Concept House.

There were in theory six therapists, six patients, Busner's parents and myself in residence. The patients were a random selection from the chronic wards that Busner had been attached to over the years. Basically he recruited for the Concept House through a mixture of fraudulence and guile. Busner was typical of experimentalists in the psychiatric and educational fields in that he blamed the failure of his methods not on their theoretical basis, but on the fact that he could only persuade wealthy parents to send their chronically disturbed children to his institution.

I participated in the exhaustive group therapy sessions, which more often than not were long periods of either silence or disjointed monamaniac ranting – usually by Busner himself. The truth was that although I felt accepted within the Concept House, it wasn't really a congenial environment. People who are severely mentally ill when they are left unconstrained tend to behave fairly badly. On reflection I suppose that is why they are diagnosed as being mentally ill in the first place. And as for the 'therapists' that Busner had recruited, they were, on the whole, fairly unstable people themselves, coming as they did from the wilder fringes of the therapeutic world. Among them were a failed holistic osteopath to naturopaths and a woman who described herself as 'seismically sentient'. Pretty stupid really. The main reason I remained was to complete the trial, added to that it was a fairly stimulating environment for debate. Busner's old cronies from Chelmsford – Harley, Sikorski and the others – dropped round at fairly regular intervals. They were all beginning to make names for themselves and they were always keen for a wide-ranging debate on all the latest developments in our various fields.

These were of course the men who were to form the nucleus of my Quantity Theory research group. Now I see what they have become I rather wish I had left them all alone, but at the time I was so pleased to be accepted by them that I suppose the dawning awareness that I might in fact be their intellectual superior was enough to make me want to stick close.

Eventually, however, I left the Concept House. It was becoming intolerable. You couldn't even eat breakfast without someone either slavering down the neck of your pullover or trying to sell you time shares in a pyramid building project. Busner himself was beginning to be taken up by the media as the prophet of some new movement and his vanity was insupportable, as was his pretension. He would sit for hours in a darkened room, thrumming mindlessly on an electric bass guitar and composing what he called 'verbal tone poems'. Let me tell you, what I could see at the time prefigured his eventual fall from grace. I knew he would end up on television game shows.

As for the trial and its findings, they received short shrift from the psychological establishment, which found both our methods and our aims quite incomprehensible. That was their problem;

and although I hadn't managed to come up with the results that Busner would have liked, I had proved, to my own satisfaction at least, that £7.00 will make someone who is significantly mentally ill feel at least marginally better.

The only person I was sorry to leave behind at the Concept House was Professor Lurie. This poor old buffer had made it to a considerable age as a happy eccentric before fatefully teetering over the brink into genuine delusional mania. Nonetheless I had spent some happy hours sitting listening to his clever, inventive fantasies of life marooned in the Amazon with a tribe of unspeakable banality.

Back to Birmingham then and the institute. My teaching, my books, my essentially lonely, but contented scholarly life. But something had changed. There was a new restlessness in the way I attacked ideas and worried at them like a terrier, a new edge to my thinking. All this came to a head as I laboured over completing the index to the revised edition of my doctoral thesis. An American college press of some obscurity[7] had agreed to publish and I knew that the work needed attention. Yet it was no longer a task that quickened my blood. Quite frankly I had long since ceased to care about the nature of academic grant application. The whole study appeared useless and fruitless to me, perhaps only interesting as the purest possible expression of the digging-out and then filling-in mentality of so much academic endeavour – especially in the social sciences. What I wanted to do was to hit upon a general explanatory theory of the relation between normal and abnormal psychopathology. A theory of the order of Freud's entire corpus of work, but, unlike Freudianism, intimately bound up with and connected to a theory of social form and change.

As I laboured on the tedious index I felt something gestate inside of me. It was like a great, warm, rounded bolus of thought. Stuck to its sides were all the insights and experiences I had had in the preceding ten years: my undergraduate days with Müeller at Oxford; my postgraduate thesis at Chelmsford; my time researching for MacLintock; my doctorate at Birmingham; my trials with Busner. All of these were now to find their rightful place, unified in the Quantity Theory of Insanity.

Drizzle over Bromsgrove. The sodden postman flobs along the pavement, pauses as if to enter by the green garden gate, and then flobs on. The damp clinging of cloth to flesh is felt across a sodden twenty-foot tangle of bindweed as he moves on past the mullions. My desk – normally a sanctuary of rigid order, a baffle against the worst of entropy – has started to decay. Curled and stained pages of typescript hold funelled within themselves soggy drifts of biscuit crumbs. Biros, cemented to one another and to balls of fluff and lint with hardened saliva are thrown into the path of the paper avalanche like so many spillikins. Hither and thither across the melamine stand ramparts of bound volumes from the institute library, Dewey decimal tags detaching from their spines and curling into Sellotape snails. I no longer have the impetus, the application, to work on the index, instead I doodle on a sheet of scrap paper, my pen describing senseless diagrams which express with a conjunction of lines and dashes the relations that obtain between a series of dots . . .

. . . And yet this particular diagram has such an appealing, cogent form. It looks as if it ought to express a genuine relationship of some kind. It is too four-square, too obviously functional, to be a mere doodle. I see in it the shape of the schematic diagram I drew to express the double-double-blind status of the Concept House trial . . . And then I see it, altogether, in one pure thought-bite; the Quantity Theory of Insanity shows its face to me.

I suppose all people who look for the first time upon some new, large-scale, explanatory theory must feel as I did at that moment. With one surge of tremendous arrogance, of aching hubris, I felt as if I were looking at the very form of whatever purpose, whatever explanation, there really is inherent in the very stuff of this earth, this life.

'What if . . . ' I thought to myself, 'What if there is only a fixed proportion of sanity available in any given society at any given time?' No previous theory of abnormal psychology had ever assumed such a societal dimension. For years I had sought some hypothesis to cement the individual psyche to the group; it was right in front of me all the time. But I went on, I elaborated, I filled out the theory, or rather, it filled out itself. It fizzed and took on form the way a paper flower expands in water. 'What if,' I further thought, 'any attempts to palliate manifestations of insanity in one sector of society can only result in their upsurge in some other area of society?'

So that was it! The surface of the collective psyche was like the worn, stripy ticking of an old mattress. If you punched into its coiled hide at any point, another part would spring up – there was no action without reaction, no laughter without tears, no normality without its pissing accompanist.

The sodden crescent at the edge of my long-since-dunked digestive biscuit flotched to the desk top like excrement. I paid it no mind. In that instant I saw whole series of overlapping models of given sanity quantities – for if each societal grouping had a given sanity quotient, then why not each sub-societal grouping? From the Bangladeshis to the bowling club, from the Jews to the Jewellers' Association. It must be so. In each model the amount of sanity available would be different and each societal model would have a bearing on the next. I saw it in my mind's eye as an endless plain of overlapping mattresses, each of a different size. Tread on one and the effect would ripple away through all the others.

That was it stated in its barest outline, but what was especially remarkable about the Quantity Theory was that it came into my mind complete with a myriad of hypotheses. Such as:

i) If you decrease the number of social class 2 anorexics you necessarily increase the numbers of valium abusers in social class 4.

ii) If you provide efficient medication for manic depressives in the Fens, there are perceptible variations in the numbers of agoraphobics on the South Coast.

iii) If you use behavioural conditioning to stop six pupils at St Botolph's primary school on Anglesey from bed wetting, the result will be increased outbursts of sociopathic rage among the ten borderline psychotics that attend the school.

And so on.

In one fell swoop I also found myself abandoning all the models of sanity and insanity I had absorbed during my years of study.

The key to the abnormal psyche lay not in a juxtaposition between the acquired and the instinctual, nor in a comprehensive model of the workings of the mind, but in an altogether purer, more mathematical direction. Traditional psychology retained the status of being a pseudo-science, its findings unable to bridge the vast gulf between the empirically testable hypotheses of neuro-physiology and the incommunicable truths of inner mental states. Just as philosophy, try as it might, cannot bind itself to formal logic. All this would end with Quantity Theory. The individual psyche would be left to discover its own destiny; psychology would be confined to the elaboration of statistical truths.

I make no bones about it, the Quantity Theory was my salvation. No one ever complains if a great artist says that he was driven to create a masterpiece by a hunger for recognition and money. But a scientist? Well, he is meant to be disinterested, pure; his ambition merely to descry the cement of the universe. He isn't meant to use it to start laying his own patio. I was saved from Bromsgrove, from Aston, from Chelmsford, from the Majestic Hotel, by the Quantity Theory. From its inception I knew that it fulfilled the criteria required by all great scientific theories: 1. It made large-scale predictions. 2. These were testable empirically. 3. The testings would really eat up cash.

That night I paced the Wilton until it smelt of singed nylon. I could not sleep, I was tormented, gripped by the fear that should I make the wrong move, should I fail to do the Quantity Theory justice, then I would be unable to claim all the credit. I knew that as a responsible scholar I should search around for some funding, do some fieldwork and then write up the results for publication in the relevant journal. But a wayward, craven part of me feared instantly that some other, some interloper was perhaps at that very moment stumbling on the same truth and about to make it known to the world – pulverising the credit due to me and me alone. I was tempted to call the national press, arrange a conference of some sort, upstage the academic community and tell the world.

Prudence got the better of me. I knew that I had to effectively gain control of the Quantity Theory. To unleash it on the world half-cocked was to ensure only that the massive industry of thought, research and practice which I could foresee would be within the domain of others. If I wanted to control I would have to plot, scheme, machinate, and above all lay my plans carefully.

Accordingly the next morning I sat down to write letters to my fellow student/analysands from Chelmsford: Sikorski, Hurst, Harley, and of course Zack Busner. (I would have asked Simon Gurney too were it not that he had given up his practice to become a sculptor.) I invited them to come to Birmingham to have dinner with me and discuss an idea which I thought might be of interest to them.

I waited for three days . . . a week . . . no word from anyone. The evening of the planned rendezvous arrived and to my surprise so did they. One after another. They had all driven up from London together in Adam Harley's car. But they had got into an argument at Toddington Services about the culturally relative perception of post-natal depression. Busner took the view that post-natal depression was an entirely patriarchal phenomenon, and that there were tribal societies where the matrilineal took precedence, that were completely free of it. Adam Harley took the view that Busner was a 'pretentious twerp' and followed up this criticism by shoving a Leviathan-burger, smothered with salad cream and dripping gobbets of part-grilled, processed shrimp, straight into Busner's face.

After arriving, I sat them down and made them tea. I wouldn't even let Busner clean up; I launched without any preamble into a description of my revelation. They were restless and barely prepared to listen, but I only had to hold their attention for a few minutes before the theory bit into them. Of course there was something in my manner that they sensed was different. Something in the way I whiffled towards the ceiling, the way I fellated ballpoint pens, the way I stood with one shoulder far, far higher than the other so that I appeared to be dangling from a meat hook, that held them, cowed them, made them realise that it was I who was to replace Alkan in their affections.

We formed a small multi-disciplinary team. The aim was to develop the Quantity Theory in relation to microsocietal groupings. Alkan's students were notable for the diversity of the paths they had followed since leaving Chelmsford; within our small group we had all the necessary disciplines represented.

We know already what had happened to Busner. Phillip Hurst, whose father had massively endowed the Chelmsford campus, had moved from pure psychology into psychometrics and statistics. His help in developing the quotient concept was to prove invaluable. Adam Sikorski had moved on from the crude behaviouristic models that he had constructed with such glee when a postgraduate. No long did he turn rats into alcoholics, heroin addicts and thieves – just to show that he could. Now he turned armadillos into anorexics, narwhals into neurasthenics and shire horses into hopeless, puling, agoraphobics. Sikorski had secured generous government funding for these experiments and his familiarity with the ins and outs of political in-fighting was to prove at the outset of great service to the Quantity Theory. Of course ultimately it alienated him entirely. As for Adam Harley – Harley the campaigner, Harley the idealist, Harley the visionary – he was the ultimate fifth columnist. He was sitting in a cold basement in Maida Vale, abasing himself before the adolescent angst and middle-aged spread of anxiety that his 'clients' laid before him. Harley, with his bloodhound eyes which threatened to carry on drooping until they made contact with his roll-neck, persuaded me of his concern, his humanity, his devotion to the very real therapeutic benefits of the Quantity Theory, but all the time . . .

Our first move was to look around for a suitably small, self-contained societal unit on which we could test the theory. We were fortunate indeed to have my cousin Sid. Sid had never been mentally ill, exactly. However, like other rather introverted children, he had had a number of 'imaginary friends'. The difference in Sid's case was that although he abandoned his imaginary friends during pre-puberty, he met them again at university. Where they all pursued a lively social life together.

Sid was now living in a small commune in the Shetland Islands, where he and his fellow communards were dedicated to the growing of implausibly large hydroponic onions. The other members of the commune were eccentric but not quite as unhinged as Sid. They believed that their ability to grow the four-foot legumes was wholly predicated on the orbital cycle of Saturn's satellite, Ceres.

For a number of reasons this commune represented an almost

perfect test bed for our research. It was remote, self-contained, and possessed a readily quantifiable sanity quotient which needed the bare minimum to assess. In addition the area around the commune contained several other examples of experimental living, left on the beach by the receding wave of the previous decade. It would be easy, therefore, to find a suitable control.

The Quantity Theory Multi-disciplinary Team set off for Shetland without further ado. Once there we would measure the quotient and then set about either exacerbating or palliating Sid. We then hoped to observe what effect, if any, this had on the other eight commune members.

It's now difficult to appreciate the then popularity of this sort of exercise in communal living, and frankly I found it difficult to appreciate at the time. I think in retrospect that all those 'alternative' modes of living were little more than exercises in arrested development. Sleeping in bags, arguing and hair-pulling. It was really all a sort of giant 'let's camp in the garden, Mummy' session. The onion-growers' camp was no exception to this rule. A huddle of bothies, caulked, in some places well and with close attention, but in others simply stuffed up with back numbers of the *Shetland Times*. When the afternoons grew dark and the wind whistled over the tedious landscape, the rain drove out of the well of darkness and shot in distinct drops through the central living area, where pasty-faced lads and lasses squatted, hooking their hair back behind their ears, absorbed in french knitting, macrame, and writing home.

In this context the team were called upon to operate just as much as anthropologists as psychologists. There was no way that the commune was going to accept us for the period of time necessary to complete our experiments if we didn't, at least superficially, show some sympathy with the ideas they espoused. So it was that I found myself night after night, the dirty denim of my acquired 'jeans' slow-burning my bent knees, as one communard or other, their minds stupidly stupefied by marijuana, attempted to discourse on ley lines, shiatsu, or some Tantric rubbish.

Of course we took our own mental profile, our own sanity quotient. Both as a group *per se* and combined with the communards. We then were able to allow for it in the context of the fluctuations we attempted to engineer. When the experiments were completed and the data collected from the 'control' commune, where Phillip Hurst had been conducting his own lonely vigil, we found that the results were far better than we could have hoped for.

The manipulations of the given distribution of sanity within the commune had, by any standards, been crude. When we wanted to palliate Sid's symptoms: his delusions, his paranoid fantasies, and especially his lively but imaginary social life, we would simply sedate him heavily with Kendal Mint Cake laced with Largactil. He stopped hearing voices, and the world ceased to resolve itself into a hideously complex, Chinese marquetry of interlocking conspiracies. Even his 'friends' went away. All but one, that is. An enigmatic welder from Weirside called George Stokes still insisted on manifesting himself.

And the onion-growers? Well, even though we had to wait to quantify the data, we could see with our own eyes that they had started to exhibit quite remarkably baroque behavioural patterns. With Sid palliated they now not only believed in the beneficial agricultural influence of Ceres, they also believed that Ceres was a real person, who would be visiting them to participate in a celebration of the summer solstice. Some of the really enthusiastic communards even sent out to Lerwick for twiglets and other kinds of exotic cocktail eatables, all the better to entertain their divine guest.

When we cut down Sid's medication everything returned to normal. We then went the other way and started introducing minute quantities of LSD into Sid's diet. The 'friends' proliferated. Sid spent all his days in the onion field engaged in a giddy social whirl: cocktail parties, first nights, openings, and house parties. Some of the imaginary friends were even quite well connected. I almost came close to feeling jealous of Sid as he rubbed shoulders with scores of influential – albeit delusory – personages, until my colleagues reprimanded me for my severely unprofessional behaviour.

Needless to say, this part of the experiment was an unqualified success as well. When Sid got madder the communards' behaviour changed again. They started wandering around the onion field in a distracted fashion. There was no more talk of the imminent arrival of Ceres – instead there was muttering about 'Going to Lerwick to see about a steady job'. And one or two disconsolate individuals even approached members of the multi-disciplinary team and asked them if they knew anyone who could help them to get into advertising.

We returned to London and conducted a full analysis of our findings. Reducing our calibrated observations and the results of the thousands of psych-profile tests we had conducted on the communards to a series of quotients, we found what we had gone looking for: whatever the fluctuations observed in the behaviour of individuals, the sanity quotient of the group as a whole remained constant.

It became time to publish. Three months later 'Some Aspects of Sanity Quotient Mechanisms in a Witless Shetland Commune' appeared in the *BJE*. There was an uproar. My findings were subject to the most rigorous criticism and swingeing invective. I was accused of 'mutant social Darwinism', 'syphilitic sub-Nietzschean lunacy' and lots worse.

In the academic press, critic after critic claimed that by proposing that there was only a fixed proportion of sanity to go round in any given society I was opening the floodgates to a new age of prejudice and oppression. Insanity would be rigorously confined to minority and underprivileged groups – the ruling classes would ensure that they remained horrifically well balanced, all the better to foment 'medication warfare' against societies with different sanity quotients.

However, the very scale and intensity of the reaction to the theory undercut the possibility of its being ignored. Added to that, my critics became sidetracked by the moral implications of Quantity Theory, rather than by its mathematics. The reasons for this became clear as the debate gathered momentum. No one was in a position to gainsay the findings until our experiments were replicated. And then, of course, they were replicated and replicated and replicated. Until the whole country was buzzing with the audible whirr of pencils ringing letters and digits on multiple-choice forms; and the ker-plunk as capsule after capsule dropped into pointed unputdownable paper beakers: the industry of thought was underway.

That would have been the end of the story. In terms of the naive model of motivation and causation I have set out for you, and then gloriously undermined, I have provided a complete explanation. But we all know what happened next. How the Quantity Theory of Insanity moved from being an original, but for all that academic, contribution to ideas, to being something else altogether. A cult? A body of esoteric knowledge? A political ideology? A religion? A personal philosophy? Who can say. Who can account for the speed with which the bastardised applications of the theory caught on. First of all with the intelligentsia, but then with the population as a whole.

Even if the exact substance of the theory is difficult to define, it's quite easy to see why the theory appealed to people so strongly. It took that most hallowed of modern places, the within-the-walnut-shell-world of the mind, and stated that what went on inside it was effectively a function of mathematically observable fluctuations across given population groups. You no longer had to go in for difficult and painful therapies in order to palliate your expensive neuroses. Salvation was a matter of social planning.

At least that's what they said. I never made any claims for the theory in this respect, I was merely describing, not prescribing. It was the members of the group I had assembled to conduct the ground-breaking research who leapt to pseudo-fame on the back of my great innovation. Busner with his absurd 'Riddle', and latterly his humiliating game-show appearances, shouting out stupid slogans; Hurst and Sikorski turned out to be incapable of anything but the most violent and irresponsible rending of the fabric of the theory, but that came later. My initial problems were with Harley. Harley the idealist, Harley the kind, Harley the socially acceptable, Harley the therapist.

Some nine months after the revelational paper in the *BJE* I received a call from Harley who asked me to meet him at his house in Hampstead. I had heard echoes of the kind of work my colleagues had been getting involved in and I had consistently been at pains in my interviews with the press to dissociate myself from whatever it was they were up to. I had my suspicions and I burned with curiosity as I strained on my foldaway bicycle up from the flat I had rented at Child's Hill to the heights of Hampstead.

The big design fault with these foldaways is that the wheels are too small. Added to that the hinge in the main frame of the machine never achieves sufficient rigidity to prevent the production of a strange undulating motion as one labours to cover ground. I mention this in passing, because I think the state I was in by the time I reached Gayton Road helps to explain my initial passivity in the face of what could only be described as an abomination.

Harley let me in himself. He occupied a large terraced house on Gayton Road. I had known that he was well-off but even so I was surprised by the fact that there was only one bell, with his name on it, set by the shiny front door. He led me into a large room which ran from the front to the back of the house. It was well lit by a wash of watery light from the high sash windows. The walls of the room were stacked with books, most of them paperbacks. The floorboards had been stripped, painted black, and polished to a sheen. Scattered here and there around the floor were rugs with bright, abstract designs woven into them. Thin angled lamps obviously of Italian design stood around casting isolated fields of yellow light. One stood on the desk — a large, flat serviceable oak table — its bill wavering over the unravelling skein of what I assumed to be Harley's labours, which spewed from the chattering mouth of a printer attached to his computer.

There were remarkably few objects in the room, just the odd bibelot here and there, a Japenese ivory or an Arawak head carved from pumice and pinioned by a steel rod to a cedarwood block. I felt sick with exertion and slumped down on a leather and aluminium chair. Harley went to the desk and toyed with a pen, doodling with hand outstretched. The whine of the machine filled the room. He semed nervous.

'You know the Quantity Theory of Insanity . . . ' he began. I laughed shortly. '. . . Yes, well . . . Haven't you always maintained that what is true for societal groups can also be proved for any sub-societal group as well?'

'Yes, that has been an aspect of the theory. In fact an integral part. After all, how do you define a "society" or a "social group" with any real, lasting rigour? You can't. So the theory had to apply itself to all possible kinds of people-groupings.'

'Parent–Teacher Associations?'

'Yes.'

'Cub Scout groups?'

'Yes.'

'Suburban philatelic societies?'

'Certainly.'

'Loose fraternities of rubberwear fetishists?'

'Why on earth not ... my dear man ... '

'How about therapeutic groups set up specifically to exploit the hidden mechanisms that Quantity Theory draws our attention to?'

'What do you mean?'

'Well, you know. Groups of people who band together in order to effect a calculated redistribution of the elements of their particular sanity quotient. Forming an artificial group so that they can trade off a period of mental instability against one of radical stability.'

'What! You mean a sort of sanity time-share option?'

'Yeah, that kind of thing.'

I was feigning ignorance, of course. I had foreseen this development, so had my critics, although they hadn't correctly located where the danger lay. Not with vain and struggling despots who would tranquillise whole ethnic minorities in order to stabilise the majority, but with people like Harley, the educated, the liberal, the early adopters.

'Well, I don't know, I suppose in theory ... '

'Have a look at this ... ' He swiped a scarf of computer paper from the still chattering printer and handed it to me. I read; and saw at a glance that Harley wasn't talking about theory at all, he was talking about practice. The printout detailed the latest of what was clearly a series of ongoing and contained trials, which involved the monitoring of the sanity quotients within two groups. There was an 'active' and an 'inactive' group. The groups were defined entirely arbitrarily. That was all, but it was sufficient. From the quantitative analysis that Harley had undertaken it could be clearly demonstrated that the stability of the two groups differed in an inverse correlation to one another.

'What is this?' I demanded. 'Who are these people and why are you gathering data on them in this fashion?'

'Shhhh!' Harley crouched down and waddled towards me across a lurid Mexican rug, his finger rammed hard against his lips. 'Do keep your voice down, people might hear you.'

'What people? What people might hear me?' I expostulated. Harley was still crouching, or rather squatting in front of me. This posture rather suited him. With his sparse ginger beard and semi-pointed head he had always tended towards the garden gnomic.

'The people who are coming for the meeting – the exclusionist group meeting.'

'I see, I see. And these?' I held up the computer paper.

Harley nodded, grinning. 'Aren't you pleased?'

Pleased? I was dumbfounded. I sat slumped in my chair for the next hour or so, saying nothing. During this period they trickled in. Quite ordinary upper middle-class types. A mixed bunch, some professionals: lawyers, doctors and academics, all with the questing supercilious air that tends to go with thinking that you're 'in on something'. The professionals were mixed in with some wealthy women who trailed an atmosphere of having-had-tea at Browns or Fortnums behind them. All of these people milled around in the large room until they were called to order and the meeting began.

It was a strange affair, this 'meeting', solely concerned with procedure and administration. There was no content to it, or perceptible reason why this particular group of people should be gathered together. They discussed the revenue of the group, where they should meet, the provision of refreshments and a group trip to Glyndebourne that was happening in a couple of weeks' time. At no point did anybody directly refer, or even allude, to what the purpose of the group was.

Eventually the meeting broke up into small groups of people who stood around talking. One of the women I had mentally tagged as 'wealthy' came and perched on the chair next to mine. She was middle-aged, svelte and smartly dressed in a suit of vaguely Forties cut. Her face had the clingfilm-stretched-over-cold-chicken look of an ageing woman who kept herself relentlessly in trim.

'Who are you?' she asked me, in a very forthright manner. Not at all like an English woman. 'I haven't seen you at a meeting before.'

'Oh, just one of Harley's colleagues. I came along to see what he was up to.'

'Adam is a marvellous man. What he has achieved here in just three months deserves to be seen as the triumph that psychotherapy has been waiting for.'

'Were you in therapy before coming to the group?'

'Was I in therapy?' She snorted. 'Is Kenton a suburb? I have been in therapy of one form or another for the last ten years. I've had Freudian analysis, I've taken anti-depressants, subjected myself to eclectic psychotherapy, rebirthing. You name it – I've tried it. And let me tell you that not one of these things has helped me in the slightest. My neurosis has always managed to resurface, again and again.'

'What form does this neurosis take?'

'Any form it chooses. I've been bulimic and anorexic, claustrophobic and agoraphobic, alcoholic and hysterical, or just plain unhappy – all until the past three months. Since I joined Adam's group my symptoms have simply melted away. I can't even remember what it was that I was so upset about. I can only recall the tortuous self-analysis and introspection that went along with my various therapies as if it were some bad dream. The way I feel now is so completely different to the way I did feel that there is no comparison.'

'Hmm, hmm. You have a relative I suppose, or a friend of some sort who ...'

'Who belongs to the other group. Yes, of course. My son, John. Well, he's always been rather unstable, I have no idea in the last analysis whether it was his shitty upbringing, or, as the more chemically-inclined professionals have said, a purely endogenous affair. At any rate John enjoys his little manic phases. He's inherited a little capital and he likes to sit up for fifty, sixty hours at a stretch watching it ebb and flow on the futures market. He's quite happy to trade an extended manic phase off against a neurosis-free period for me. I suppose some people might call it perverse. But to me it seems the eventual, loving coming together of mother and son after so much discord ...'

I don't know whether the above is a verbatim recollection of what the woman said, but it certainly captures the substance. I was horrified. Here was the incarnation of all I sought to avoid. The recasting of Quantity Theory as a therapeutic practice designed to palliate the idle sorrows of the moneyed. I left the house without speaking to Harley again. The rest of the sad story is familiar to us all. Harley is here at the conference, along with his disciples. His Exclusionist Therapy Movement has grown in the last five years by leaps and bounds. And Harley has, to my mind, diminished as a person in direct proportion. I don't know exactly what has happened to him. Perhaps he has simply got the wrong end of his own therapeutic techniques, spent too long in the wrong group. But his affectation of some bizarre tribal costume, his disjointed and facile mutterings – which are taken as gospel by his disciples – these seem to me to be the logical result of his meddling with the natural order of sanity quotients.

Incidentally, I did find out what happened to the awful woman I met at Harley's house. Her son died of a heart attack, brought on by asthma during one of his manic phases. Needless to say the woman herself is now safely institutionalised.

And as for the rest of them, those tedious souls who I saved from a lifetime of near-obscurity, they all proved unworthy of the gifts conferred upon them by their proximity to genuine theoretical advance. Hurst was at least predictable, even if his actions were in some ways the most odious.

It was about nine months after the afternoon I spent in Hampstead that I first read an item in the newspaper which confirmed my worst suspicions about him. Short and to the point. It said that Phillip Hurst, the noted statistician and psychologist, one of the originators of the Quantity Theory of Insanity, had been appointed by the government to head up a new bureau loosely attached to the Central Office of Statistics, but charged with a novel task – a sanity quotient survey of the whole country. The aim was to develop an effective measure of the quotient so that central government could accurately fix and concentrate its deployment of palliatives, in the form of funds spent on mental health, to create a fair and weighted distribution of aberrant behaviour throughout the realm.

I stopped waiting for more news. I knew it would be bad. I took the first academic job that I could lay my hands on that would take me as far away as possible from the onrush of the demented juggernaut I had spawned. In Darwin, in the Northern Territory of Australia, I sat and I waited. On Saturday mornings

I would climb into my Moke and drive down to the Victoria Mall where the only good newsagent in Darwin kept newspapers, three and four days old, from around the world.

So it was, standing amongst men with elephant-skin crotches of sweated, bunched, denim shorts, that I read, while they scratched at Tatsalotto cards, the plastic shavings falling around their thongs. The news was all of strange theatrical events of extreme violence. The newspaper editors published programme notes, replete with heavy black arrows, and the sort of drawings of men wearing windcheaters and carrying machine pistols you would expect to find on Letraset sheets.

As for the government's attempts to arrive at an accurate way of measuring the sanity quotient, these were dogged by problems that on the one hand seemed to be purely semantic – and which on the other appeared as worrying, aberrant, unknowable.

First one measure of sanity, then another, and then several more were developed in an effort to arrive at the definitive. The problem was that the straightforward measure S_1 was arrived at by a number of calculations – the rate in the increase of schizophrenic diagnoses was indexed against the rate of increase in the population – which were themselves open to different methods of calculation and hence interpretation.

Even when the various warring 'experts' (who were these people? Where had they been when I was crouching in bothies in the Western Highlands, or roaming the toilets of central London?) could agree on a given measure, it soon manifested mathematical instabilities which rendered it unworkable, or incalculable, or both.

S_9 had quite a vogue. It involved adding together all the doses of Valium, or other related sedative drugs, prescribed in the country over a given period of time. Dividing the sum by a base unit of 5mg and then dividing that figure by the incidence of advertising for stress-relief products on each regional television network. Musselborough, at one time a swingeing and totally unsympathetic critic of my work on job reductivism, did his best to associate himself with S_9, which for a while had a considerable following, measuring, its proponents claimed, not only the base sanity quotient, but also assessing the direction and rate of change of that quotient throughout the society. But the figure itself would fluctuate over quite short periods in such an alarming way as to throw serious doubts on the validity of the data being assembled.

I watched from Millarrapulla Road with detached amusement. The life there was a good one. Every month or so the director at the local college where I taught invited me for a barbecue, and together with other men in short-sleeved shirts, pressed shorts and white kneesocks I would stand out on the lush lawn and listen to the flying foxes as they whistled into land chattering in the mango trees. The other men were bland, white, tolerable. They lived in a society where constant rates of sanity had been achieved by the creation of a racial underclass which was killing itself with alcoholism. Actually, the overclass was killing itself with alcoholism as well, but there were remarkably few sufferers from any of the major pathologies.

Simon Gurney came to visit me for a while. He was convivial company; I would come back from the college in the evening and find him sitting with a small group of Groote Eylandters as they deloused one another on the veranda. Gurney worked hard and at the end of his visit presented me with a six-foot-high featureless basalt slab which I have to this day.

The spectacle of a growing, centralised bureaucracy, labouring to implement centralised policies based on the findings of Quantity Theory, filled me with amusement. As did the news that university department after department found it necessary not only to incorporate the theory into its undergraduate syllabus, but also to seek funding for all manner of research based on the possible applications of Quantity Theory to areas as diverse as North Sea oil production and the training of primary school teachers.

From time to time a journalist or a doctoral student would seek me out. I suppose I had the cachet of being the 'founding father', but in practice this meant very little. I think that when these people arrived, toiling up suburban roads, driven into psychosis by the heat, they found someone not altogether to their taste, someone not prepared to present them with an easily definable and analysable set of personal characteristics. The theses and profiles, when in due course they appeared, reflected this difficulty. Put simply: they just didn't know what to make of me. I clearly wasn't a bohemian and yet I had dropped out.

I had no charisma to speak of, I had gathered no disciples around me and yet I was by no means eccentric. I wasn't even eccentrically ordinary; a Magritte found in his own tropical Brussels.

Inexorably my reputation began to grow. Mostly, I think, as a result of the failure of my former colleagues to retain any kind of unity with their opinions whatsoever. So, although at the beginning of the Quantity Age my name was seldom if ever heard, within five years or so Busner, Harley, Hurst and even Sikorski, were driven into mentioning my name as representing the benchmark of orthodoxy, in opposition to the wholly misguided views of one another. I suppose there was a strange sort of satisfaction in this success-for-all-the-wrong-reasons. Certainly the large cash sums from royalties on dusted-off and republished papers came in handy; and I was also shrewd enough to bargain up my price for an interview.

When the offer came to take a job with PiggiBank I seriously considered it. They flew me by private jet from Darwin to Tokyo. A bizarre seven-hour drive took me so slowly from the airport to my destination (a 'country' inn outside the conurbation, of which the chairman was a fanatical patron) that I felt despotic, borne at shoulder height through the press of so many tens of thousands of short people.

I appreciated the chairman's meeting place. The inn, sited in a counterpane fold of green land, sweeping down from the conical peak of a hill which stood out against the dirty blue of a static sky, was horned and crouching, its roof a crisp pile of upturned toast-corners curling and calcined. Behind the inn towards the hill was a petrol refinery, or a chemicals plant, or some such thing – a twisted root of tangled knots of pipe.

'Wal!' The chairman's greeting was as effusive as a baby's fart through a muted trumpet. He and his people moved around the room, gesturing, giving me morsels, getting Japanese servants to give me morsels and drinks; and to give them morsels as well. They went out into the garden through the screen doors and then came back in again. Their movements around the room, with its polished block floor, lacquered furniture and paper walls, were lecherous. They molested the space. Every time their pink hands clutched at it, or their coarse faces rubbed against it, it shrank into itself, a little more hurt, a little more damaged.

Vulker himself wore a kimono so large that it diminished even his vast frame, completely upsetting what already distorted sense of proportion I had had on entering the room.

'Wal,' said Vulker, 'I think we had better address ourselves to the implications of sanity quotient fluctuations within the context of a more collectivist, potentially static situation.' He barely glanced at me; the comment seemed addressed rather to the morsels of fish smeared across his palm. I grunted noncommittally. I knew what I really thought: namely that the size factor was going to have a far more significant and widespread influence on world society than any specific internal reaction or attitude towards mental illnesses with defined pathologies. When all those really short oriental people got right out into the West they would begin to suffer from a nagging sense of inferiority. The impact of this on world sanity quotients could be catastrophic. But why should Vulker be told?

'See here?' One of Vulker's aides handed me a report bent open out of its celluloid backing. I idly scanned the columns of figures, concentrating only to relate an asterisk in the text to Harley's name at the footer. So that was it, they had started without me. I made no excuses, but left. Fourteen hours later I was back in Darwin.

So Harley became Sanity Quotient Adviser to PiggiBank. And it was afterwards rumoured that he served some useful function for the chairman himself. I would have nothing of it. Was it pride? I think not. I think it was a growing awareness of the direction that events were taking. Just as the inception of Quantity Theory itself had a dreamlike, inspirational quality, so now I felt myself drifting into a creative kind of indolence in which I saw things for what they really were.

Denver Airport. And the mountain air pushes me naked into a white, tiled bathroom. Dagglebert struggles with the suitcases. It isn't until two days later that standing on the campus field, looking towards the ridge of blue and white mountains, that I realise that I have never been to America before. This is unimportant – the reason for my presence here is to confirm a suspicion. They are all here as well: Hurst from Hampstead, Harley from New York, Busner from Montreux where he has been receiving a television award. I am not here to confront but to bear witness.

Cathcart, the resident purveyor of the theory, who has taken the time to organise this celebration, is a lively man in his early fifties, mysteriously kinked at the waist as if caught midway in some mysterious, lifelong act of mincing. Despite his fluting voice and preposterous clip-on sunglasses Cathcart proves amiable and, more to the point, respectful. He has allocated me a secluded but comfortable cabin in a distant corner of the university grounds. Over the last couple of days I have shown myself sufficiently around the campus concourse, in the faculty building, and on one evening in a Denver bistro frequented by visiting academics, to counter any possible charges of snobbery or stand-offishness.

When I have run into my old colleagues I have done my best to be courteous and pleasant. I know they regard me as a fearful prig, but why should I descend to embrace the pseudo-cultural fallout that has surrounded my lifetime's work? Why should I allow my very thought to become a creature of fashion?

And so up on to the podium, and to the lectern. Introduced by Cathcart I stand looking out over the upturned faces. Now is my moment, now is my chance to ensure that posterity has some inviolate record . . . I hesitate and then begin to speak; the coloured lights process across my crotch. Dagglebert salivates below me.

My address is a triumph, a *cause célèbre*. Or so I think. At any rate I am very well received. But then I didn't try anything fancy, I confined myself to areas that are well known. I didn't trouble my audience with complexities, or give them any real idea of what tremendous conceptual heat is required within the crucible of creation. In a word my address – to my own mind – was anodyne.

Towards the end of the morning, as my eyes scanned still more distant prospects in an effort to avoid contemplating the crumpled, impotent visages of my colleagues, I saw a flicker of white moving in and out of the trees at the edge of the stretch of lawn that bounded the auditorium building. It came and then went, and then came again. Until it resolved itself into the figure of a young woman, perhaps in her early twenties, clad in a loose hospital gown, who ran hither and thither, arms outstretched, or in her hair. She pirouetted and thrust herself, as if brutally masturbating, against the trunks of the stately Douglas firs. In time she was joined by more figures, some similarly attired, some dressed in fragments of surgical garb, others girt with appliances for restraining the deranged, still others naked but for either torn sweaters or cast-off trousers.

While this cavalcade, this strange fiesta, made its way out of the trees and on to the lawn, I went on speaking, automatically. I knew what was happening, I had heard rumours. My suspicions were confirmed when a tall figure appeared in the wake of the dancers. He stood head and shoulders above them, naked to the waist and below that clad only in harlequin tights and an absurd, priapic codpiece. His beard jutted towards the auditorium, his eyes flashed and even from a distance of several hundred metres, seemed to search mine. I had been joined by the last of the original team. Sikorski had arrived, along with his Radical Psychic Field Disruptionists.

If Hurst represented the therapeutic corruption of Quantity Theory, Sikorski had done his best to effect a political corruption. Sikorski's first published paper in the wake of our work together had contained a lively refutation of the idea of sanity quotients being measurable within the context of social groupings. For him the very idea of 'society' was a fallacy. 'Society' could not be quantified, but a physical area could. Sikorski proposed, therefore, what he called 'psychic fields' – not really a difficult concept to grasp, he simply meant 'areas'. Within each of these psychic fields there was, of course, a given sanity quotient. It was in the interests of the establishment, he went on to say, to create a complex and sustainable pattern of such fields, which would ensure that the principal burdens of depression, schizophrenia, alcoholism, mania and depression, fell primarily on the disadvantaged: the working class, the ethnic minorities and so forth.

Clearly this fascism of the very animus had to be counteracted. Sikorski, scion of a wealthy East Anglian landowning family, at one time a brilliant clinician with a promising career in orthodox medicine ahead of him, took the plunge and followed the path dictated by his own convictions. After the initial Quantity Theory multi-disciplinary team broke up Sikorski disappeared. Later, there were rumours that he had had himself sectioned; that he had undergone more than twenty ECT treatments, that he had been overdosed with Halperidol. And later still that he had been partially leucotomised . . . privately . . . by a friend.

He emerged two years later on the fringes of the metropolis. By now he was at the head of a ragged band, which styled itself as 'the Radical Psychic Field Disruptionists'. The aim of this collection of university dropouts, druggies, actors and other assorted social deviants was to act as a kind of emergency oil rig capping team in the context of mental health.

Like a method acting workship they refined and perfected their assumption of symptoms of mental illness. (Occasionally members of the troupe would appear on one of the regional news-feature programmes to give the folks at home a demo.) Then, they would descend to picket day-care centres, long-term asylums, secure wards for the criminally insane and of course analysts' and therapists' offices. Lounging, squirming, ranting, collectively deluding, over a two- or three-year period the Radical Psychic Field Disruptionists became a familiar sight around Britain. They had the same sort of cachet – as a bizarre diversion threading their way through the conformist crowd – as the Hare Krishnas had had some ten or so years before.

I had always had a kind of a weakness for Sikorski. He was such an attractive man, and so enthusiastic, given to large passions. Very Slav. He was really the Bakunin of psychology, asexual and subject to borrowing large amounts of money that he couldn't possibly hope to repay.

Now he stands. And then struts back and forth on the sward. Arms outstretched, he clutches up divots and presses them to his brow. His mouth opens and closes, but I can't hear what he's saying. Apparently he has been invited to Denver as a gift to the municipality from the conference organisers. The Radical Psychic Field Disruptionists are going to practise their strange arts in the vicinity of the state mental hospital and ameliorate the conditions of the inhabitants . . . that's the idea at any rate.

Plenty of people, some of them quite respectable thinkers believe implicitly in the efficacy of Radical Psychic Field Disruption. What a joke! These people haven't a clue what Quantity Theory is really about. Quantity Theory is not concerned with total physical cause, it operates at the level of the signifier. People are willing to come forward in droves and claim that they have been helped by the actions of Sikorski and his followers. And it is considered slightly hip by the intelligentsia to piggyback on a field disrupting trip in order to obtain relief from some trying neurosis or other – to shuck off a co-dependant relationship, or 'deal' with some emotion or other. I have been told that nowadays it's virtually impossible to pass a mental institution of any kind at all, without seeing a little ersatz ship of fools moored by the main door and in the shadows, lurking, a pasty-faced scion of the Sunday Review benefiting obscurely from the local field disruption.

As soon as my address is over and the ovation has been tidied away I stride out of the auditorium. Walking across the concourse I turn to Dagglebert, outraged.

'What the hell are these people doing here? Why have the conference organisers allowed them into the precincts of the university?'

'Oh, them,' says Dagglebert – and as he speaks I see once again the utter stupidity of employing a research assistant who drools – 'They're here by invitation of the conference, as a gift to the municipality of Denver . . . '

'I know that, I know that!' I turn away from Dagglebert and head towards the cafeteria, which lies on the far side of the precinct. Dagglebert, undeterred, follows me, drooling the while.

Safely ensconsed behind a chest-high arras of plastic bamboo shoots I watch the ebb and flow of conferees as the swarm coming from the auditorium runs into the traffic on the precinct and the Radical Psychic Field Disruptionists enter from the outside. Rocking and dribbling they stand here and there talking to former colleagues, half-remembered through a fog of tranquillisers.

I see my own former colleagues there as well. Zack Busner stands with a tall, shrouded girl, nervously rolling and unrolling the end of his mohair tie. Phillip Hurst has his briefcase propped open on one knee, foot up on the rim of a concrete shrubbery container as he riffles through notes for the benefit of a stocky individual, who flexes and reflexes his muscular arms. I see Adam Harley deep in conversation with Janner, the anthropologist, who I know vaguely. Janner is wearing what looks like a second-hand Burton overcoat and carries a plastic bag emblazoned with the logo of a popular chain of South London convenience stores. Janner is a repellent individual, with something of Alkan about him – the way he tilts his head back in order to slurp the catarrh down his throat is especially striking. I have no idea why he has chosen to be in Denver.

And here and there dotted around this space are other familiar figures. Faces from the past that split and reform with speech. A manic, Jewish type who looks like an accountant clutches a sheaf of marketing brochures under his arm, and stands engrossed, while Stein, that millenarian charlatan, lays down his new law. Sikorski is moving among the throng. There's something hilarious about the way his false penis quests ahead of him. Especially if you know, as I do, that he's completely impotent. He stops to shake hands and chat with well-wishers. However he hasn't knocked off work altogether. A slowly rotating strand of spittle still threads through his tangled, fair beard, twisting this way and that, catching and refracting the sunlight streaming through the skylights above.

And as I observe Sikorski and his cohorts the nervous irritation that has gripped me since I arrived in Denver starts to fade away. I am left with a sense that this conference, this scene, is a watershed for Quantity Theory. A heaven-sent second opportunity for me to re-establish the school of thought at the correct level with the correct emphasis. Where has Quantity Theory gone wrong? In its application. In its development as a therapy? As a method of social control? As a tool of radical psychiatric policy? In all and yet none of these areas. The truth, as ever, comes to me purely, in one flash of instant realisation. I knock over the styrofoam beaker full of tepid coffee that Dagglebert has placed at my elbow as I fumble through my pockets for pencil and notebook. I start to jot down a first attempt to express the realisation in some form of notation:

$$Q(Q><[Q]) = Q(Q><[Q])$$

Of course it would be possible to qualify this. It may be that this is itself too blindingly, elegantly simple and that the value

'Q' may have to be defined with some reference to a value external to itself. But for the moment it stands happily to explain what I see around me.

The Radical Psychic Field Disruptionists; the American students dressed in puffy, autumnal sports gear; the heads of a dozen university faculties gesturing with passion over a subject they neither know nor understand. And all of them, mark me, all of them, confined within definable societal groupings.

The Quantity Theory of Insanity has reached its first great epistemological watershed. Like theoretical physics it must now account for the very phenomenon it has helped to identify. It must reconstruct the proof of its own ground on the fact of its own enactment. Clearly, by concentrating so many aberrant and near-aberrant people in one place or series of places, the very fact of Quantity Theory has been impacting on the sanity quotient itself.

The task now is to derive an equation which would make it possible to establish whether what I suspect is true. Namely that as more and more insanity is concentrated around educational institutions, so levels of mental illness in the rest of society . . .

Select Bibliography

Ford, Hurst, Harley, Busner & Sikorski, 'Some Aspects of Sanity Quotient Mechanisms in a Witless Shetland Commune', *British Journal of Ephemera*, September, 1974.

Ford, H., 'Teaching Stockbrokers Ring Dancing', *Practical Mental Health*, January, 1975.

Ford, H., *The Quantity Theory of Insanity*, Publish Yourself Books, London 1976 (limited edition).

Ford, H., 'Repressing People Who Laugh Alone: Towards Effective Public Transport', *The Bus*, October, 1995.

Harley, T., 'Shamanism and Soya Futures', World Bank Research Briefs, September, 1979.

The Quantity Theory of Insanity

Hurst, P., 'Nailbiting in Bournemouth versus Bed-Wetting in Poole: Action and Amelioration', *Journal of Psychology*, March, 1976.

Hurst, P., 'General Census of Sanity Quotients in the UK', HMSO, January, 1980.

Sikorski, A., *'Daddy, Mummy's Mad.' 'Good.'*, Shefcott and Willer, London 1976.

Mono-Cellular

I used to play a game as a child. Well, not so much a game, it was more of a pastime. Lying in bed, if I squinted at the shafts of light that streamed in through the curtains they became solid. Solid tubes of brightness. I could extend and contract these tubes simply by the degree to which I squinted. It was a sensation of the most incredible kind of control, a control of a peripheral world that lay behind the thin sham of mere workaday appearances. A secret world. Lots of things happened to me during my childhood. It wasn't happy or unhappy, it was eventful, but what I remember best are those solid tubes of brightness.

I remember them best because they're back, albeit in a different form. I'm sitting in the living-room and there are these solid tubes of brightness wreathing just about everything in sight. A blue haze runs over the back of the leather three-seater sofa against the far wall. It shimmers across the carpet, six inches above the surface of the Wilton twistpile, mimicking, in a ghostly kind of a way, the diamond patterning. Purple haze round the pelmets. Green haze pulsing gently in front of the wall unit. And through the double doors, with their distorting pains of toughened glass, I can see my misbegotten children in the dining-room. They are lying in orderly rows, their backs humped at angles, a militaristic school of miniature cetaceans. Above each one there is a little corona of black light. If I squint I can harden the corona to a cloud. If I strain it fades out to almost nothing, a faint retinal after-image, nothing more.

You see, my feeling is this: I'm going to sit here for some

time. Probably for the next three hours. You see, if I move, there's a little sort of wart of pain – a hard little thing – stuck in the crook of my arm. And I hate the way it bobbles and jostles me when I move. It does it even when I perform a very simple action like taking a sip of beer. God knows what it would do to me if I walked through to the kitchen and fried up some spicy mushrooms. That would be a real mistake.

It's a mistake I don't intend to make. I have adjusted my environment. I've erected a little bubble here. I'm like one of those children that are allergic to everything. I cannot leave my bubble. I would be risking death. The wrong sort of stimulation could be fatal to me at this point. I mark down especially the spicy mushrooms in this context. Although I am not subject to those mushrooms in any real sense. Nor their foil container.

There are a lot more of my children upstairs. They are sleeping quietly. When the morning comes and Gavin calls . . . they will be taken away from me. Into Care. Yes, I like that 'Care'. With a capital 'C'. They're sleeping up there swathed in robes of bubbled plastic, girded with corrugated cardboard. But for this wart, this worrisome wart, I would join them. Lie for a while, in the small back bedroom. Go into the second bedroom and then disport myself in the master bedroom. Lie among them like a patriarch. Actually, I could do this. If I really wanted to. But I don't. I want to be right here when the dawn makes the railings across the road fizz. When an aureole projects out from the statue of the naked woman at Henley's Corner. When Gavin rings . . .

Actually. Actually, I think, I think Gavin will ring quite soon. It's nearly 6.00 a.m. and there's the time difference to consider. I'm worried about something, no, let me tell you. I'm worried that you think me needlessly cryptic: children, warts, spicy mushrooms, purple pelmets . . . but let me do it my way. Because I've already finished. As far as I can see, each sentence, each clause I utter contains the whole story. Beginning, middle and end. If I were to be true to my vision I'd shut up now. I could always shake my head and subside in a snowflake whirl of fragmented light . . . so let me be cryptic. If I hold out I can pretend that I haven't finished telling the story and that makes it worth telling, you see.

There are a lot of books lying around this chair. It's like a little village. They are all half open, spines upward. Little houses of knowledge. I've always liked books about How To Do Things. *How To Do Economics, How To Do Finance, How To Form a Company, How To Enamel Jewellery, How To Build a Boat.* Within the past hour or so I've looked at each of these books in turn. And in the next hour or so I'll do it again. I've done the same thing with the swathe of magazines and newspapers in the wedge of space between my chair and the wall. I'll come to the records later.

I look at each of the books in turn. I read a sentence or a short paragraph. And then, that's it. I've built the boat. Made the pendant. Floated the company. I have the same problem as I do with my own story. Everything is contained within everything. But I don't despair, I continue to pick up each of my books in turn, riffle through it, seize on a paragraph and then abandon it. Early on in the night the same was true of other rooms in the house. In the kitchen, before the spicy mushrooms gained their grip, I read cookery. In the toilet, humour. Upstairs it was novels. I daresay the books are all still there, abandoned villages.

I search the books and the newspapers for one fact, one piece of information, that will provide the key . . . but I already know it. What I've neglected to tell you is that I'm old, really old. Inhumanly old. I'm as old as a long-buried culvert. Bricks fall from my walls and expose the mud. I'm a huge wrinkled finger. I've been in the bath too long. My flesh hangs on me in wattled pouches. Every part of my clothing is a sweaty gusset. And I haven't mentioned the pulsing sound. Or the booming sound. The great wash of the ocean that pulls my head around on my neck.

And then again. That's better. Good to pull taut the clothesline. It's awfully depressing to see those grey many-times-washed aertex shirts. Trailing their cuffs in the dirt. Ha! Ha, ha . . . We bought a company, off the shelf. I like that 'off the shelf'. Makes me think of neat wire boxes full of miniature executives, all stacked on racks. Not quite like that. Our company, that is, Gavin's and mine: Ocean Ltd. Formerly trading as plankton farmers, for fish food, you see. Pet fish. Estuary – somewhere. Now, ours. And fitted out with new directors: Gavin, myself and Mr Rabindarath. Unwittingly in this last instance. He never leaves his room except to pick up his prescription. Gavin kindly relieves him of the bother of reading any of the correspondence relating to Ocean Ltd. And, indeed, of his responsibility as Financial Director thereof. Good of Gavin. Mr Rabindarath is a hopeless neurotic. He would worry.

I feel a lot better. Well enough to take on the kitchen. The purple edging around everything has stopped furiously oscillating. Either that or it now vibrates with such frequency that it appears static. At any rate, objects have achieved a crystalline purity of line. This beer can, for example. Have you ever seen a purer beer can than this? Why, the drawing of the Castlemaine Brewery in Brisbane is so sharp, one might be standing right outside of it. I drink. That flat taste. Absolute purity of line.

I lift myself from the chair. A little stiff. To be expected. Cigarette ash forms a network of lines pointing to my crotch. It's a crotch rubbing! Ha! Ha, ha . . .

Walking, like most other human activities, requires a great deal of assurance. If you want it to look right you have to undertake it with tremendous confidence and verve. You can usually spot a young or inexperienced walker by their lack of style, or their assumption of a style which is too old and complex for them. Pretentious walking can be a real problem. But here, I stride into the hall quite naturally. I'm on my way to the kitchen . . . 'Spicy mushrooms,' you say? Well, to hell with them, is my reply. You were taken in by my bullshit.

There is no discontinuation of floor covering between the front room and the hall, which is comforting. The careful two-cornered ascent of the staircase in the corner is reassuring as well. I bought this watercolour, hung centrally on the wall, over the oval hall table, in Betys-Y-Coed. It depicts a stone cottage, in the mid-ground. In the foreground there is a field and a dry-stone wall; in the background, clouds. It's tremendously homey, this watercolour, as is the table, bought in Beccles, which looks dark and woody in the light that spills through from the front room. It imparts a mahogany, old solidity to my house, which it doesn't really deserve.

Even the children, the fruit of my labours, look innocuous enough here, viewed in receding twos, marching up the treads of the staircase and huddling around the door to the cupboard under the stairs. They've lost their militaristic mien. I can pause here, tent my hand casually on the oval table, pinning down some junk mail, and recount.

Gavin says that this house is a cluttered little cabinet of lower-middle-class knick-knacks. That it betrays my yearning for respectability. All I know is that I could never be comfortable in his minimal environment: spotlights, wire-wooled mouldings, varnished wood, little rugs, that's all.

When I bought this house, a necessary bit of deficit financing for Ocean Ltd, I was determined that it should be a place of real respite. At the time I was spending almost all day sitting up against freestanding baffles covered in sheeny grey fabric, talking to men whose hair pointed and whose gestures were punctuated by little stabs with aluminium ballpoints. Coming back to this house was an escape. I've only lived here a few months, but it really feels like home.

Setting up lines of credit for Ocean Ltd was the easiest thing in the world. Gavin was utterly convincing; there is nothing forced in his manner, he simply makes people want to be his friend. As a consequence people are his friends, and the way friends do, they do Gavin favours. He talks to them with his confident mellow voice, which has only the faintest aftertone of social superiority. It's all in the aftertone; people don't hear it, but they absorb it subliminally and respond. Ocean Ltd effortlessly borrowed its operating capital.

'Not everyone responds to a glossy brochure,' said Gavin, nudging his whiskey sour with an extended finger – I noticed the tuberous bulge of plastic flesh where the cuticle should have been – 'but it has to be there.' Ocean Ltd had a glossy brochure: receding panels of textured paper, spot-varnished duotones of our babies looking sleek, tiny squares of copy and typefaces pulled this way and that, and the Ocean Ltd logo: one of the babies, stylised with ripping lines.

There's a nasty ripple in the air here, in the hall. It's too close, that's the problem. I'm becoming absorbed with detail. Gavin tells me that that's my problem. 'You're a classic anal-retentive,' he says, 'tirelessly absorbed by minutiae, anankastic in the extreme – it's lucky you have to deal with the broad sweep of things, to do the abstract thinking.' That may be so, but Gavin's abstract thoughts have led to remarkably concrete things, like

the Bloomsbury flat, the Oyster Perpetual, the suits from Bromsgrove, shirts from Barries. While my concrete mentality, my eye
for detail has lead me . . .

. . . to the kitchen. Yaaah! . . . Bloody fool. A white flash of
light. I punched the wall switch, the strips flickered once in
too-late warning and then sprung into full, flat light, hammering
down on my tissue-paper retinas. I am a pin-hole camera. Ugh!
. . . Everything is lit up. The dresser is exposed in the corner –
an old woman taking her clothes off. There are spice jars here
like the moon, one side silvered, the other buried in perpetual
darkness. Everything in the kitchen is lunar, polarised. On the
rectangular melamine table sits last night's supper; those devilish
spicy mushrooms crouch, warbling in their foil. In the flesh they
are far less terrifying than I had imagined. I feel a slackening
off, my heart surfaces from the bottom of the empty stomach-
pool that it jackknifed into when the light went on. I'll just go
to the sink and get a glass of water.

Hu, hu, heu, ggh . . . I'd forgotten. I'm gagging. I can barely
contain myself. I feel a bitter sewage-gorge rising up my neck. I
can only seize a can from the fridge, hit the light and retreat back
across the hall to the front room and my seat by the window. I'd
forgotten the tandoori chicken wings, they were lurking on the
draining board. Just the sight of those bent red limbs in filmy
bondage, wet turmeric paste pressed all around. It was enough
to destabilise me. I'm sitting in the chair. And nothing makes
any sense. Any more. I'm sitting vertiginously. Tipping forward.
Looking down on the looking down, looking down. And how I
regret those purple pelmets. And the malignant wart, that little
hard nodule of pain in the pit of my arm is throbbing fit to bust.
It's no simple organic pain, this is a pain the insidiousness of
which undercuts the very idea of flesh; it's a pain that speaks of
a future when we will have all evolved into cybernauts; the wart
is a bolt screwed into the template of my arm, casually mashing
rusted tendon cables . . .

'As you were, as you were.' I must drill this transitory army of
occupation and then set them at ease with myself. When they
arrived yesterday afternoon their custodians couldn't quite
believe where they were to take up residence. Standing in their
pseudo-denim windcheaters, company names emblazoned on

their breasts, the men squinted at my semi and then rang the descending chimes. One of them held in his solid mitt the flapping sheaf of onion-skin invoices.

With the unhurried ease of labourers everywhere, who seek, on a daily basis, to escape the winding down of their own bodies' strength, they brought the children in from the truck and stacked them all over the house. Box after box, one hundred gross in all, laid out in all the rooms. After they had gone I amused myself for a while by taking them out and playing with them, forming patterns, marching them up and down, and when that palled I lined them up in ranks. Especially next door in the dining-room where, at this moment, four companies are drawn up in tight formation under the table.

When they'd all been unloaded and the various invoices signed I wanted to stop the three men as they moved off to their orange truck. I felt a terrible sense of abandonment and strangeness. The whole grey afternoon possessed an awful thin reality that might slice into me. I wanted to call them back, but could think of no pretext. The air brakes hissed and they roared up through the gears and away towards the North Circular.

You see, I'm not convinced any more by Gavin. That's the root of it. I'm suspicious. When we met David Hangleton two weeks ago for a 'little Italian dinner' in Hampstead, he was so much more convincing. I've never pretended to know anything about this. It was never my job to supply front or charisma for Ocean Ltd. I was the back-room boy who would square things away and make them look right on paper. But next to Hangleton, Gavin seemed insubstantial. It was as if, with Gavin, I had witnessed a clever pastiche of the real thing. Everything Gavin did, the gestures he made, the things he said, the suits he wore, was forced, it was a performance. Hangleton on the other hand was clearly a real entrepreneur, he meant it all. He was natural and unforced and his bragging related to funds that were, if not entirely his own, at least not subject to punitive rates of interest.

'Buy something very cheap, with someone else's money and then sell it, quickly, not so cheap.' That was Gavin's maxim and the motto of Ocean Ltd. He even made me get a little sign made up with this written on it and hung it over the computer.

'Then we can pay off the loans.'

'Then we can pay off the loans.'

'And the credit cards.'
'And the credit cards.'
'And the current accounts.'
'And the current accounts.'
'And the charge cards.'
'Yeah, and the frigging charge cards.'
'And pile the capital back into a real enterprise.'
'Of course, this isn't simply a stupid sting, is it. We're businessmen, entrepreneurs.'

Businessmen, entrepreneurs. Gavin had certainly looked and acted the part. At least I had thought so to begin with. He was so good-looking for a start, with his neat sandy hair, his regular, even features. He had a nose that had such a tight little bridge, not like my flat lump of clay; and a flawless complexion, so flawless that I wouldn't have been surprised to find a seam running down the back of his neck.

When Gavin and I first became colleagues he took me out with him to meet his friends. They all had the same kind of manner as him, a sort of unforced and facetious ease. It was the kind of charm that I've always found myself a victim of. Gavin and his friends, with their minor public school slang, their games of backgammon and their saloon-car races round London's arterial roads, reminded me of the *nouveau riche* kids I went to school with. They had the same consumer's attitude to the business of living. Like Gavin they went straight to the bottom line without troubling to check the balances. I suppose the difference was that Gavin brought to the whole thing the strong implication of ultimate solidity, a four-square Virginia Water kind of security. Redolent of retrievers and women with seriously quilted clothing. He also had the knack of elevating you, making you feel special: 'I'm telling you this because I know you can keep a secret and . . . ' Lengthy pause, 'well, because I suppose I regard you as one of my closest friends.' Eyes downcast to denote embarrassment and then briefly flicked upwards into your own to indicate complete faith.

Actually, you know, I'm wrong to rubbish Gavin like this. I'm wrong and I'm stupid. Very stupid. He's out there alone in a hotel room, he's staked everything he has on Ocean Ltd. I never had anything to stake to begin with. He's been a friend to me – if a little capricious. But maybe that's what friendship is, a slap and then a tickle. I suppose I'm nervous because I'm expecting the call and because the last thing I read in *How To Form a Company* was 'Business partnerships can be very thorny indeed, even close friends should ensure that partnership agreements are vetted by an experienced solicitor.' But of course we don't have a partnership, we have a limited company, with directors. Mr Rabindarath and, of course, Sandy – although his identity could be said to be problematic.

I can see the corner of the garden out of the corner of my eye. Dawn must be coming. Gavin should call. It's damp out there, a little wetness glistens in the orange light, on the privet and the flattened grass. In here it's the same. My chair. The sofa. The wall unit, the triangular area between the side of my chair and the wall, full of loosely piled newspapers. The miniature landscape of the newspaper, up column and down advertisement. Who is to say that it's really smaller than the room, the garden, or the world? If I rub my hand up and down the arm of the chair the pile on the cover moves from flat to prickily upright, to flat again. Co-ordination is the key here, foolish to look for wisdom in books, because they have nothing new to say. They contain everything in their one long sentence. Everything and nothing. Whereas in this simple ritual – rotating the chair-cover pile with the flat of my hand, whilst rhythmically breathing and, at the same time, running my eye carefully over the newspaper hillocks – I achieve control. I create a tiny ordered universe, which means that Gavin will call. He must call because the universe is ordered. The solid beams can be made to expand and contract in tight ranks. The children have all gone to bed quietly. The mushrooms lie swaddled in batter, the chicken wings subside into the polystyrene mattress. And the wart starts up as a dot, that flares into a portal. A ghastly do̶ ̶ ̶ ̶ ̶ *beautaneousness*. Urghh . . . its *layeredness*. I hate th̶ ̶ ̶ ̶ ̶ ̶ ̶ ̶ ̶ ̶ because they're all over and beneath the̶m̶ ̶ ̶ ̶ ̶ Someone has sprinkled sand between th̶ ̶ ̶ ̶ ̶ And the beer is flat again. And I have he̶ ̶ ̶ ̶ times. Where is my control . . .

Actually, there's nothing particularly ̶ ̶ ̶ ̶ has a kind of folksy innocence, a w̶ ̶ ̶ ̶ ̶ my current mood. It could be ironic̶ ̶ ̶ ̶ looking, I think, rather dapper for someone who's been up the whole night. My clothes have a rather billowy aspect to them, perhaps it's the light quality. I sit in the pool thrown down by the standard lamp, washed by the orange from the street lamp and tinged with the palest of grey flushes from the coming dawn. And the beams, those solid beams, which elsewhere in the living-room are orderly and controlled, dance and hum around me, weaving in and out of one another; I am their focus.

I am like some small, brightly coloured fleck of life, caught under a microscope. Beautiful, weightless, shrunk beyond the force of gravity or the effect of the sun, I swim in the amniotic air of the living-room. The wallpaper gently susurrates. And then, without warning, a hostile beam enters the room, plunges through the cornice, a beam unlike the others, not subject to my optical control: a beam of pure anxiety. Which probes me with its needle tip, touches me just once. Pokes a single time, into my soft midriff, the heliotrope heart of my pathetically simple organism. And I contract. I seize up. I clench and ball into a little jelly fist. Slowly, slowly I relax again, blob out, float in the limpid fluid that magnifies my transparent body. It happens again and again. I am but a single-celled creature capable of one, giant, knee-jerk reflex. This is a bit of a digression from my main area of concern, or at any rate the area of discussion, founded, as it were, on words like 'pallet' and expressions such as 'bill of lading' and 'pro-forma invoice'. This area is coextensive with tarmac aprons bordered by chain-link fences. The world which Ocean Ltd inhabits is an active world of quantifiable phenomena, not some amoebic fantasy concocted in a suburban living-room at . . . getting on for 6.30 a.m.

And who exactly is to say that Sandy, Mr Rabindarath's arthritic old labrador, with greying muzzle and shambolic walk, is not entitled to his place on the board of Ocean Ltd? Even if his identity had to be constructed for him, pieced together from headstone to birth certificate, to passport, to bank account. Mr Sandy Eccles is an accomplished fact now. His name appears on ur letterhead. He is casually referred to by one and all and red periodically in the eyes of numerous minds, powering xhall down great swathes of motorway, listening to Shirtsleeved, his jacket dangling from a hook behind his head, confident that he's going to close that sale . . .

I must say that I congratulate myself . . . well done, old chap! This living-room is a bold testament to your struggle against anxiety. Everything seems to be right in its place, there's nothing that jars the eye. The village of books, the chair set at a precise angle, the wedge of newsprint, the fan of album covers, all good rugs of media. Nicely offsetting the restrained beige of the carpet. Magnolia may not be an inspired choice for wall-covering but it is restful. And as for the furniture, surely it is the right decision to play it down, keep it modern, but not too . . . After all, the shape of the room, the metal-divided, six-pane windows, none of it would support anything but angularity and pastels.

This folk song. I really hate it, it says nothing to me. But steady now, I've tried jazz, flirted with the classics, run through a gamut of rock, reggae, fusion and soul. They didn't work; they all skittered out of the speakers as so much senseless timpani. I cannot hear rhythm or melody, I must confine myself to songs about battered children and alcoholic old men. They might be real. No time to change the record, anyway. It's time for what the papers say . . .

And looking first of all this morning at last month's *Hendon Advertiser* we see that St Peter's Mount held a Bring and Buy Sale that was hugely successful and raised £176.000 for Great Ormond Street Hospital for Sick Children. Especial congratulations go . . . apparently . . . to Mrs Tyler, for organising the event and for baking no less than twenty ginger cakes. Hmmmn, hmm, a powerful lead story, strongly backed by items on new bus shelters, a mobility scheme for the elderly and the retirement of a long-serving school dinners lady. There she is on page five, beaming over an ornamental barometer. Editorial? Let me see . . . riffle, riffle, riffle. A-ha! Dog mess, as I suspected. That perennial and coiled question. It won't go away, will it. It effects the polity of the Finchley municipality much as the Irish Question dominated late nineteenth-century Britain.

But the real news is at the very back of the paper. After full-page ads for shock absorbers and such, we find the small ads; and here is the full pathos of life. Pathos than inheres not just in the advertisements themselves:

Travelling suitcase, hardly used, clean inside and out. £3.00.
671 0042 after 6.00 pm

or,

MFI shelving units. Seven 5' x 1'6".
£15.00. Will consider part-ex for coffee table/similar.
229 5389 (days)

and

Tit Bits, Nos 148 – 546. Suit Collector.
£40.00 ono
229 4917 after 8.30 pm

but also in one's attitude towards them. I betray myself here.
Gavin would never read the small ads in the *Hendon Advertiser*.
He glances only at glossy spreads where women with hips so
high they must know Dr Moreau undulate down the Promenades des Anglais, selling smelly water, Euro-box cars,
whatever . . .

The serrated edge of the type on these little advertisements.
It drags me down, and what's worse is that I can see myself
reading them and see myself seeing myself. All too vertiginous
again. I'll have to abandon the papers. And pick up a book . . .
How To . . . How To . . . something . . . With a blue cover and
white dots. The Dewey decimal system used for bullet points
that shoot between my tired eyes. I've been up for too long to
absorb:

1.21 Infrastructural debits cannot be handled by a day-to-day spreadsheet analysis.

Quite so . . . quite so . . . and it follows, so it does, that:

1.22 Invisibles must be separated prior to any medium-term
strategic plan.

That's been my mistake. Not separating those damn invisibles. Here am I, in a position of responsibility, a board member of a fairly substantial import/wholesale outfit, a certified accountant and I'm still really letting those invisibles get to me. Invisibles and intangibles – like the wet, iron-tasting squish of turmeric paste, or the small ads' pathos, this is a retching matter. And I'm the man for it, with my inexhaustible supplies of salty bile, with my cheddar gorge. I can feel my diaphragm undulate ... come now, not in front of the children, *pas devant les engafangas*. Concentration on some apparently useless but therapeutic task is what I need to pull me through. Rearrange the autodidactic village, so that all the roofs are parallel and rake up at the same angle. Yes, I can just reach them all from my chair. The blood is rushing to my head as I lower my miniature crane of a claw of a hand. Fucking wart! A pox on you wart! Hell's bolt on my arm, an arm saturated like a sponge with seeping watery infection. The senselessness of the task. Don't you realise I'm in pain here?

'I'm not worried about security for this loan at all.' The Child Banker sat behind the angled blotter, his face worryingly unlined.

'Everything seems in order as far as already established collateral is concerned and ... ' Coffee cooled uselessly in Star Trek beakers. Gavin shifted in his chair, his suit a vague swathe of blue in the Rembrandt brown of the Child Banker's office, his attaché case propped open on the corner of the desk. Inside it a miniature world: memo pad, filofax, brochures for Ocean Ltd, keys, pens and some of our different kinds of children. Currently fostered but, with the Child Banker's assistance, scheduled for – albeit temporary – adoption. I watched as the Child Banker drew a pad towards him and affectedly added columns of figures with pretty strokes of his fountain pen. A little girl in a pinstripe suit floated in the gloom over his right shoulder, flicking digits on to a green screen that from time to time scrolled upward in bright streaks. The Child Banker turned the sheets of foolscap round so that we could see what he'd written; the bottom line was thirty-eight per cent. Thirty-eight per cent. We would have to bring those children up and send them into the world so fast, so bloody fast.

'There's no problem.' Gavin unlocked the green door and we stepped into the clammy passageway.

'Look here ... ' Mr Rabindarath and Mr Eccles' post was

loosely stacked, leaning up against the wall, on top of the ply-wood housing that covered some hernia of the aching house, the gas or electricity meter, bursting from the bellied wall. Gavin snapped open the envelope and scanned the letter.

'They're on their way, one hundred gross. The paperwork is with the shipper at the terminal. They'll be here the day after tomorrow.'

Mr Rabindarath came footing round the bend in the stairs. Sandy, aka 'Mr Eccles', padding by his side. Mr Rabindarath wore a very long gaberdine mac that covered him to his feet. He headed on down and passed us, blank eyes recessed into his grey, eroded face. His prescription was clutched in one hand and in the other he held a child's blue plastic spade which bore Mr Eccles' toothmarks.

'Not so good I'm afraid,' Gavin was reading a letter addressed to Sandy in his capacity as marketing manager of Ocean Ltd, 'they seem to be getting rather cold feet in Hamburg, I'll have to go over. I'm sure they'll be no trouble once I get there, Horst just needs a little babying. You stay here, transship the goods. No sense in warehousing them, it'll simply eat into our profits. Keep them at your place. It'll only be for a night . . . '

We left the house and walked down the North End Road. Gavin seemed not to notice the oppressively low sky, or the sad juxtaposition of tatty mullioned windows with dirty sheet glass. He was erect and going somewhere. But the city held me to it, like some dried and crusty discharge mirroring the Artexed wall, above the meter, where Mr Rabindarath and Mr Eccles' post had lain.

Gavin took me to the Savoy for a farewell tea and we ate crumpets and drank Earl Grey at the bottom of that great sunken swirl of carpeting. Waiters came and went with the softest of footfalls, bringing and taking thick crockery and heavy, stainless steel vessels. The crisp, white linen of the tablecloth and the crisp, white linen of my napkin, folded into each other on my lap. Gavin talked about Ocean Ltd and his sex life as if they were one and the same and chopped the air vigorously with his hands. Stubby hands with spatulate fingers and recessed nails, Gavin's hands were like someone else's shoulders.

I couldn't concentrate. I became fixated by the details: the underside of a leaf on a rubber plant, the ridged rubber rim of a waiter's shoe, the precise three-button belly bulge of a fat man at an adjacent table, and eventually by the green-gold pelmets capping the great swathes of drapery at the end of the room. A pelmet isn't a piece of furniture, but nor, on the other hand, is it merely decorative. These pelmets were vast, adult versions of my little purple pelmets at home. The curtains cascaded down from them to the floor. They were fringed with hooks of gold thread. Gavin waved buttered toast about and I couldn't wait to get home, to my chair and my bubble and the quiet part of the night.

That was thirty-six hours ago. For thirty-two of them, or thereabouts, I have sat here. Excursions to the toilet, the fridge, to supervise the unloading of the children. There has been one phone call from Gavin: everything is going well. I'm just to sit tight and wait for his call and then fill out the pro forma invoice which coils out of the old Unwin on the dining-room table. An undemanding way to make a living, or so I think. I'm privileged in my house, which is only superficially attached to the other houses strung out alongside an isolated rectangle of green in the midst of the suburbs. My truncated garden is backed up by another, the same and the same to east and west. My house is built into the next one, but only brick deep. Inside it is a tardis, far larger than anyone can imagine. It is an island, separated from the rest of Brent, floating in a viscous bath of salty, crusted fluid.

Damn it all, I should make an EEC declaration when I transfer objects from one room of this house to the next, or even mental objects within my own head. Yes, that's it. Declarations of intent: stating the purpose of the thought, its resale value and so on. The problem is not to attach such a declaration (in triplicate) to each thought. It is simply that there is no one there to check it, no customs men. Nothing new, except mile upon mile of dun-coloured tundra, unrolling under a sky that matches it, for flatness, for billowing featurelessness, excepting for here, and there, the brackish open sore of a peaty pool, fringed with sedge.

Breakfast television starts in half an hour. I've just checked my watch. There's two certainties. Two pieces of evidence . . . that add up to . . . my control: real evidence of my control over

my environment. There's a certain homeliness about a cardigan
... at 6.30 in the morning, worn by an avuncular man ... on
a screen. It's the kind of assurance that I need. I must find that
bastard child the remote controller ... a complete misnomer.
There's nothing remote about the control I exercise with it, one
push of the soft stud and the television will spring into life ...
I can check out the test card and the occasional notices they
issue at this hour of forthcoming programmes.

Where is the bastard child? My fingers skate nervelessly over
the carpet, sketching out the faint raggedy afterimage of those
once firm and solid purple bars. Gone ... gone ... gonnie!
Nothing now but the grey wash of near dawn and the fading
yellow pool around my chair, marking the limit of my bubble.
The pictures on the opposite wall, which through the long night
appeared thoroughly appropriate ... full of meaning ... in
good taste, are now old postage stamps and curling posters on
an adolescent's bedroom wall: Snoopy, woman in tennis dress
scratching her naked buttock and worse. The colour scheme in
here is as anonymous and inhospitable as a supermarket aisle,
or the neglected lobby of a large corporation.

My hand is heavy with blood. I long to clutch its slim, cool
blackness and feel the play of soft studs ... so unlike ... the
wart! Which throbs in my inner elbow, a hard stud that promises
nothing but pain. Imagine pressing it ... eugh! Jesus Christ!
Jee-suss Kerist! Hard, but squishy ... and if I pressed it ...
what then ... not control ... but less control. Less control ...

Well, bastard child. So here you are, snug in my hand, as if
you'd never left, and the preview screen undulates gently across
the room. 6.45 a.m., *Good Morning Britain*. And good morning
to you ... I say. A simple salutation. To breathe freely I have
opened the window and a fresh draft of privety air is wafting in
from the front garden. In the distance I can hear the swish and
roar of artics as they make up for lost time along the North
Circular.

It is dawn ... If I stretch out from my chair the bubble that
encloses me comes too. Stretching stickily around my hand.
Cling-film adhesion that turns me into a Cyberman. Time to
stand up again, free my clothes where they've melded to my
body, move around the room a little, gently shaking my limbs.

Another night . . . another dollar. What a doddle. Huh! Futile really to read so many books on self-improvement . . . Here . . . I'll gather them up now and put them away on the shelf. What we need in here is a certain orderliness with which to face the morning. Ch-onk. They fall on to the shelves . . . and I'll gather up these album covers that are fanned out over the floor . . . and stack them here . . . and now the free newspapers that silt up the wedge between my chair and the wall . . . *voilà*. Now all I can see is a conventional room in a conventional house, with breakfast television about to be watched, by me: Company Director.

We went out on the town. That is, those directors of Ocean Ltd who weren't rocking spasmodically in their rooms, or slavering over blue plastic spades. We had just finished opening the last line of credit we required in order to make the big purchase, and Gavin and I were in high spirits. We were just two more young men out on the town. There's nothing quite like it, is there? That feeling that you're somehow connected, at the centre of things. You're walking down Old Compton Street and this is your burgh, your village.

We fell in with some girls at a pub on Cambridge Circus, the way that sailors on leave do in Hollywood films. It had never happened to me before . . . I put it down to Gavin. They were red and brown in tailored suits and didn't make a habit of this kind of thing and laughed a lot and had conspiratorial nods and catchwords which passed between them. And Gavin and I were interested in them and talked to them about their jobs and their flats and got to know them, because this was our night already and we were young bucks, as it were, loose on the town.

And I remember going on from the pub. This less concretely than before, everything still funny, but with an edge. One of the girls said, 'What do you do then?' And I said that we had this company, Ocean Ltd, and gave her my card – stupid really – because she wasn't in business. Sitting in La Capresa scrunching on breadsticks and drinking red wine that grabbed at my throat. When they went off to the toilet – and God knows why I remember this because it really isn't important – Gavin asked me to sign a guarantor release on the Ocean Ltd fund account. At least

I'm pretty sure that's what it was. At the time I just signed it. He was always giving me things to sign in my directorial capacity, and on this occasion, being a young Turk, it seemed the right thing to be doing in La Capresa, taking out my thick fountain pen and snaking my bloody signature across the hair-lined box . . . and then . . . that's it. The rest of the evening was the rest of the evening. And I know I didn't go home with one of those girls, because I never do . . . and I know that Gavin probably did, because he always does. And I don't know why this business of signing the form is swimming at me now out of my memory, because it really isn't important at all, is it?

Standing now on the oblong of stairway that is the half-landing. Appalled by the little banks of fluff that have accreted in the gap between the nap of the carpet and the corrugation of underlay. Appalled also by the thin dustfall on my children that dulls them. I'm a pale face at a window on a half-landing . . . I'm a half-remembered surreal poem, learnt by rote in school, years ago. I'm on my way upstairs to make a tour of inspection, but I can't get further than this. Transfixed again by a miniature world, where the brass rods that hold tight the tread are Nazca lines on the floor of some delusory desert. Because everything, as it were, contains everything. And this half-landing has as much right to be considered the world as any other, wouldn't you agree? That's a rhetorical, rhetorical question, maybe the first of its kind, tee-hee! As long as you can be miserable in good surroundings.

Hoo . . . It might be a mistake to go upstairs, there's something a little strange about the giant tortoise that my bed has become, stacked as it is with the fruit of Ocean Ltd's labours. And I don't think that I'll be able to repeat my book-tidying act. I don't want to be upstairs when Gavin rings, because I hate having to run to answer the phone. As it is I can float downstairs. I feel sustained by lines of credit, that flow like the purple bars, like the bright bars of my childhood, but lighter, filmier, wavier. I float downstairs at the centre of a net of lines of credit, they undulate slackly around me and then gather me together and whisk me back into the living-room. Breakfast television is on the cards and Gavin may phone at any moment. I can see him in my mind's eye. He's wearing lederhosen and standing in an international phone booth that looks like a giant, porcelain-sided stove. We're in split screen: me in my chair, he in his stove; and he pushes his phone card – emblazoned with a double-headed eagle – into the cast-iron fissure ... Clinks and ker-cherunks and whirrs as the line springs into action triggering circuitry across and over the continent ... but no ... no ring here. Perhaps he'll ring in a little while.

Here's the studio swimming into view. And it makes me feel nauseous. The unreal quality of that manufactured space, intended only to contain posturing presenters. Chipboard pouffes encased in oatmeal twistpile, turquoise striped banquettes ... It is a slab for displaying human fish ... I can't bear to watch them swim into view and 'O' at me fatuously ... I've more pressing problems, like flatness of taste ... and the malignant wart ... Have you met one another? I say here – and mark this – that this wart is cancerous. It represents a new and virulent form of cancer that is peculiar to me. This is an implosive cancer, other cancers infect cell after cell in a chain reaction, but this cancer works in on itself, nullifying cells which turn into heavier and heavier dead matter, glutinous matter, nailed into the pit of my elbow. The symptoms? Well, flatness of taste for one, flatness of mouth taste, eye taste, ear taste. Smell? Ferrr-geddit. The only palliative is chemotherapy ... and the side-effects can be disturbing ...

What I need to consider, as the television wetly observes me, is some kind of strategy that will make Gavin phone me, now. I'm sick of waiting. I'm aware that there are certain rituals that I can perform which will make him phone me. Never underesti-mate the power of magic. We may think that cause and effect are billiard balls that strike one another, but we know that we can tip the table. And that's what I'm going to do, I'm going to tip the table.

What is it that keeps me here, sitting, stiffening, in a repro Queen Anne chair, bought from a mail-order catalogue, when I could be asleep. I could be lying in between warm, brushed cotton sheets, enjoying that special, infinitely sweet, morning sleep, that turns one's aching body inside out like a sock. Instead, I'm rigid, upright, staring, waiting. I'm going to compile a list of the things that stop me sleeping and act upon them forthwith:

1. The wart
2. Lack of appetite
3. Waiting for Gavin to ring

Appetite and the wart and Gavin are all intimately linked. I realise this now although it's been staring me in the face all night. If I can do something about the former, the latter will fall into place. (I'm just kidding about all of this – really, believe me – just to keep me occupied. I don't really think I can influence Gavin by acts of magic, but it's a nice thought, isn't it?) I see the wart as a hungry thing . . . actually as a hungry entity. You notice that I can speak quite openly and casually about the wart at this stage? That's because the wart isn't hungry at the moment. The wart is the bivalve that determines my cycle, my expansion and contraction. What I need to do is give it some real nourishment, something that will completely assuage it. Since the wart owes its very existence to the founding of Ocean Ltd, the act of sating its relentless hunger will necessarily bring about the completion of Ocean Ltd's business. You have followed me so far I hope?

The wart takes in matter and massively condenses it. If you like, it is the biological equivalent of a black hole, infinitely heavy. And what about the meal it requires? Well, this must be a combination of real food: spicy mushrooms, tandoori chicken wings, stale bagels, morello cherry conserve, squares of processed cheese – and material relating to Ocean Ltd. To whit: invoices, bills of lading, delivery notes, customs declarations, spreadsheet analyses and a couple of brochures, one for the product – the children's scrapbook – and one for Ocean Ltd itself.

I will have to travel to assemble the ingredients of my spell. Into the dining-room to fetch the Ocean Ltd material and then to the kitchen to get the food. Before I go, let me take stock. Is this the only course of action left open to me? Or can I get by with a plainer, more matter-of-fact view of my world? I say 'my world' advisedly, the truth of the matter is, can I make my world elide gracefully into being 'the world' again? A world of housecoats, washing-up brushes, bilateral agreements, tax returns, sexual encounters and stand-up comedians. Can I?

No. Emphatically not. Things have gone too far. I never

should have started that nonsense with the solid tubes of brightness. I've made my epiphenomenal bed, now I'll have to stand in it. Up. And to the dining-room. Gather the necessary papers and continue walking with an easy and unhurried, a supremely natural gait, into the hall. 'Good morning, watercolour.' 'Good morning, table.' The kitchen is quite light now but I have to see what I'm doing so I'd better put on the strip light. Aha! The mushrooms warble a greeting, the chicken wings hunch on the draining board. Off with their packaging!

I have everything assembled now. Lain out in a pattern on the table top. One question remains . . . how to eat it. Oral intake is inconceivable. For one thing there is the flatness . . . the wart's fault . . . and for another the gorge which continually deposits freight lift-loads of metallic saliva in my mouth. No, I'll have to absorb the potion through my skin. Sandwich a spicy mushroom between two invoices, package it like some strange dim sum and press it into the hollow of my neck, rub down its crinkly, greasy softness. Open my tired shirt . . . take squares of processed cheese and feel them bind into the spindly hairs on my chest . . . not long now . . . stale bagels are to be ground up in the hand and the crumbs dropped down the front of my trousers, together with torn squares of laminated 275 gsm art board . . . morello cherry conserve on my forehead . . . nothing is sticky when you immerse yourself in it . . . plaster the triple-leaved invoice on to the gungy mess . . . the best till last . . . the wart itself . . . the chicken wing . . . like a foetal arm . . . roll up the sleeve and spread the turmeric paste on to the wart . . . Jesus, that hurts! But yes it feels good . . . it feels good . . . What's that! A trill in the living-room . . . a 'spung' and then a trill . . . the phone is ringing . . . it worked . . . I rush out of the kitchen . . . I can feel crumbs falling down around my crotch . . . the conserve gums up my eyes . . . emulsifiers and E207 additives are speedily imploding into the wart . . . I only have a limited amount of time . . . in the living-room the first peal is sharp, hectoring, insistent . . . that was quick! I made it from the kitchen to the living-room in the time it took the phone to fully connect . . . but where is the phone . . . Where is the phone! . . . I can't see it anywhere . . . I haven't used it for two days . . . I don't know where it is . . . Stop. Where's the ringing coming from . . . Not in here at all . . . I can hear it through the floorboards . . . It's coming from the bedroom upstairs . . . And I'm up there before the thought has even taken form . . . but I can't find the phone anywhere . . . The ringing is coming from the testudo that covers the bed . . . it's one of the children! I tear the packaging from its sylvan form with scrabbling nails, the plastic bubbles pop between my fingers . . . the corrugated cardboard is strangely slick . . . My Children . . . with their buttons and their bows . . . with their little rubberised penises . . . one of them is calling to me . . . But which one? Not this one . . . not this one . . . not this one . . . I tear off jacket after jacket . . . And now another one starts . . . and another . . . and another . . . Upstairs and downstairs . . . in the living-room . . . in the kitchen . . . in the hall . . . in the back bedroom . . . until all hundred gross of them are pealing away in a synchronous cacophony . . . pulsing like some insane electronic cicadas . . . pulsing in and out . . . expanding and contracting . . . expanding . . .

Waiting

'I can't stand this any more, I'm getting out of here.' Jim was cradling the plastic rim of the Ford Sierra's steering wheel in his forearms and staring blankly through the windscreen. I noticed, completely inconsequentially, that his forearms were angled as if they were part of the car's controls – perhaps some kind of overarching indicator levers. And then he was gone; he elbowed the door open, slid sideways and jackknifed his feet out of the car with a suddenness that sent the rest of his body pivoting after them. After that he was off and running. He vaulted the grooved steel barrier that divided the carriageways and bolted across the eastbound side of the motorway, narrowly evading the oncoming traffic which was whipping through the long, low chicane as if to purposefully taunt the banked-up vehicles not heading west. There was a chorus of Dopplered hoots which rose and then fell and he was gone into the close darkness.

The door rocked gently on its hinges and wafted a little more petrol and diesel fumes into the passenger compartment. The night was as warm and as vinyl as the interior of the car. It was as if the motorway, the central reservation, the screed, unfinished banks – all of it – were enclosed in some larger, staler, automotive interior. The sky was flatly two-dimensional; an all-encompassing, bug-smeared windscreen, stippled with dried, dirty droplets.

For a full three minutes after Jim had got fed up with waiting I thought that things might still pan out. By rights in a situation such as this, left, unable to drive, in the passenger seat of a car hopelessly jammed on the M25 in the middle of the night, the scene ought to fade out. It was a natural ending. But after three minutes the traffic started to edge forward and I panicked. Eventually, irate fellow motorists – family men, stock controllers and solicitors' clerks – in beige leisure wear and patterned Bermudas, got out of their cars and pushed the Sierra across the two nearside lanes and on to the hard shoulder. Then they got back into their hatchback Daihatsus and Passat estates and ground off, with infinite pains, towards the tangle of striped cones and panting JCBs which marked the genesis of the jam.

I was left sitting. The knob atop the steering column of the Sierra clicked on and then off – what a drama queen – sending a false message of hopeful hazard, nowhere.

Two hours later a truly fat man buckled the belts round the car's axles, pulled the lever on the back of the pick-up and an electric motor whined. The cable pulled taut and yanked the front of the Sierra up in the air. We got into the cab and started off towards scored and grooved exit roads, ranged around the orbital road like the revetments of some modern hill fort, marking our way back into the Great Wen. The AA were unsympathetic; the nominated garage man wanted cash. It was almost 3.00 in the morning when I woke Jim's wife up. The source of the trouble was crouched, looking crippled on the steep camber of the road, its knob still clicking. To give her credit she paid up without a murmur. The truly fat garage man went on his way. Jim's wife, Carol, gave me a blank look of sad resignation and shut the door quietly in my face.

Jim and I had spent the day up in Norfolk. 'I like flat places,' said Jim, 'places where the sky has a chance to define the land. I'm fed up with the tiny proscenium arch of the Home Counties. If I wanted to act on my day off I'd join an amateur theatre company.' He tended to talk like this – in the form of a series of observations, which hammered out a Point Of View. One that couldn't be argued with, only acknowledged, or assented to. We had spent the afternoon wandering from village to village. Jim took a lot of photographs with his new camera. He was a good photographer, his photographs were always artfully uncomposed; they were visual asides. He only took pictures where objects in the foreground could insidiously dominate the scene. He wasn't interested in people, or nature for that matter.

Naturally enough, Jim had a view on photography as well: 'It doesn't mean fuck all. It's a toy – that's all – not some potent weapon for transforming reality. You point it at an object, you press the button, and a few days later you see the "thing", and can't resist a little gasp of wonderment.'

We started the drive back at about 10.00. As darkness fell, the promised cool of the evening failed to materialise. Instead, the sticky, humid afternoon, gave way to a hot, close night-time. The first part of the drive was relaxing and apt. We swished across the Norfolk plane, our tyres whispering to the tangled verges, the Sierra's boxy suspension flatly reporting over the potholes.

I sat rocking on the car's offside, absorbed by Jim's concentration as he drove. He sat low, the car seat raked backwards and at an angle. His disproportionately long arms gripped the bottom of the wheel at the unrecommended position of twenty-five minutes past seven. His eyes seemed to be roughly at the level of the top of the instrument panel. He was more intent on the green and red lights inside the car than those ahead. But he drove well, with an unforced and intuitive ease, as if the car's controls were natural extensions of his own limbs.

However, by the time we reached the A45, things had begun to change. It was as if we were being sucked into some giant vortex of traffic. Although we were still over fifty miles from London I could feel the magnetic pull of the city. The cars that passed and repassed one another along the sections of dual carriageway were like iron filings, unwillingly coerced into flowing lines, all heading in the same ultimate direction. It felt as if we were no longer in a car at all, but in some miniature, mono-carriaged train. The track was laid out ahead of us. We could increase or decrease speed, but it was impossible to change direction. And when we reached junctions or roundabouts all the points had been switched in advance. We howled through the tight curves, wheel rims straining against the track, and on.

Thirty minutes later we pulled off the A11 into a petrol station. As Jim filled up the tank I continued to stare blankly through the windscreen. The forecourt was brightly lit. A sales display of garden furniture was set out near the cashier's window, flower-patterned chairs and recliners with frosted aluminium arms and legs. There was a coming and going of leisure wear and Bermudas. A high octane stench combined with the wash of orange halogen light, spreading across the stained concrete pan. It was like some parody of recreation.

Jim paid with his company petrol card. He threw the crumpled-up counterfoil into the back seat where our jackets lay and we wheeled out on to the road. He let the Sierra pull us up quickly through the five long, low gear ratios and then hunkered down into his seat again.

We had long since ceased to speak when we neared the intersection of the M11 and the M25. I could feel Jim's indecision in the way the car held the road. He was calculating routes back to south-west London. I knew he hated the M25, 'The stupidest thing about it is its name. If a road is described as "orbital", it's a sure-fire guarantee that when you get on to the thing you're bound to feel as if you're in outer space.'

The alternative to the M25 was to keep straight on and join the North Circular at Gants Hill. Jim tensed at the wheel in a peculiar way. A body tenses up before receiving an expected blow. Jim tensed as if to ward off the heavy traffic congestion at the roundabout where the A404 meets the Great North Road. The Sierra skittered a little, and then it was done, we plopped off on to the exit road. There were two seconds when it was too late: one when we were on the exit road and the next when we saw the great yellow hoarding with its familiar legend, 'Delays possible until late '91'. There was nothing for it now. It was as if we had been determined. The Cynics were correct, the sense of freewill is only that feeling which we have when we take the necessitated option that most appeals to us. Nothing for it now, but to regard the motorway furniture with a baleful eye as we cruised gently to a halt and rocked into stasis at the back of the stack of cars snaking through the long, low, flat chicane.

'A three-lane jam at midnight on a Sunday! I can't fucking well believe it. I can't believe it. I do not believe it. Look at these people.' Jim gestured wildly at the yellow profiles receding into the distance like a frieze of minor Assyrians. 'They simply don't know what they are doing. They are waiting. Do you understand me? Waiting. And while they wait nothing is happening, and when they stop waiting nothing will happen either, and while they have waited nothing will have occurred – except, perhaps, for the collapse of some more carbon molecules. Mmmmm!

Breathe it in, man.' Jim encompassed some air with another ham gesture and drew it into his nose and mouth. 'Finest destruction of the ionosphere, most perfect winding down of fossil fuel reserves. I love it! I love it! God speed, you future patina of grey chemical soot on the leaves of municipal gardens in Osterley, Eggham, and for that matter, Stockholm! Mmm, my air sacks have never felt so good!

'Hello! Hello! How are you? How about a little personal interaction here. After all, we're all stuck in this together. Why don't we break down some barriers here? My name is Jim. What's yours?' Jim was talking to the profiles, but they wouldn't hear him, they sat on, acquiring verdigris in the wash of light from their fascia. 'Hi kids, wanna play? Why don't we start a game of cricket on the central reservation? Six runs if you can hit the ball off the motorway.' But the kids didn't want to play cricket. Their little budding mouths were glued to parental shoulders, grouted with congealed Tango and Sprite. And the parental shoulders were set square towards the future. Whenever the steel testudo unbuckled and coiled its way forward a few feet, all the drivers reverted to form and tried to switch lanes to gain the tiniest advantage available – because it was there.

Jim gave up on his attempts to foster communication. He took out his camera and rested it on top of the steering wheel. He squinted through the viewfinder while continuing to murmur under his breath, 'Very slow exposure and we should get the picture. I'll be damned, a three-lane jam on the M25 at midnight; this is it. This-is-it. Strained and ruckled, bumper to bumper, immanence and imminence. It's all here. It's all here . . . ' He was clicking away, his voice tending towards falsetto.

I swivelled in my seat and looked back. We had reached the bottom of the depression that the chicane had snaked through and there were as many cars piled up behind as in front of us. I had the strange feeling that there was absolutely no depth to what I could see. In both directions there was simply the flat pattern formed by car shapes. The traffic in the oncoming carriageway grew larger and diminished without extension. The cars were so many globs of multicoloured oil, expanding and contracting in a giant version of one of those risible Sixties lamps. Jim and I were the tiniest slivers of humanity, pressed in the microscope slide of the Sierra.

Jim turned to me, 'You know why I like this car so much?' The question was rhetorical. 'Because of its quiddity, its what-ness. It has no other quality; it is. It has no need to come into being – it is already utterly mediocre. They've sold 25,000 of these cars in the past year. Twenty-Five thousand! We could be in any one of them. We could still be on the production line inching forward. Any moment now an operative is going to come along and start bolting new prostheses on to you, new forms of biological engineering that you could never imagine. This car is not waiting. Do you understand that? This car has already arrived. We are where we're going, this . . . ' He gestured at the Assyrians, the Daihatsus, the Passats, the orange night, 'is home.'

He sat cradling the wheel for a while, inching forward with the rest. Tirelessly performing the heel-toe dance step of slow locomotion, and then: 'I can't stand this any more, I'm getting out of here,' and he was gone.

I worked about two streets away from Jim and the following day I walked over to his office during my lunch hour. I was determined to confront him over his behaviour of the night before. Everybody has a certain leeway with everyone else. Everyone is entitled to the odd bout of craziness. But Jim's stunts were becoming habitual. I had witnessed his preoccupation with 'waiting' grow from the occasional rant – always amusing and good value as a party piece – into a full-blown obsession, and like all kinds of obsessional behaviour it was beginning to hurt other people. Jim was becoming a self-centred and destructive egotist. If our relationship was to continue he was going to have to recognise last night for what it really was: a neurotic, knee-jerk reaction. Rather than for what he would have it be: some profound statement concerning The Way We Are and The Way In Which We Live.

I found Jim at his desk, he was taking copy over the phone. The receiver was wedged between his shoulder and his ear, leaving both hands free to type. His fingers riffled over the keyboard at tremendous speed. He grunted into the mouthpiece and occasionally read back a line to check it. When he had finished and hung up he swivelled round to face me and held up his hand.

'Stop. Don't say it. Because I know, and I can tell you in advance that I'm ashamed and I'm sorry. I've been behaving like a self-centred egotist. I've become obsessive and my critique of The Way In Which We Live is nothing but the cynical, sour grapes of an emotional child.'

'Has Carol been at you already?'

'Yeah, man. She's not a happy woman, but she accepts the truth of what I have to say.'

'Oh, she does, does she. Well I for one don't want to lose a friend in order to become an audience.'

'Stop being such a sententious tosser. Come on, I'll buy you some lunch.'

But I had to wait another ten minutes for lunch. The features editor of Jim's rag appeared with an obese piece of copy that needed a crash diet. Jim obliged. He was the fastest sub I've ever seen at work. It was almost as if he could photograph a whole sheet of text mentally and then work on all the separate parts of it simultaneously. His knowledge of the twisted rules of English usage was also superb; he knew when to judiciously skate away from the received in order to achieve clarity, and how to make sure that every clause was just so.

Wherever Jim worked he soon became an invaluable practical asset, but unfortunately at the same time a devastating emotional liability. He could never hold a job down for long and now he'd managed to outstay his welcome with most of the nationals and was on to magazines.

'To tell you the truth, I prefer working for *Bicycling*,' Jim said as we clattered down the stairs to the street. He paused a few steps below me and struck an attitude. 'Do you want to know why?'

'All right, Jim. Why?'

'Because I don't have to wait, silly. All the way up to press day I'm keying copy into that little terminal there and I only have to walk around the corner to see it all nicely laid out on another screen. Even at Wapping I had to wait hours to see a completed page. But here it's all format work. The hacks write absolutely to fit and I know what a page is going to look like even before I've started working on it.'

'But Jim, that's no fun at all, you might as well be subbing catalogues.'

'Catalogues, mmm ... you might have a point there. I've never thought of catalogues before, there's a certain purity in them.'

I pushed the bar of the fire door and we fell into the street. High Holborn was pulsing and groaning with lunch-time traffic, wheeled and legged. The air was blue with exhaust fumes. People shouldered their way along the pavement and in and out of the cars as they inched towards New Oxford Street. Clerks and secretaries formed straggling knots of protein lacing the arterial strip, constantly harried by cruising antibody-streams of data-processing managers, bank tellers and shop assistants. Looking first up and then down the crowded thoroughfare, I had the same impression that I had had the night before on the M25. It was as if the whole scene were two-dimensional. I existed at a point that had no extension. Either side of me were flat slabs of pulsing colour.

Jim was in his element. He did a little pirouette on the curb.

'Look at this. Do you know what these people are doing?'

'They're having their lunch hour.'

'Yes, yes. Of course they are in a manner of speaking. But what are they really doing? Look.' He held up his hands to conduct an imaginary orchestra. His fingers extended to catch the most delicate modulations of the crowd. He held them there for a beat and a half and then brought them straight down. A forelock of brown hair flipped over his forehead and pointed down directly at the pavement. The passersby paid not the slightest attention.

'There you have it.' Jim was triumphant. 'For that beat and a half I held them, I gauged them. The whole lot of them. I interrupted the cadence of the crowd; they were waiting.'

'Waiting!' I snorted. 'Waiting for what?'

'For the end of the lunch break, for a nuclear war, for the poisoning of the earth, for old age, for the millennium, for the last judgement, for their hair to turn grey, for retirement, for a big gambling win, for a strange sexual experience, for the hand of God to touch them, for their children to support them, for the right person, for a new car, for the interest rate to fall, for the next election, for their bowels to get back to normal. What does it matter? I've said it once, I don't care if I say it a thousand times – everyone is waiting.

'There are only two great feelings left in the late twentieth century. Two great feelings that have eaten up all the other, little feelings like love, loyalty, exaltation, anger and alienation; as surely as if they were krill being sucked into the maw of a whale. Immanence and imminence, immanence and imminence. Everyone is convinced that something is going to happen, but they don't know what it is. Some people suspect that whatever it is will be some implosion of the numen, some great exposure of the transcendent. The rest don't know . . . yet. But they will, they will.'

'Jim, we were going to have lunch, and you promised to cut down on the ranting.'

He recovered himself and we went to get a drink and a sandwich at the Mitre. Jim was quite reasonable throughout lunch and I was almost prepared to forgive him his outburst in the street. There was no talk of waiting at all, even though the bar service was pretty appalling and there was a five-deep press of double-breasteds around the bar. On the way back over the viaduct I said to Jim that I'd see him around.

'Yeah, you'll see me around. Around 6.00 at Houghton Street; we're going to a lecture.'

'A lecture? What lecture?' He shoved a crumpled A5 flyer into my hand. It was blue-bordered and had the University of London shield at the top. It read as follows:

Meaning and Millenarianism
Transition to Another Era
An open lecture by Richard Stein, Emeritus Professor of
the History of Ideas at the LSE.
6.00 p.m. The Old Lecture Theatre
&c.

'All right, I'll come.' Jim looked shocked. 'It'll be a pleasure to hear someone else give a lecture besides you.'

I left Jim outside the doors to his office and walked on up towards the Central School on Southampton Row. I turned back at the corner to wave goodbye, but Jim didn't notice. He was deep in conversation with two despatch riders whose bikes were pulled up to the curb. One of them was short and ginger-haired with a slack, gap-toothed mouth. The other was black and angular, with his hair shaved into a tight triangular wedge on top of his head. Both of them were dressed in the couriers' uniform: ribbed leather jackets, leather trousers and high rubberised boots, complete with ridges and crenellations. I studied them for a while. It was clear that Jim knew them well. The way the three of them stood, gestured and smiled indicated friendship; and yet I knew Jim well, I was a close friend, but he had never mentioned his despatch rider friends. I turned and walked back to my office.

Both phone calls and Post-it notes have a life cycle of their own. They are not mere servants of man, but clever parasites that use human industry to further their own growth as a species. That at any rate is the way I felt by the time I reached Houghton Street to meet Jim after work. I found him standing outside the Australian High Commission. He was standing at the tall, plate-glass window, staring into an aquarium of humans, as they snaked slowly towards the visa application counters.

I was expecting some kind of tirade, but he desisted and instead lead me across the Aldwych to Houghton Street. However, rather than turning left into the main lobby of the LSE, he turned right into the Students' Union Building. He walked as if he knew the place. Rounding a corner we came to a lift with a difference.

It was more like a vertical escalator than a conventional lift. A series of compartments moved slowly but continually past the landing where we stood. All we had to do to get on was jump through the opening. To the left the compartments descended, to the right they ascended. We stood for a couple of minutes in silent contemplation of this mechanical oddity, then Jim turned on his heel with a vague gesture and said, 'No waiting.' We started back towards the entrance.

The Old Lecture Theatre must have been purpose-built as such when the Houghton Street building was erected in the Thirties. It was far wider than it was deep, and curiously wedge-shaped, like a slice of cake a compulsive eater might cut themselves. The lecture was sparsely attended; up in the gallery I could just see the round heads of a few diligent students, already bent and scribbling, while the scattered audience we sat among in the stalls seemed to consist of an odd assortment of octogenarians and the kind of slightly featureless black and brown men who one can tell immediately are perpetual students from the developing world. Men who have been spending years on writing doctoral theses on public policy in Coventry, while diligently sending a proportion of their grant money home to the family in Bangladesh.

Professor Stein and the academic who was to introduce him were already seated up on the podium when Jim and I came in. The podium took up the whole front of the theatre and was faced in the same dark brown wood as almost every other surface in sight. The overwhelming impression was one of enclosure and stultification. A dusty decanter of water and a cut-glass vase of wilted flowers stood on the podium table, behind which the Professor regarded the audience with mild, mournful brown eyes as if he were a cow with no milk to give. In the hard, cramped, tip-up seat I tried to compose myself for sleep.

The chairman rose to his feet. 'Errumph ... It's er ... 6.15 and it doesn't look like we'll have too many more people coming so I think we'll make a start.' My eyelids felt gummy and heavy. 'Most of you are, no doubt, familiar with Professor Stein's work. For those of you that aren't I must apologise at this juncture. The Professor has asked me especially to refrain from a long recitation of his publications and the academic positions he has held and confine myself purely to those works that have a direct bearing on the lecture he is going to give us this evening. That being so, let it suffice for me to say that since Professor Stein retired from the chair here at the LSE some three years ago, he has spent the vast bulk of his time on organising, administering and teaching at the Centre for Millenarian Studies which he himself founded at Erith Marsh. His publications during this period have reflected his preoccupation with the coming end of our era; I refer to his paper "Wittgenstein and the Arterial Road System in the South-east of England" and, of course, "Mirror Image: Reductive Cultural Identity in Late Twentieth-century Britain", both published in the *BJE**.

'The occasion of this particular lecture is to give us all an opportunity to, as it were, preview Professor Stein's new book *Meaning and Millenarianism*; and to hear from the author himself some of the arguments he puts forward in the book, in

---

* *British Journal of Ephemera*

183

advance of its publication next week. I'd like to say at this juncture that there will be an opportunity for questions and discussion at the end of the lecture, but this period will of necessity be circumscribed as we need to clear the lecture theatre for the Students' Drama Society, who, I believe, are rehearsing for a production of *Oklahoma*. Err . . . Professor Stein.'

The Professor mooched over to the lectern and stood for a while several feet behind it, regarding his audience with baleful eyes. I was shocked to see that he was dressed rather nattily for an emeritus professor in a sharp Italian suit with the narrowest of chalk stripes. He was also quite a bit more virile in appearance than I had at first supposed. Although over sixty his hair was still intact and ungreying, his jaw was set and two veins rode up his temples and seemed to visibly throb in the wan light of the lecture theatre. He hovered over the lectern as a surgeon might an operating table. He carried no notes.

'Picture the future. Picture it like this.' His voice was sonorous, insistent and persuasive, more spiritual than academic. 'An orderly phalanx of flagellants some four hundred in number march down off the Marylebone Flyover. They chastise themselves with the precise, timed strokes of their leather lashes. They take up the entire inside lane of the road. The chastisement is considered and vicious. Each stroke on each back brings forth blood, which spatters the windscreens of the cars that are backed up in the two offside lanes, all the way from Lisson Grove. The morning air is full of a pink, frothy spray as the passive commuters put on their water jets and windscreen wipers in an attempt to stop their windscreens coagulating.

'Or, if you prefer, picture this: Speaker's Corner is in full swing on a Sunday afternoon. There are the usual crop of eccentrics – cranks and people with extreme political views – but on this Sunday, to their chagrin, they are wholly eclipsed by bands of ragged men and women wearing filthy grey shifts. These people move among the crowds enjoining them to enter a state of grace immediately and to throw off the restrictive chains of mere human morality.

'"Rejoice! We are already saved!" they cry. They shamelessly roll on the ground, fighting, copulating, and drinking to prove their point. Together with other adherents they are forming a secessionist commune in Hyde Park, dedicated to the anticipation of the Apocalypse.

'Can you picture this? Or is it beyond your comprehension?' Stein paused and raked his meditative gaze over the darkened theatre. I could imagine it all right, I was rapt. I hadn't expected anything like this. Jim was clearly imagining it too, he sat hunched forward on his seat, panting. I looked round the rest of the audience: the octogenarians still slept, the perpetual students took notes. Stein continued, 'My purpose in this lecture is to briefly outline the central argument of my forthcoming book. Obviously time will mean that this outline will be incomplete, but nonetheless I hope to make it reasonably clear that the kind of scenarios that I just asked you to envisage are not accurate predictions of the way millenarianism will effect the populations of Western societies as we move towards the third era since the death of the Christ-figure. These things may have occurred in the past, but I believe that there are now certain overriding factors that make a recurrence of such phenomena distinctly unlikely . . . '

And there I lost him. The rest of the lecture became increasingly involved, turgid and difficult to follow. Stein didn't help matters by continually digressing from his central argument in order to inveigh against other academics in the same field. The digressions themselves had digressions. As far as I could gather they related specifically to the difficulties involved in the exegesis of certain recondite texts, penned in the closing years of the ninth century by monks scattered across Europe. Stein raised his voice, he moved out from behind the lectern and came to the front of the stage, as if intending to embrace his audience like an ageing singer having a Las Vegas comeback.

For me, it was all to no avail. The sheer weight of detail eroded my attention. His digressions began to resolve themselves into a series of Post-it notes stuck fluttering in my mind . . . I began to tune out. When I tuned back in again it was 6.50 and Stein was summing up.

'. . . To sum up: The existence of the possibility of the destruction of the world by men themselves, in a number of different forms – nuclear war, ecological disaster, man-made pandemics – means that although in a sense we live in a time that is more acutely aware than ever before of the possibility of some form of the Apocalypse, nonetheless that Apocalypse is no longer in any sense evidence of the immanent; it is merely possibly imminent. In the past, the ending of an era, or even a century, was viewed with great fear and a spontaneous move towards salvation in one form of another, a move that can only be understood solidly in the context of the Judaeo-Christian cultural dialectic. The end of this current era will, I believe, be met with at worst indifference and at best with some quite good television retrospectives.'

Before the chairman could get to his feet and ask whether there were any questions, one of the perpetual students was already on his and asking. He was a grey-black man, tall and rangy in a slightly unravelled raglan sweater, with three neat fish-shaped scars on either cheek.

'Professor Stein. Sir, to what extent, sir, can the arguments you have just presented, sir, be held seriously. In view of the *fact*', particular emphasis on 'fact', 'that such arguments have themselves been present in other cultures during the end of other eras. Does not the fact, sir, that this is not the first time that people have believed they had the power to destroy their own world to some extent invalidate your argument? Well, sir, what do you think of that?'

The cicatrised African sat down as abruptly as he had stood up. There was an uncomfortable pause. Professor Stein was straining forward. From the expression on his face it was quite clear that he hadn't heard a word the African had said. At length the chairman leant forward and whispered into his ear. Stein nodded several times and then rose to his feet.

'I think the answer is no. As to why, the answer is that although previous cultures have thought that they possessed the power to destroy the world themselves, they in fact didn't. We are dealing in this instance with a reality which can be empirically verified.'

I was aware of Jim batting about in the seat next to me. He was sweating profusely and his long, mechanical arms gripped the back of the seat in front of him as if he wanted to rip it off the ground and throw it at the podium. Jim didn't give the African a chance to respond to Stein's reply – he was on his feet.

'Professor Stein. You say that the difference between this and previous eras is that humankind now possesses the real ability

186

to destroy the world in which we live – and that this fact means that the wilder manifestations of millenarianism are unlikely to occur as we move towards the 21st century. However, could this lecture itself not be said to be an even wilder manifestation in its own right? This surely is the first era in which the historically literate have felt free to say "Well, in the past people got over-excited about the millennium and expected Armageddon and all sorts of other terrible things, but we're beyond that." Is this not the purest form of hubris? Do you not agree that there is an aching feeling in our society, people are desperately waiting for something – anything to happen! Look at these people,' Jim swept an arm around the lecture theatre to embrace the ancient Fabians and the perpetual students, 'aren't they waiting for something to happen? I don't think your lecture, your calm, measured reasoning will serve to dampen down the great currents of expectation which are bound to flow with increasing strength throughout the population. Well, what do you think of that?'

Jim sat down, still quaking and sweating. I wasn't sure that what he had said could altogether be classified as a question. However Stein seemed to be taking it seriously enough. As Jim sat down, the Professor set down his pen and scrutinised us.

'What you say has a good deal of emotional force, young man. And I think you may be right – but only in a very limited sense. The involutions of thought and reflection you draw our attention to are just that: thought and reflection. They bear no real relation to the motivation of the great mass of people. A few years ago when the Strategic Arms Limitation Talks had ground to a halt and before the rise to power of the current General Secretary, there seemed to be some real cause for alarm and the manifestation of some fringe political groupings was undoubtedly millenarian, but now, pshaw! All the political crises of the past forty years have served only to underline the fact that the dialectic imposed by technological advancement is irrefutable, unstoppable; more primary than thought itself. Although you express yourself eloquently, young man, I am more inclined to view the seeming irony you draw our attention to as a perception of marginalised youth, contemplating the grey power of middle age. It is an attitude rather than a timely perception. And perhaps for that reason it is all the more to be admired.'

Jim didn't wait for the end of Stein's answer. He was already disappearing through the brown swing-doors. It was left for me to inch my way out of the row of seats where we were sitting, grating past, and offering my bunched crotch to a number of disapproving faces. The last thing I saw as I went out the door was the chairman doodling with a finger on the dusty tabletop.

Jim was pacing back and forth in the lobby, in front of a noticeboard covered with a tatter of posters, flyers and hand-lettered advertisements. A flyer for next week's open lecture was prominently displayed. 'An authoritative exposition of recent developments in the Quantity Theory of Insanity'. Obviously the School's policy was to offset one dull, minority interest lecture, against another, popular, general interest one. It was strange, it hadn't really occurred to me before, but for a culture that was supposedly unaffected by the end of an era we certainly showed a lot of interest in esoteric theories. Jim shot an angry glance at me and shrugged. 'I didn't expect anything better from him.'

'Oh, I don't know, it didn't seem like such a bad lecture to me. Admittedly I dozed through a lot of it.'

'Oh yes, Stein is clever all right, but he just doesn't understand. He's an academic. Even if he does study contemporary events, he still renders them microscopic by looking at them through the wrong end of his theoretical telescope. Waiting isn't like that. It's an immediate, physical experience. If he saw Carlos in action, then he'd understand.'

Jim turned on his heel and walked off towards the exit. From behind I noticed how strange he looked, with his long muscular torso and silly little legs. He reminded me for a moment of nothing so much as a PG Tips chimp. His millenarian rants could easily have been a voice-over. Perhaps the real Jim had just been going, 'Ooh, ooh, ooh! Ahh! Ahh!' His tartan shirt was coming out of his trousers and the collar was dandruffy. He wasn't looking after himself. I followed him out through the lobby feeling guilty, as if Jim had heard my thoughts about him.

Outside on the pavement. In the cold, dark, night-time canyon of Houghton Street, I found Jim standing with the two couriers I'd seen him with at lunch. Ginger was expostulating as I came up, while the character with the triangular hairdo stood back, arms folded. They were all too preoccupied to notice me. I heard the following:

'Carlos doesn't want anyone else in on it. Carlos couldn't give a fuck about anything but the job.'

'But he's exactly the kind of person we need to convince. Sooner or later Carlos will need to reveal himself . . . and then . . . '

'And then, cobblers!'

'I'm not waiting around to listen to this bollocks.'

This was hairdo. He had a peculiar falsetto voice for such a large man. As he voiced the sentiment, he picked his helmet up off the saddle of his bike and pushed it down over his head, with a hermetic 'plop'. This was effectively the end of the conversation. Ginger put his helmet on as well. And without any farewells the two of them turned over their engines and peeled off, out on to Aldwych. Leaving behind an acrid smell.

'What was all that about?' I asked Jim as we turned out of Houghton Street and walked down towards the Strand tube station.

'Nothing, really. Nothing worth talking about.'

'Come off it Jim, you owe me an explanation. Those blokes weren't doing a late pick-up. At least I didn't see you sign for anything. They were talking about me.'

'Yeah, well I did tell them that you might be interested . . . '

'In what? Interested in what?'

'In meeting this Carlos fellow.'

'I don't even know who he is. How do you know I'd be interested in meeting him?'

'Well, you were interested in Stein's lecture. And Carlos isn't dissimilar, excepting that he's something of a leader, as well as a teacher.'

'Leading what? Who does he teach?'

'This little group of motorcycle couriers. I suppose you'd think it was all a little bit cranky. Another facet of my overriding obsession. But these bikeys have cottoned on to almost the same set of ideas as I have myself.' He paused. 'They're fed up with waiting.'

'Well, I'd be fed up with waiting if I were a despatch rider. It must be an incredibly frustrating thing to do. Doesn't it have one of the highest occupational death rates? I'm sure that's because they get frustrated and then they make mistakes.'

'You don't understand. These people are operating at the limit.' Jim was getting worked up. He was going into rant mode. He stopped in the middle of the pavement and turned to face me, arms akimbo, twitching. 'They're shooting methedrine, or basing coke, or snorting sulphate. They're driving at all hours of the day and night, existing at a level of frayed neural response that we can only faintly imagine. They're operating not at the level of other traffic, a straightforward level of action and antici-pation, but at the level of nuance, sheer nuance. They perceive the tiniest of stimuli with ghastly clarity, and respond. Think of it, man. Weaving your way through heavy traffic astride a monstrously overpowered motorcycle, always pressured to meet a deadline, the ether plugged into your helmet. They have to mutate to survive!'

After this little outburst we carried on walking in silence for a while. We were going down Essex Street past one of the world's largest accountancy firms. Between the slats of a three-quarters-closed Venetian blind I could see a man in shirtsleeves. Still crouched, at this late hour, over a flickering monitor in the pool of an Anglepoise. As I glanced at him he pushed a button and the figures on the screen scrolled upwards in a stream of green light.

Jim was breathing heavily, but he'd calmed down a little. I didn't know what to say, I was curious but I didn't want to provoke him. For the first time I had the sense with absolute clarity that Jim had teetered over that fine, fine line between eccentricity and madness. Eventually I spoke. 'These despatch riders, Jim, do they believe in "waiting" as well?'

'Of course, of course, of course. They are the real waiters. Waiting is ground into them. Every moment could be an arrival, at a pick-up or drop-off, or the ultimate drop-off, death itself! No wonder they understand what is happening. They exist at the precise juncture between the imminent and the immanent! Carlos has seen their potential. He is a man of extraordinary powers, he understands that the future will belong to those who clearly articulate the Great Wait!'

We were standing in the forecourt outside the tube. A few late office workers mingled with the eddy and flow of tourists, who moved in and out of the entrance in their bright pastel, stretchy clothes. It was a clear night and the neon sign above the National blipped its message across the flat water. I took Jim's upper arm in what I hoped was a firm, avuncular sort of a grasp.

'Jim, don't you think you're letting all this rather get to you? I think you're overtired and overworked. I'm sure you're not spending enough time with Carol. Why don't you take a rest for a few days? If you'll forgive me for saying so, the world will wait for you.' His response surprised me.

'Well, yes, er . . . you could be right. She has seemed a little distant recently. She can't cope with my insomnia, you know. Perhaps you are right. But even so, you should meet Carlos, he isn't a crank, or a freak. His powers are real enough, believe me. I've never had any truck with any kind of cults or mystical twaddle, have I?'

No, he never has, I thought to myself, after we had parted and gone our separate ways. And perhaps there is something in what he says. My eyes flicked across the tracks, between which lay the typical refuse. I picked out Jim's figure at the far end of the platform. His shoulders were hunched and he'd inserted his body between a dangling sand bucket and a coiled, canvas hose in a wooden cabinet. It was as if he was trying to restrain himself. It was clear from his posture and his blank stare what he was doing. He was waiting for a train.

I tried not to think about Jim for the next couple of days. If he was having a breakdown of some kind there was probably very little I could do for him – and if he wasn't. Well, after Norfolk and Stein's lecture I didn't really want to see him for a while, anyway. I needed a change of company; I needed to spend some time with people who were a little less heavy. I went out in the evenings to films and parties, I got tipsy, I had yelping conversations with people I had just met. Conversations in which each yelp seemed, at the time, a touchstone of empathy. At the time, that was.

But try as I would I couldn't shake Jim. He nagged at me and I knew it was because I should at least try and help him. The image that stayed with me most clearly – appearing as a flickering ghost when I switched on my terminal in the morning – was of Jim in the old lecture theatre, his arms clutching the seat back, his face distorted.

After a week I was really anxious. Jim hadn't been in touch, which was unlike him. I resolved to go and see Carol, his wife. After all, I reasoned, before the whole 'waiting' thing took off we used to see quite a lot of one another. I had been in the habit of regularly having dinner at their house. Childless couples have a tendency to adopt single people and try and feed them up and marry them off. And this is the way it had been. Carol had invited me to a series of Tuesday evening affairs where I'd eaten spinach and tomato lasagne and met a number of her female colleagues.

After a while the Tuesdays had petered out. I missed them. I missed the atmosphere of somewhere where people cooked on a regular basis; and I missed seeing Carol, who I liked. And who, despite my failures as a potential pair-bonder, never seemed to judge me. She was one of those people who had a tremendous sense of containment about them, her physical presence constantly emitted the quiet message that she was fine just as she was, she was content to do x or y, but it wasn't really necessary. When she and Jim had married their friends had called it 'a marriage of opposites'. It was significant that over the years no one had seen fit to add to this observation.

Carol worked at home as a freelance editor. So I could be sure of finding her in if I called unannounced. I took the morning off work and the train out to Wandsworth. Their house was across the Common from the station. As I walked over I felt the morning's catarrh slop and gurgle in my chest. I had a bitter, old iron taste in my mouth and felt considerable premonition.

Jim's Sierra was crouched on the steep camber of the road outside their flat, like a beetle redesigned by committee. I walked up the tiled path along the privet hedge and pushed the intercom buzzer. After a while there was a crackle on the speaker.

'Who is it?'

'It's me, Carol. I need to talk to you, about Jim.'

'Hang on a minute, I'm not up yet.'

I wanted for more than a minute. But when I saw, through the glass door panel, the door of their flat swing open, it wasn't Carol who emerged. It was a young man. A tall young man, who came to the door, opened it, and walked past me with a cheery nod and a cheerier 'Good Morning'. He tucked his arms energetically into his windcheater and jauntily walked off down the road, implying that he was off for a day's hard work. One that he was looking forward to.

A few minutes later Carol came and let me in. She was wearing a dressing gown patterned with pastel blooms. She was superficially groomed but there hung about her the subtle, sour smell of someone who's been making love in the morning. I followed her down the corridor and while I sat at the kitchen table she made me a cup of coffee.

'So what about Jim?' Carol panted, vigorously depressing the stainless steel plunger of the cafetière.

'Just that I think he's having a breakdown, Carol. I think he needs help of some kind. I haven't seen him for the past week; the last time I did he was absolutely raving.'

'I haven't seen him either. I haven't as much as clapped eyes on him. You know he's cabbing in the evenings now?'

'Cabbing? What on earth for? Not for money, surely.'

Carol laughed and pulled a twist of inky hair away from her face. 'Oh no, not for money. To relax him. That's why he does it. He says it relaxes him.'

'He's mad.'

'Maybe, maybe, but you can't help someone who doesn't want to be helped, believe me.' She said this earnestly, and sat down opposite me, an identical coffee mug cupped in her hands.

I believed her. Whatever part the young windcheater played in her life there was no doubting her affection for Jim. If she couldn't influence him, no one could.

'He comes back from work every evening and goes straight out again. I don't think he actually takes a lot of money. He's more intent on keeping in touch with his friend Carlos.'

'So you know about that.'

'Oh, yes.'

'And the despatch riders. What do you think?'

'Well, strictly speaking, I suppose he could be right, but it strikes me that there's enough that's obviously wrong with the world without becoming obsessed by the intangibles.'

I took the train back into town. I had a couple of hours to kill before I was expected at work. I thought I might walk into

Soho and drink some espressos at the Bar Italia. The clear, sharp light of the morning had given way to the kind of intense sepia tone and gritty air that precedes a summer storm in London. The sense of rising barometric pressure was tangible. I felt oppressed and confused by my talk with Carol. I still couldn't accept that there was nothing to be done for Jim. It was if those who loved him were just waiting for something awful to happen.

I trailed my damp, stinging feet along Oxford Street and turned into Soho Square. There was a gust of wind and a peppering of grit flew into my eyes. For a moment I was blind. I leant against a wall while the tears gathered and flowed down my face. When my vision cleared I saw Jim.

He was standing, leaning on the inside of the door of his car, talking to another despatch rider. This despatch rider was even more singular than the others I'd seen with Jim. He had the regulation jacket and bright, vinyl tabard. But instead of boots and leather trousers he had on baggy, green cords and battered trainers. He was propped on his bike, a battered, black 250 MZ, regarding Jim with slight disdain. His head was quite repulsive. He looked like a failed albino. His hair was the palest of gingers, his face putty-white, his features were soft and vestigial, his eyes the pinkiest of pinky-blues.

I crossed the street and hailed them. The failed albino turned to look at me, I could see his hand clutching the handlebar. It was as flat as a skate, the nails – dirty little crescents of horn – were deeply recessed into the flesh.

'I was just at your house, Jim, and I saw the car outside. Were you there all the time?'

'No, mate, I was out on the Common doing my exercises. I just went back, picked up the car and came into town to meet Carlos.' He indicated the failed albino with a twist of his hand.

'Why aren't you at work, Jim?'

'I could ask the same of you, mate.'

There was something rather light and cheery about Jim's manner that I found reassuring. I suppose in retrospect I should have been scared by the change in him. After all, the last time I'd seen him he'd been utterly driven, but, despite the mood swing and the weird company he was keeping, I was pleased to see my friend looking a little more like his old self.

'Carlos is taking me on a run today. Do you want to come along?'

But before I could reply, Carlos broke in, 'Can he come along, James? May he please come along? That is the question.' Carlos had a high, fluting voice and spoke with the accents of a comic Welshman. It was immediately clear that he always spoke facetiously and that all his questions were rhetorical.

'Carlos, this is the man I was telling you about. My old friend. He's the one I went to Stein's lecture with. He knows most of it already.'

'There's a difference between knowing and seeing, isn't there, James? Now I don't suppose you'd deny that, would you?'

I wasn't really paying that much attention to this exchange. Carlos struck me as a ludicrous figure. I had to get back to work. I was suddenly angry with Jim. Everything he said was clearly a manifestation of what I now saw as an illness. It was strange, but I could feel falling back down my throat the level of choked emotion I had invested in Jim. I should never have tried to help him. He was someone I knew only vaguely. I could do without Jim. He was receding fast.

'What are you waiting for, man?'

'What's that?'

Carlos was addressing me. 'Why don't you come and see, then? I value Brother James's opinion very highly, very highly indeed.'

'Look, Carlos. I don't really know what you and Jim are talking about. All I know is that my friend here', a jerk of the thumb and special, heavy emphasis on 'friend', 'has developed a dangerous and cranky obsession. He has tried to draw me into the fantasy world that he's constructed around this obsession, but I'm not interested – I think he needs help. Apparently you are an active player in this fantasy world. Therefore, I can only choose to adopt the same attitude towards you.'

As soon as I'd finished speaking I felt ridiculous. The words had sounded all right as I was saying them. But now, as they hung in the air unwilling to disperse, they constituted a reproach. The failed albino and my twitching former friend stood there, both of them still propped up by their vehicles. Jim's hazard lights clicked. In the square, female office workers, hobbled by tight, mid-thigh-length skirts, lay on the grass eating sandwiches, their legs free from the knee down. They were like some species of crippled colts. Jim and Carlos regarded me quizzically.

'Come and look.'

The pink, flaccid Welshman had a voice of insidious, quiet, insistent command. We walked in single file up to Oxford Street. Standing on the inside of the pavement, grouped stiffly together, the three of us formed an odd little protuberance, around which the great stream of pedestrians flowed. Carlos leant up against the window of Tie Rack. He'd left his helmet on the bike, and his pale hair fluffed out around his ears. As he pressed backwards, his plastic tabard rode up above his shoulders. His eyes seemed to disengage; they unfocused, slid out of gear, and became simply oval, colourless blobs stuck down on to his blurred, colourless face. Jim and I stood either side of him, awkward and still.

After a while sweat began to well up from Carlos's temples. His eyes quivered. I had never seen anyone sweat like this before – the sweat coming straight out of the exposed skin, rather than trickling down from the hairline. It was as if a boot had been ground down into a peaty, boggy surface. The sweat ran down his temples, milky against the pale flesh. I felt utterly nauseous and afraid. Then, as quickly as Carlos had gone into the trance he snapped out of it with a chilly shiver.

He turned to me.

'How good is your knowledge?' I was taken aback.

'Good enough, I suppose. I know my way around.'

'How quickly do you think you could drive from here to the Hornimans Museum via Shootup Hill?'

'Well . . . ' I looked around me. It was nearly 1.00 and the streets were thick with lunch-time traffic. The stodgy air boiled with blue exhaust. I computed routes, thought about the ebb and flow of cars, transit vans, lorries and buses. I tried to visualise the roads I would travel down. 'If you were lucky you might do it in an hour and twenty minutes, but I'd allow an hour and a half.'

'We'll do it in forty-five minutes.' Carlos was emphatic. He wiped his temples with a big red handkerchief and turned on his heel. Jim and I followed him back to the square. A traffic warden, neat in dark uniform and fluorescent sash, was tucking a ticket behind the Sierra's windscreen wiper. As Carlos mounted his MZ Jim tore it off and shredded it. The traffic warden shrugged. The central locking chonked and I took my place in the passenger seat, immediately conscious of the interior of the car as another, separate place.

We peeled away from the curb and followed Carlos off round the square, turning left into the alley that leads to Charing Cross Road.

'Pay no attention to the Secret Police of Waiting.' It was a flat statement. Jim made it through hard-pressed teeth. I paid no attention. I was stuck in a kind of torpor, all I could focus on were the flapping sides of Carlos's corduroy trousers as he moved ahead of us through the traffic.

Jim drove with his habitual, flattened ease. The boxy modern car clumped and tchocked through the streets. Carlos hovered ahead on his bike. It was as if he were attached to us by some invisible, umbilical cord. He didn't lead us through the traffic, we moved in concert.

Across Gower Street and then right, past the Royal Ear Hospital, to the top and then left and right, on to Tottenham Court Road. There was no delay at the Euston Road lights, we went straight up through the estates behind Hampstead Road. I noticed idly that the council, instead of pointing some of the older blocks, had taken to cladding them with caramel slabs. Our little convoy accelerated through the half-circuit of the Outer Circle. Nash terraces were reduced by speed to a single, tall, thin house. We skittered across the bridge that led out of Regent's Park. Down Belsize Road; for a moment we were poised alongside an old Datsun 180D, bulbous, red and rusting. It plunged with us towards the elbowed bend, where the road narrows to one lane. The cord tightened between the MZ and the Sierra. We pulled ahead of the Datsun. In the wing mirror, the surrounds of its blind headlights, conjunctival with rust, were sharp and then gone. We tore through the aggressive signing of the one-way system between Finchley Road and West End Lane. Then dropped down the other side into a trough of squats and second-hand furniture shops that in turn disgorged us on to the great, raddled, calloused, Kilburn High Road.

I registered all these junctures, but only vaguely. There was an unreal, static sensation to the journey. The long London roads were panoramic scenery wound back behind us to provide the illusion of movement. The MZ and the Sierra stood still, occupying a different zone.

We reached Shootup Hill in about seventeen minutes. The facility with which Carlos had led us was unnatural. At every juncture where there was an opportunity for a choice, he took the right one. Time and again we turned one way and I saw in the rear-view mirror that if we had gone the other, more obvious way, we would have been frozen in a tail-back, eroding synchro-mesh for five minutes or more. Even stranger than that was the realisation that the idiosyncratic directions we did take, always took time off our journey. Carlos had not only apprehended every road, he had anticipated every alleyway, every mews, every garage forecourt and the position and synchronization of every traffic light. He could not possibly know what he seemed to know – the only way he could have seen the route we took was from the air, and even then he would have had to have made constant trigonometric calculations to figure out the angles we seemed to have followed intuitively.

We were going up Shootup Hill towards Kilburn doing about forty, when suddenly Carlos put his right leg down and yanked the bike round in a tight turn. Jim followed suit, without even looking at the oncoming traffic, and before I'd had time to register the extent of the risk we'd run, we were heading back down and under the railway bridge.

The swish of an underpass, the whirr of an overpass, a long row of wing mirrors reaching out to us, the rise and fall of identically gabled roofs. Jim's arms – the inside of the forearm pressed against the wheel – insectoid and manipulative. The child's counterpane world of London's roads – where a turned corner can mean a distant prospect, a sudden impression of pillows in the distance, or a dip into a hollow can completely enclose you in a tiny world where the light quality never changes and spindrifts of sweet-wrappers chase one another in a tireless pavane.

As we crossed Blackfriars Bridge, the water glinted for a second; to the right a glimpse of banked-up buildings, circum-stantially pompous – an encrustation of administration which could belong to any city on earth – and then gone, back into the homogeneous, the undifferentiated London, where twee shopping parade succeeds arterial road, in turn flanked by the dusty parade ground of a municipal park where single, silent figures stand, tied to stuffed dogs.

No frenzy, no hurry. No giving anyone the finger. Carlos weaved and we weaved with him, cutting up whole files of traffic, ignoring feeder lights, insinuating ourselves on to round-abouts. The outward stretch to Shootup Hill had presented itself as an elegant piece of geometry. The downward swipe to Horni-man's Gardens was guile and outrageous nerve. I felt chilly in the stuffy, corrupted car. Chilly and scared.

Through Dulwich Park the Sierra's engine phutted into the cleaner air and Carlos's trousers dappled in the sunlight that fell through the trees.

We pulled up at the Hornimans Museum exactly forty-five minutes after we had started from Soho Square. Carlos banked his bike on to the tarmac lip that curled up from the road and we followed suit. Behind us the prospect opened out for the first time since we had crossed the river. In the middle distance a ridge of crenellated, oblong buildings stood out above the sea of tree- and rooftops. Beyond them London washed away towards the northern horizon, bluer and greyer.

Carlos was pulling off his gloves as I jackknifed myself out of the door of the Sierra in an attempt to jerk myself out of the strange trance. Carlos wore two gloves on each hand. The cheap vinyl of the outer glove had worn away exposing the tufts of the wool gloves inside. For some reason these worn patches fixated me, they were somehow anatomical. The blood rushed to my temples – I stared at the gloves. I felt sick. Carlos leant up against the signboard advertising the museum's exhibits.

The irritating Welsh voice: 'You see boy, when I trance like that,' he rolled his eyes back in his head exposing a network of veins under the pink ball, 'I assess the flow, at one location, for one brief moment. But because I know, you see, I know so much about this,' he gestured towards the horizon, 'it means that all the movement stands still. I know ev-ery-thing.' He rolled out the syllables with fluting emphasis. 'All the tail-backs, all the hold-ups, every burst water-main and dropped lorry load in the metropolis – at that moment I realise them all. Take me to any street, any street in London whatsoever where there is a constant traffic stream and just by looking at it I can know the state of every other road in the city. Then there's no waiting. You understand? I never have to wait.'

The albino's leeched brow moved to one side, exposing the signboard. A poster was tacked on it, advertising some forthcoming exhibition of Amazonian artefacts. A double-decker bus laboured up the hill from Forest Hill Station. I looked at my watch, it was 1.50. The dreamlike state I'd been in since I met Jim and Carlos in Soho fell away as suddenly as stepping out of a bath. I started running for the bus.

'Don't you see!' Jim was shouting after me, 'He doesn't have to wait! Don't you understand, he's beyond waiting; however far he travels he's already arrived! Oh, you bloody fool . . . '

The last words were a scream. I paid no attention and swung myself up on to the platform of the bus as it pulled away from the stop and started the long descent to East Dulwich.

A week passed and then a month. There was no news from Jim and I made no attempt to contact him. Then a Post-it note appeared stuck to the keyboard of my computer. It asked me to ring a Mr Clifton at a Camden-based legal practice. Before I could respond, Clifton called me. He had an appalling phone manner, breathy and inaudible and his legalese sounded put on.

'It's concerning our client Mr Stonehouse.'

'Oh, yes. Jim. What's he done?'

'He has been convicted of failure to stop; one count and two counts of aggravated assault.'

'Did he do it?'

'He made a statement to that effect to the police, he appeared before the magistrates' court at Highgate who have passed the matter of sentencing over to Snaresbrook.'

'I see, I see. That's a bit rough. Still, I can't say I'm surprised.'

'Surprised?'

'Well, he had been behaving rather erratically lately.'

'That's just it. It would appear that the best course of action for Mr Stonehouse would be for us to apply for further psychiatric evaluation.'

'What if you don't?'

'It could be three to six years.'

'I see, I see . . . What I don't see is where I come into this . . . '

'Well, as you said yourself, Mr Stonehouse has been behaving erratically recently and you've been a witness to this. A statement in court from someone like you, with your position, could be the deciding factor.'

'That's it then – you want me to turn up in court?'

'And supply us, if possible, with a written statement.'

'Presumably you want that on a letterhead.'

'It may well be a decisive factor.'

'Can you tell me exactly what happened?'

'I'm afraid not, it would be up to Mr Stonehouse to tell you the details. Were we to say anything, it would be in direct breach of client confidentiality.'

Jim called later that morning. He was wholly unrepentant.

'Just a little bust-up coming off the Marylebone Flyover. It's absurd really that the thing's got as far as Crown Court.'

'Your brief says that he wants you remanded for psychiatric observation.'

'Yes, well, err . . . it does seem the best course of action. Personally, I don't mind – I mean I could use a few weeks' rest. You know, making ashtrays and rapping with some jejeune shrinks.'

'What happened, Jim?'

'Well, I was coming in to work. I'd stayed the night with Carlos in Acton and it was only about half-seven. I was on the Westway and everything told me that I'd be clear to go the full length and come off at Marylebone rather than taking the Paddington exit. But when I got to the top of the Marylebone Flyover the traffic was backed up solid, at half-seven in the morning! I don't know, I guess I just felt humiliated. I sat in the stack waiting to get off for about five minutes. It was infuriating, the sense of being contained to no purpose, and it was all the fault of an intellectual decision. If I'd tranced the way Carlos taught me, I'd have been all right.'

'What happened, Jim?'

'Well, I was coming off the end of the flyover at last, when this character tried to muscle in from the left, from the slip road that leads to the Edgware Road. He was a short, fat creep driving one of those midget Datsun vans. I remember it distinctly, it had a dirty cream paint job and a badly stencilled sign saying, "Exodus Fruiterers, Crouch End & Stanmore", then a phone number. This character was all pushy and hunched over the little wheel. A bundle of senseless dingle-dangles swinging from his rear-view mirror, rinky-dink bazouki music blaring out of the window, eugh!

'I'd been in that jam for five full minutes! So I just sort of herded this little van man with my front bumper, just sort of herded him . . . across on to the side of the road. I didn't damage his stupid van at all, just a scrape of paint, really, but he went absolutely mad, came out of it like a sweaty little grub. "Why you do that! Why you do that!" Over and over and poking me as well. I told him, "Because I felt like it." And this enraged him more. He was a nothing, he was a Waiter, he meant nothing. So eventually I hit him, just to shut him up.'

'Just to shut him up . . . ?'

'Like I say, he was a Waiter, he was a nothing.'

'So explain why you're pleading insanity?'

'Well, when the police took my statement I told them the truth and they started grinning at each other and making silly faces – so it sort of suggested itself, logically, as it were. Let me tell you, this could be a lot more than a stupid assault case. This could be the end of waiting for a lot of people.'

There was a lot more of the same before I managed to get shot of him. I wasn't convinced. I was becoming more and more inclined to think that he was bad rather than mad. The bizarre trip I'd been on with Jim and the fluting failed albino stayed in my mind as something sinister. I didn't like Carlos and I didn't like his influence on Jim. Jim was becoming twisted and distorted; he was a personality viewed in a 'fun house' mirror. His mechanical arms were getting longer, his epicene hips wider and fuller.

I resolved to write Jim his reference, but not to turn up at Snaresbrook, unless he showed a willingness to break with Carlos and the whole perverse philosophy of waiting that he had built up. I wanted Jim to admit that he needed help – and use it.

Over the next couple of weeks I called Jim a number of times, both at home and at his office. He was always out. Carol was very distant, but not unsympathetic. I think she felt as I did, but with the added twist of having shared a bed with the man for five years. I modified my position and told her that I would write the statement, but I still wouldn't turn up in court unless Jim showed some willingness. I told her to give Jim the message. He never called back. I left messages for him at his work; he must have ignored them. Eventually, I washed my hands of the whole thing.

Mr Clifton wrote and thanked me for my statement – which stated quite clearly the way I felt about Jim Stonehouse – and told me the date he was due to appear and the court number. I did my best to forget this information. But on the morning itself I sat in my office completely distracted. I wandered around the room picking up the Post-it notes that were stuck to every available surface and mashing them up into thick wadges of yellow paper and tackiness. I knew I was right not to go to court, I knew it was the strong – and ultimately caring – thing to do. At 9.30 Jim called up.

'Just called to say goodbye, I don't expect I'll be seeing you for a while.'

I was choked with salty guilt. 'Jim, I'm sorry about this . . . ' I was about to relent.

'No, don't be sorry. Clifton's got his own little ideas, but, really, I'd positively like to go down. Carlos was inside for a couple of years and he says it was the formative experience that really made him fully understand the nature of the millennium. It's waiting in a class of its own!' There was an exultant, manic edge to his voice. He was laughing when we said our goodbyes and hung up.

As soon as I'd put the phone down it rang again. This time it was Clifton.

'I really would like to make one last appeal to you. Ignore what my client says; he is undoubtedly an unstable man. I have personal reasons for believing that he has fallen under the influence of people who are . . . ' his voice trailed off '. . . evil. I urge you to come to Snaresbrook for 10.30. Mr Stonehouse needs help. He is not a man who will adjust well to prison.'

When Clifton had rung off, I sat at the desk spasmodically ripping up my wadded Post-it notes. After a while I looked at my watch, it was 9.50. I ran out of the office and down into the street. I was on the Gray's Inn Road before I managed to find a cab.

'I need to be at Snaresbrook Court by 10.30 – do you think we'll make it?'

'Hard to say, mate.' It was a flat, laconic statement. The cabby's hand circled lazily and brought the cab neatly into the traffic stream. 'We could do it, it really depends on getting through past Clapton.'

'Why not head north and cut across the Marsh to Leyton.'

'Nah, nah, not worth it.'

'But ... '

'Trust me. Anyway, what's the hurry?'

'It's a friend, he needs me as a character witness, he could go down.'

'Oh, I see.'

We sat in silence. The cab juddered its way through the morning traffic, purring noisily like a vast, bronchitic panther. I fidgeted with my lip, my cheeks. Smoked and flicked, squinted out the window at the façades of buildings growing and retreating. The cabby took my advice after all. We turned off Green Lanes and cut across Stoke Newington to Tottenham High Road. The rows of semis and villas gave way to unfinished areas of warehousing and light industrial premises as we dog-legged round on to the Lea Bridge Road. It was 10.25. I sat forward in my seat, willing the traffic ahead to part for us.

'What'd he do then, this friend of yours?'

'He got fed up with waiting.'

'Ha! If that was a crime we'd all be bloody banged up, wouldn't we?'

'Yeah, well, I suppose so. He reacted rather drastically though. He shunted some bloke's van and then took a poke at him, then when the Bill came to get him he took a poke at them as well.'

'I bet he did. Listen, that's nothing. I was at this wedding on Saturday down the Roman Road, and one of the guests took a knife to the bride's father 'cause he couldn't stand waiting for a drink.'

'Really ... ?'

'Straight up. Gave him it in the neck. Poor man's still in a coma. The bloke then ran out into the road. But some of the other guests caught up with him. They held him down and then one of them ran him over in his car. Now he's in a coma too.'

'Too?'

'Like the bride's father.'

'Nice friends you have.'

'Well, they weren't anything really to do with me. The groom was a mate of my son's. I just went along for the hell of it.'

'That sounds about right.'

We relapsed into silence again. The cabby was doing his best. Every time we got mired in the traffic he got his *A–Z* out and started looking for a shortcut. It wasn't his fault that this part of north-east London was one tortuous, twisting high street after another. There were hardly any alternatives.

It was 10.30. We were stuck in a jam on Leyton High Road. I'd more or less given up. There was sixteen quid plus up in red on the meter. An artic was stranded across the intersection. A roar from behind us and a file of motorcycles came dodging through the stalled traffic, very fast. A blur of dayglo faring, leather shoulders, dirty visors, vinyl tabards and in front, already fast disappearing, the flapping flares of some familiar corduroys.

There was a jolt in the queue. The lights changed and two minutes later we were pulling up outside the court. I leapt out and shoved some bills at the cabby. Jim was being sentenced in Court 19, in the modern annexe. I ran through the car-park and into the building. I slowed to a walk going up the stairs, labouring to capture my breath. In the upper hall a tall black man with a wispy beard approached me. It was 10.40.

'You must be . . . ?'

'Yes, yes . . . '

'I'm Clifton.' He extended his hand. It was Jim's brief. Carol was in a corner with a knot of people standing around a robed barrister.

'But the case . . . ?'

'We've had to ask for a slight postponement. Mr Stonehouse isn't here yet.'

'Isn't here! Then where the bloody hell is he? The judge is going to take a pretty dim view of this.'

'I should imagine he will.'

I went over to the corner where Carol was talking to the barrister – a rather hepatitic-looking woman.

'Oh, hello,' said Carol and introduced us.

'Didn't Jim stay at home last night?'

'No, I was just saying. He's more or less moved in with Carlos now. He'll have been coming from Acton. It's a long haul across town.'

'I hope he's at least managed to put a suit on for the occasion.'

At that moment, the devil we spoke of appeared at the end of the room and walked down it, erect, head swivelling mechanically from side to side. He beamed contempt at the motley bunch of defendants, lawyers, plaintiffs, witnesses and police who waited their turns.

'Sorry I'm late. Got stuck in the lift. I had to wait for an hour before they let me out.'

Just at that moment the swing-doors from the courtroom swung open and a small throng appeared. The hepatitic barrister pressed through and I saw her lean over and talk to the clerk. I turned to Jim. 'It looks like we're on.' We passed through and into the courtroom.

Jim took his place in a rather long dock to the right of the courtroom. In fact the dock stretched the whole width of the room; there was enough space in it to contain terrorist and stock market multiple defendants. Carol and I took our place at the back of the four rows of tip-up seats immediately to the right of the door we came in by. Together, the seats and the dock faced off two sides of the court. Opposite the dock was the bench; and in the main area, the pit of the court, were rows of desks for the lawyers. The whole place was well lit by flat, flickerless, strip lighting. Every surface – the front of the dock, the lawyers' desks, the witness box, the bench – was fronted with a light varnished wood. It reminded me of the Old Lecture Theatre at Houghton Street, except that there, all was dark with obscurity. Here, everything was light: truth, the panelling seemed to say, albeit of a particular, restricted, keyline-boxed variety, is about to be pursued.

The presiding judge gave a diffident tap with his little mallet and the court was in session. The clerk of the court rose and read the charges:

'. . . that you on the 21st of August did wilfully cause damage to the vehicle belonging to Mr Takis Christos of 24 Rosemount Avenue, Crouch End; that you did thereafter assault Mr Christos; that you did fail to report the accident or to stop after the accident; that you did assault a police officer who came to interview you concerning the accident on the 22nd of August at your place of work. How say you to these charges, guilty or not guilty?'

'Guilty.' Jim sounded like a large plastic doll, the word 'guilty' wheezed out of him in a breathy, strangulated voice about an octave higher than I'd expected. It was clear that all his bravado had deserted him, he was frightened. A sharp toothpick of compassion entered my heart. My friend was on trial. It was painfully ridiculous.

'Mr Stonehouse.' This was the judge, a dormouse figure perched up on his high chair. He was little and pink; a quivering snout quested out from under his wig, his pink eyes blinked as if they had been recently washed in tea. 'Can you tell the court why you were late arriving here this morning?' The judge had an incongruously weighty and judicial voice. Imposing and threatening in equal measure, he must have practised a lot when he was by himself.

'I got stuck in the traffic, your Honour.'

'I see. Where were you coming from?'

'Acton, your Honour.'

'And at what time did you set out?'

'8.30, your Honour.'

'I see. It took you nearly three hours?'

'There were extremely bad road-works in Hackney, your Honour.'

'I see, I see.'

The prosecution counsel came to Jim's assistance.

'There were indeed bad tail-backs through Hackney, your Honour, I was caught in them myself.'

'All right, all right. This is a court of law not an A A incident room, let's get on with it.'

The prosecution set out its case. Counsel, the policemen and even Mr Christos kept things brief and to the point. I sensed from the manner in which they gave their evidence that they all believed that Jim was cracked and didn't really want to see him go down. There was little vindictiveness in the way they spoke about him, it was rather that they were all playing their part as subsidiary cogs in a well-oiled machine. At each juncture the QC asked the judge if he wanted to ask further questions – the only time he did ask one, it was addressed to Mr Christos.

'I have a note here from the police saying that you have been unable to present your own license and insurance documents, Mr Christos. Is that correct?'

'It is true, yes, but I have them, but in the post like I say to them, from Swansea, like I say.' Mr Christos was a very short individual, globular with tufts of hair protruding irregularly from a balding scalp. It was very difficult indeed to visualise him as a representative of that great, quiescent multitude which Jim believed to be awaiting the onset of the millennium in a lather of spiritual anticipation.

'See that you present your documents as soon as they become available.'

'Of course, of course, like I say . . . ' The judge cut him off with a paw gesture. The fruitier rejoined his friends who were sitting in the row in front of me. They were a couple of sharpish young men who looked like estate agents; and a plump woman in late middle age wearing elephantine slacks and a CND sticker on her raincoat.

I had no time to consider the implications of this. The hearing rolled forward. Jim's hepatitic barrister got to her feet and looked yellowly around the courtroom, checking no doubt that all her witnesses were in place. The witnesses turned out to be me and a Dr Busner from Heath Hospital. Busner was the psychiatrist who had been charged by the Highgate magistrates with the job of assessing Jim's state of mind. Busner took the stand.

'You are Dr Busner, a consultant psychiatrist at Heath Hospital?' There was a pause. Busner was an ageing hippy with grey, collar-length hair. He wore a striped poplin suit and a tie like a rag. I vaguely recognised him, but couldn't pin down the recollection. I'd never seen him in the flesh before, of that much I was certain, but perhaps on television. He'd have to be a pretty damn good witness to justify turning up in court in that rig. If I was the judge I would have sent Jim down just on the basis of his expert witness's apparel.

Busner stroked his chin, and for a ghastly minute it looked as if he was going to launch into some philosophical analysis of the question of his own identity, but he pulled himself together and answered, 'I am.'

'Would you like to give the court your professional view of

the defendant's mental state, insofar as it relates to the plea of mitigation on grounds of diminished responsibility.'

'I have seen Mr Stonehouse for three hour-long sessions over the past month. During that time I have built up a fairly comprehensive picture of him as an individual. He has spent most of these sessions expounding in great detail a series of views he holds concerning the probable impact of the millennium on our society. Views he characterises as "Immanence and Imminence". It is Mr Stonehouse's contention that the two assaults on Mr Christos and PC Winch, and the damaging of Mr Christos's van, were necessary revolutionary acts in terms of the propagation of his ideas.'

Busner paused again. At least it seemed like a pause to begin with, but after the pause had run on for a while it became clear that that was all he was going to say. A susurration of unease ran around the courtroom. The policeman Jim had hit, and who had already given his evidence, began whispering, quite audibly, to one of his colleagues. The judge, who was scrutinising Busner's written assessment, didn't notice that Busner had stopped speaking.

Jim's barrister was obviously taken aback. Eventually she pulled herself together. 'Is it your view, therefore, Dr Busner, that Mr Stonehouse was in full possession of his faculties when he committed these crimes?'

'It's difficult to say; either he's right in what he says, in which case he was fully *compos mentis*, or else he is the victim of an extremely complex delusionary state, in which case he is clearly not morally responsible for his actions.'

The judge started at the words 'morally responsible' and began to pay attention to the proceedings again.

'Well, is he or isn't he?'

'What, your Honour?' queried Jim's barrister, sensing that the battle might be lost.

'Is he morally responsible?'

'We think not, your Honour.'

A long sigh from the bench.

'Mr Stonehouse, we have gone to considerable lengths to hear all the evidence in this case. We have heard from Mr Christos how you drove into his van and when challenged by him laughed and said,' the judge scrutinised his notes, ' "I'm fed up with waiting." We've heard from two police officers how you exhibited the same contempt towards the law when they came to interview you as you showed to Mr Christos's possessions and person. All in all your behaviour has been reprehensible, immature and criminal. However, I'm swayed by the arguments put forward by ... by ... '

'Dr Busner, your Honour.'

'Dr Busner – and it is to him that I will entrust you for further psychiatric assessment and treatment if applicable. I will defer sentencing for three months pending reports. Mr Stonehouse, is there anything you wish to say?'

This was Jim's opportunity to really louse things up for himself. I waited for him to take it. He stirred uneasily in the dock; his mechanical arms reached out and grabbed hold of the top of the barrier in front of him; he swept a lock of hair back from his forehead.

'Only that I'm grateful to the court for giving me the opportunity to sort myself out for a while. I really have been under a lot of pressure recently.'

Only Carol and I and possibly Clifton and Busner could have known how unnatural Jim's voice sounded when he said this. As far as the rest of the court was concerned it was an honest statement. But I knew that voice, Jim was bullshitting.

The court rose and we went back out into the ante chamber. I walked over to where Clifton stood with the barrister, at the plate-glass window, looking out over the car-park.

'Congratulations, that was quite a result, and you didn't even need me to say my piece.'

'Yes, I'm sorry you had to take the trip.' Clifton brushed the tangle of hair on his lip with the top of a stack of papers. 'But I'm afraid it really had nothing to do with us. Snape can't afford to send anyone else down this session. Mr Stonehouse has evaded imprisonment because there isn't enough room in it for him at the moment, not because of the merits of the case.'

'Well, I hope you don't tell him that. Hopefully this whole experience will help him to see some sense.'

From where we stood I watched as Carol came out of the main door of the court building and began to work her way across the car-park, threading her way in between the parked cars. As I watched she gained the outer edge of the tarmac, moved on to the grass to avoid a gaggle of motorcycle couriers who were standing around their machines smoking, and headed off towards the main gates. I turned away from the window.

Jim came up to me, pulling off his jacket and rolling up his sleeves. He was grinning broadly. He took in the group of us – Busner had now idled over – and launched into a rant.

'Well, that fixed them. I thought about it and decided that what waiting had to be done could be done more profitably out here. I will go to prison eventually, but for the moment it's more important that I improve my knowledge. For this opportunity I thank you all . . . ' He began to bow stiffly from the waist, but paused in mid-salaam, and looked round at us. 'Where's Carol, didn't she come out with you?'

I glanced down into the car-park again. Carlos was looking up at me. His pink head was glowing faintly in the flat sunlight. A withered roll-up dribbled from his lip; his vinyl tabard rode up around his shoulders. I turned back to Jim. 'Yeah, she was here Jim, but I think she got fed up with waiting.'